PENGUIN BOOKS

MOON TIGER

Penelope Lively grew up in Egypt but settled in England after the war and took a degree in History at St Anne's College, Oxford. She is a Fellow of the Royal Society of Literature and a member of PEN and the Society of Authors. She was married to the late Professor Jack Lively, has a daughter, a son and six grandchildren, and lives in London.

Penelope Lively is the author of many prize-winning novels and short-story collections for both adults and children. She has twice been shortlisted for the Booker Prize: once in 1977 for her first novel, *The Road to Lichfield*, and again in 1984 for *According to Mark*. She later won the 1987 Booker Prize for her highly acclaimed novel *Moon Tiger*. Her other books include *Going Back*; *Judgement Day*; *Next to Nature, Art*; *Perfect Happiness*; *Passing On*, which was shortlisted for the 1989 *Sunday Express* Book of the Year Award; *City of the Mind*; *Cleopatra's Sister*; *Heat Wave*; *Beyond the Blue Mountains*, a collection of short stories; *Oleander, Jacaranda*, a memoir of her childhood days in Egypt; *Spiderweb*; her autobiographical work, *A House Unlocked*; *The Photograph*; *Making It Up*; *Consequences*; *Family Album*, which was shortlisted for the 2009 Costa Novel Award; and *Life in the Garden*.

She has also written radio and television scripts and has acted as presenter for a BBC Radio 4 programme on children's literature. She is a popular writer for children and has won both the Carnegie Medal and the Whitbread Award. She was appointed CBE in the 2001 New Year's Honours List.

By the same author

FICTION

Going Back
The Road to Lichfield
Nothing Missing but the Samovar and Other Stories
Treasures of Time
Judgement Day
Next to Nature, Art
Perfect Happiness
Corruption and Other Stories
According to Mark
Pack of Cards: Collected Short Stories 1978–1986
Moon Tiger
Passing On
City of the Mind
Cleopatra's Sister
Heat Wave
Beyond the Blue Mountains
Spiderweb
The Photograph
Making It Up
Consequences
Family Album

NON-FICTION

The Presence of the Past: An Introduction to Landscape History
Oleander, Jacaranda: A Childhood Perceived
A House Unlocked
Life in the Garden

PENELOPE LIVELY
Moon Tiger

PENGUIN BOOKS

PENGUIN BOOKS

UK | USA | Canada | Ireland | Australia
India | New Zealand | South Africa

Penguin Books is part of the Penguin Random House group of companies
whose addresses can be found at global.penguinrandomhouse.com.

First published by André Deutsch Ltd 1987
Published in Penguin Books 1988
Reissued in this edition 2018

004

Printed and bound in Great Britain by Clays Ltd, Elcograf S.p.A.

A CIP catalogue record for this book is available from the British Library

ISBN: 978-0-141-04484-2

www.greenpenguin.co.uk

Acknowledgements

I am grateful to Tim Tindall and to Andrew Wilson for correcting me on military matters.

For material on the desert war I acknowledge the help of Alan Moorehead, *African Trilogy*; Barrie Pitt, *The Crucible of War*; Correlli Barnett, *The Desert Generals*; Keith Douglas, *Alamein to Zem Zem*; Cyril Joly, *Take These Men*; and the photographic, film and art archives of the Imperial War Museum.

I was born in Cairo and spent my childhood there during the war. I have also to acknowledge the contribution of that *alter ego*, understanding little but seeing a great deal.

I

'I'm writing a history of the world,' she says. And the hands of the nurse are arrested for a moment; she looks down at this old woman, this old ill woman. 'Well, my goodness,' the nurse says. 'That's quite a thing to be doing, isn't it?' And then she becomes busy again, she heaves and tucks and smooths – 'Upsy a bit, dear, that's a good girl – then we'll get you a cup of tea.'

A history of the world. To round things off. I may as well – no more nit-picking stuff about Napoleon, Tito, the battle of Edgehill, Hernando Cortez ... The works, this time. The whole triumphant murderous unstoppable chute – from the mud to the stars, universal and particular, your story and mine. I'm equipped, I consider; eclecticism has always been my hallmark. That's what they've said, though it has been given other names. Claudia Hampton's range is ambitious, some might say imprudent: my enemies. Miss Hampton's bold conceptual sweep: my friends.

A history of the world, yes. And in the process, my own. The Life and Times of Claudia H. The bit of the twentieth century to which I've been shackled, willy-nilly, like it or not. Let me contemplate myself within my context: everything and nothing. The history of the world as selected by Claudia: fact and fiction, myth and evidence, images and documents.

'Was she someone?' enquires the nurse. Her shoes squeak on

the shiny floor; the doctor's shoes crunch. 'I mean, the things she comes out with . . .' And the doctor glances at his notes and says that yes, she does seem to have been someone, evidently she's written books and newspaper articles and . . . um . . . been in the Middle East at one time . . . typhoid, malaria . . . unmarried (one miscarriage, one child he sees but does not say) . . . yes, the records do suggest she was someone, probably.

There are plenty who would point to it as a typical presumption to align my own life with the history of the world. Let them. I've always had my followers, also. My readers know the story, of course. They know the general tendency. They know how it goes. I shall omit the narrative. What I shall do is flesh it out; give it life and colour, add the screams and the rhetoric. Oh, I shan't spare them a thing. The question is, shall it or shall it not be linear history? I've always thought a kaleidoscopic view might be an interesting heresy. Shake the tube and see what comes out. Chronology irritates me. There is no chronology inside my head. I am composed of a myriad Claudias who spin and mix and part like sparks of sunlight on water. The pack of cards I carry around is forever shuffled and re-shuffled; there is no sequence, everything happens at once. The machines of the new technology, I understand, perform in much the same way: all knowledge is stored, to be summoned up at the flick of a key. They sound, in theory, more efficient. Some of my keys don't work; others demand pass-words, codes, random unlocking sequences. The collective past, curiously, provides these. It is public property, but it is also deeply private. We all look differently at it. My Victorians are not your Victorians. My seventeenth century is not yours. The voice of John Aubrey, of Darwin, of whoever you like, speaks in one tone to me, in another to you. The signals of my own past come from the received past. The lives of others slot into my own life: I, me, Claudia H.

Self-centred? Probably. Aren't we all? Why is it a term of accusation? That is what it was when I was a child. I was considered difficult. Impossible, indeed, was the word sometimes used. I didn't think I was impossible at all; it was mother and nurse who were impossible, with their injunctions and their warnings, their obsessions with milk puddings and curled hair and their terror of all that was inviting about the natural world – high trees and deeper water and the texture of wet grass on bare feet, the allure of mud and snow and fire. I always ached – burned – to go higher and faster and further. They admonished; I disobeyed.

Gordon, too. My brother Gordon. We were birds of a feather.

My beginnings; the universal beginning. From the mud to the stars, I said. So . . . the primordial soup. Now since I have never been a conventional historian, never the expected archetypal chronicler, never like that dried-up bone of a woman who taught me about the Papacy at Oxford time out of mind ago, since I'm known for my maverick line, since I've infuriated more colleagues than you've had hot dinners, we'll set out to shock. Tell it from the point of view of the soup, maybe? Have one of those drifting floating feathery crustaceans narrate. Or an ammonite? Yes, an ammonite, I think. An ammonite with a sense of destiny. A spokesperson for the streaming Jurassic seas, to tell it how it was.

But here the kaleidoscope shakes. The Palaeolithic, for me, is just one shake of the pattern away from the nineteenth century – which first effectively noticed it, noticed upon what they were walking. Who could not be attracted to those majestic figures, striding about beaches and hillsides, overdressed and bewhiskered, pondering immensities? Poor misguided Philip Gosse, Hugh Miller and Lyell and Darwin himself. There seems a natural affinity between frock coats and beards and the resonances of the rocks – Mesozoic and Triassic, oolite and lias, Cornbrash and Greensand.

But Gordon and I, aged eleven and ten, had never heard of Darwin; our concept of time was personal and semantic (tea-time, dinner-time, last time, wasting time . . .); our interest in *Asteroceras* and *Primocroceras* was acquisitive and competitive. For the sake of beating Gordon to a choice-looking seam of Jurassic mud I was prepared to bash a hundred and fifty million years to pieces with my shiny new hammer and if necessary break my own arm or leg falling off a vertical section of Blue Lias on Charmouth beach in 1920.

She climbs a little higher, on to another sliding shelving plateau of the cliff, and squats searching furiously the blue grey fragments of rock around her, hunting for those enticing curls and ribbed whorls, pouncing once with a hiss of triumph – an ammonite, almost whole. The beach, now, is quite far below; its shrill cries, its barkings, its calls are clear and loud but from another world, of no account.

And all the time out of the corner of her eye she watches Gordon, who is higher yet, tap-tapping at an outcrop. He ceases to tap; she can see him examining something. What has he got? Suspicion and rivalry burn her up. She scrambles through little bushy plants, hauls herself over a ledge.

'This is my bit,' cries Gordon. 'You can't come here. I've bagged it.'

'I don't care,' yells Claudia. 'Anyway I'm going up higher – it's much better further up.' And she hurls herself upwards over skinny plants and dry stony soil that cascades away downwards under her feet, up towards a wonderfully promising enticing grey expanse she has spotted where surely *Asteroceras* is lurking by the hundred.

Below, on the beach, unnoticed, figures scurry to and fro; faint bird-like cries of alarm waft up.

She must pass Gordon to reach that alluring upper shelf. '*Mind* . . .' she says. 'Move your *leg* . . .'

'Don't *shove*,' he grumbles. 'Anyway you can't come here. I said this is my bit, you find your own.'

'Don't shove yourself. I don't want your stupid bit . . .'

His leg is in her way – it thrashes, she thrusts, and a piece of cliff, of the solid world which evidently is not so solid after all, shifts under her clutching hands . . . crumbles . . . and she is falling thwack backwards on her shoulders, her head, her outflung arm, she is skidding rolling thumping downwards.

4

And comes to rest gasping in a thorn bush, hammered by pain, too affronted even to yell.

He can feel her getting closer, encroaching, she is coming here on to his bit, she will take all the best fossils. He protests. He sticks out a foot to impede. Her hot infuriating limbs are mixed up with his.

'You're *pushing* me,' she shrieks.

'I'm *not*,' he snarls. 'It's you that's shoving. Anyway this is my place so go somewhere else.'

'It's not your stupid place,' she says. 'It's anyone's place. Anyway I don't . . .'

And suddenly there are awful tearing noises and thumps and she is gone, sliding and hurtling down, and in horror and satisfaction he stares.

'He pushed me.'

'I didn't. Honestly mother, I didn't. She slipped.'

'He pushed me.'

And even amid the commotion – the clucking mothers and nurses, the improvised sling, the proffered smelling salts – Edith Hampton can marvel at the furious tenacity of her children.

'Don't argue. Keep still, Claudia.'

'Those are *my* ammonites. Don't let him get them, mother.'

'I don't *want* your ammonites.'

'Gordon, be quiet!'

Her head aches; she tries to quell the children and respond to advice and sympathy; she blames the perilous world, so unreliable, so malevolent. And the intransigence of her offspring whose emotions seem the loudest sound on the beach.

The voice of history, of course, is composite. Many voices; all the voices that have managed to get themselves heard. Some louder than others, naturally. My story is tangled with the stories of others – Mother, Gordon, Jasper, Lisa, and one other person above all; their voices must be heard also, thus shall I abide by the conventions of history. I shall respect the laws of evidence. Of truth, whatever that may be. But truth is tied to words, to print, to the testimony of the page. Moments shower away; the days of our lives vanish utterly, more insubstantial than if they had been invented. Fiction can seem more enduring than reality. Pierre on the field of battle, the Bennet girls at their sewing, Tess on the threshing machine – all these are nailed down for ever, on the page and in a million heads. What happened to me on Charmouth beach in 1920, on the other hand, is thistledown. And when you and I talk about history we don't mean what actually happened, do we? The cosmic chaos of everywhere, all time? We mean the tidying up of this into books, the concentration of the benign historical eye upon years and places and persons. History unravels; circumstances, following their natural inclination, prefer to remain ravelled.

So, since my story is also theirs, they too must speak – Mother, Gordon, Jasper . . . Except that of course I have the last word. The historian's privilege.

Mother. Let us take, for a moment, Mother. Mother retired from history. She withdrew, quite simply. She opted for a world of her own creation in which there was nothing except floribunda roses, ecclesiastical tapestry and some changeable weather. She read only the *West Dorset Gazette*, *Country Life* and the periodicals of the Royal Horticultural Society. Her greatest anxieties were concentrated on the vagaries of the climate. An unexpected frost could cause mild consternation. A bad summer was matter for gentle complaint. Fortunate Mother. Sensible, expedient Mother. On her dressing-table stood a photograph of Father, trim in his uniform, eternally young, his hair recently clipped, his moustache a neat shadow on his upper lip; no red hole in his stomach, no shit no screams no white singing pain. Mother dusted this photograph every morning; what she thought as she did so I never knew.

History killed Father. I am dying of cancer of the gut,

relatively privately. Father died on the Somme, picked off by history. He lay in the mud, I have learned, all one night, screaming, and when at last they came for him he died on the stretcher, between the crater that had been his last bed and the dressing-station. Thinking, I imagine, of anything but history.

So he is a stranger to me. An historical figure. Except for one misty scene in which a poorly defined male shape stoops to lift me and puts me excitingly on his shoulder from whence I lord it over the world including Gordon down below who has not been thus favoured. Even then, you note, my feelings towards Gordon predominate. But whether this undefined male is Father or not I can't be certain; it could be an uncle, a neighbour. Father's course and mine were not long entwined.

So I shall start with the rocks. Appropriately. The rocks from which we spring and to which we're chained, all of us. Like wretched thingummy, what's-his-name, him on his rock . . .

'Chained to a rock . . .' she says. 'What's he called?'

And the doctor pauses, his face a foot from hers, his little silver torch poised, his name in gilt letters pinned to his white coat. 'Sorry? What did you say, Miss Hampton?'

'An eagle,' she states. 'Pecking out his liver. The human condition, d'you see?'

And the doctor smiles, indulgently. 'Ah,' he says. And he parts her eyelids, with care, and peers. Into her soul, perhaps.

Prometheus, of course. Mythology is much better stuff than history. It has form; logic; a message. I once thought I was a myth. Summoned to the drawing-room, aged six or so, to meet a relative richer and more worldly than Mother, of whom Mother was in awe, I found myself swept up, held at arms' length by this gorgeous scented woman, exclaimed at: 'And here she is! The little myth! A real delicious red-haired green-eyed little myth!' Upstairs, I examined my hair and eyes in the nursery mirror. I am a Myth. I am Delicious. 'That'll do,

7

Claudia,' says nurse. 'Handsome is as handsome does.' But I am a Myth; I gaze at myself in satisfaction.

Claudia. An uncharacteristic flight of fancy on Mother's part; I stood out like a sore thumb amid the Violets and Mauds and Norahs and Beatrices. But I stood out anyway, with my hair and turbulence of mind. Other families' nurses, on the beach at Charmouth, quailed when we hove in sight, and gathered their charges around them. We were nasty rough children, Gordon and I. A shame, really, with Mrs Hampton such a nice person and a widow too ... They tutted and watched us with disfavour, playing too noisily, too dangerously, an unkempt, unruly pair.

A long time ago. And yesterday. I have still a chunk of Blue Lias from Charmouth beach in which hang two grey fossil curls; it has acted as a paperweight on my desk. Two *Asteroceras*, adrift in a timeless ocean.

Perhaps I shall not write my account of the Palaeolithic at all, but make a film of it. A silent film at that, in which I shall show you first the great slumbering rocks of the Cambrian period, and move from those to the mountains of Wales, the Long Mynd, the Wrekin, from Ordovician to Devonian, to Red Sandstone and Millstone Grit, on to the lush glowing Cotswolds, on to the white cliffs of Dover ... An impressionistic, dreaming film, in which the folded rocks arise and flower and grow and become Salisbury Cathedral and York Minster and Royal Crescent and gaols and schools and homes and railway stations. Yes, this film blooms before my eyes, wordless and specific, homing in on a Cornish cliff, Stonehenge, Burford church, the Pennines.

I shall use many voices, in this history. Not for me the cool level tone of dispassionate narration. Perhaps I should write like the scribes of *The Anglo-Saxon Chronicle*, saying in the same breath that an archbishop passed away, a synod was held, and fiery dragons were seen flying in the air. Why not, after all? Beliefs are relative. Our connection with reality is always tenuous. I do not know by what magic a picture appears on my television screen, or how a crystal chip has

8

apparently infinite capacities. I accept, simply. And yet I am by nature sceptical – a questioner, a doubter, an instinctive agnostic. In the frozen stone of the cathedrals of Europe there co-exist the Apostles, Christ and Mary, lambs, fish, gryphons, dragons, sea-serpents and the faces of men with leaves for hair. I approve of that liberality of mind.

Children are infinitely credulous. My Lisa was a dull child, but even so she came up with things that pleased and startled me. 'Are there dragons?' she asked. I said that there were not. 'Have there ever been?' I said all the evidence was to the contrary. 'But if there is a word dragon,' she said, 'then once there must have been dragons.'

Precisely. The power of language. Preserving the ephemeral; giving form to dreams, permanence to sparks of sunlight.

There is a dragon on a Chinese dish in the Ashmolean museum in Oxford, before which Jasper and I once stood, eight months or so before Lisa was born. How should I describe Jasper? In several ways, each of them deficient: in terms of my life, he was my lover and the father of my only child; in terms of his own, he was a clever successful entrepreneur; in cultural terms, he was a fusion of Russian aristocracy and English gentry. He was also good-looking, persuasive, potent, energetic and selfish. I have Tito to thank for Jasper; I met him in 1946 when I was working on the Partisan book and needed to talk to anyone who had had anything to do with the Jugoslavian business. I dined with him on a Tuesday and we were in bed together the following Saturday. For the next ten years we sometimes lived together, sometimes did not, fought, made it up, parted and were reunited. Lisa, my poor Lisa, a silent and pasty little girl, was the tangible evidence of our restless union, and an unconvincing one: she never looked or behaved like either of us.

Unlike her father, who nicely manifested his ancestry. His good looks and his cavalier approach to life he inherited from his Russian father; his unshakeable social confidence and sense of superiority from his mother. Isabel, heiress to a chunk of

Devon and centuries of calm prosperity and self-advancement, had had a rush of blood to the head in Paris at the age of nineteen. Defying her parents, she married the irresistible Sasha. Jasper was born when she was twenty-one. By the time she was twenty-two Sasha had got bored with life as a Devon squire, Isabel had come to her senses and recognised a disastrous mistake, and a discreet divorce was arranged. Sasha, paid by Isabel's father to remove himself from the scene and give up all but residual rights in Jasper, retired without complaint to a villa at Cap Ferrat; Isabel, after a decent interval, married a childhood friend and became Lady Branscombe of Sotleigh Hall. Jasper spent his youth at Eton and in Devon, with occasional excursions to Cap Ferrat. When he was sixteen these sorties became more frequent. He found his father's life-style stimulating and an agreeable antidote to hunt balls and shooting parties; he learned to speak French and Russian, to love women and to be able to turn most situations to his advantage. In Devonshire, his mother sighed regretfully and blamed herself; her husband, a man of stoical tolerance who was to die on the Normandy beaches, tried to interest the boy in estate management, forestry and stud farming, all without success. Jasper, as well as being half Russian, was clever. His mother apologised still further. Jasper went to Cambridge, dabbled in everything except sport, got a double first and made a great many useful friends. Afterwards, he sampled politics and journalism, had a brilliant war as the youngest member of Churchill's staff, and emerged from it ambitious, well-connected and opportunist.

Thus, in general, Jasper. In my head, Jasper is fragmented: there are many Jaspers, disordered, without chronology. As there are many Gordons, many Claudias.

Claudia and Jasper stand before the dragon on the Chinese dish in the Ashmolean, Jasper looking at Claudia and Claudia at the dragon, inadvertently learning it for ever. There are two dragons, in fact, blue spotted dragons confronting one another, teeth bared, their serpentine bodies and limbs wonderfully disposed around the dish. They have what appear to be antlers, fine blue manes, tufts of hair at the elbows and they are crested from head to tail. A most precise definition. Claudia stares into the case, seeing her own face and Jasper's superimposed upon the plates – ghost faces.

'Well?' says Jasper.

'Well what?'

'Are you coming with me to Paris or not?'

Jasper wears a brown duffel coat, a silk scarf instead of a tie. The briefcase he carries is incongruous.

'Possibly,' says Claudia. 'I'll see.'

'That won't do,' says Jasper.

Claudia contemplates the dragons, thinking of something quite other. The dragons are backcloth, but will last.

'Well,' says Jasper again, 'I hope you will. I'll phone from London. Tomorrow.' He glances at his watch. 'I'll have to go.'

'One thing . . .' says Claudia.

'Yes?'

'I'm pregnant.'

There is a silence. Jasper lays a hand on her arm, removes it. 'Ah,' he says, at last. Then – 'What would you . . . like to do?'

'I'm having it,' says Claudia.

'Of course. If that's what you want. It's what, I suppose, I would prefer.' He smiles – a charming, deeply sexual smile. 'Well . . . I must say, darling, the one thing I don't see you cut out for is motherhood. But I daresay you'll display your usual power of adaption.'

She looks, for the first time, at him. At the smile. 'I'm having it,' she states, 'partly out of inefficiency and partly because I want it. The two possibly are not unconnected. And I'm certainly not suggesting we get married.'

'No,' says Jasper, 'I don't imagine you are. But naturally I shall wish to play my part.'

'Oh yes, you'll stand by me,' says Claudia. 'You'll be the perfect gentleman. Are children expensive?'

Jasper watches Claudia, who has been abrupt all afternoon,

11

as only Claudia can be. She stands at a glass case, absorbed, apparently, in Chinese ceramics. She is handsome in an emerald green tweed suit; a blue dent in the second finger of her right hand tells Jasper that she has been writing that morning.

'Would you like to come with me to Paris next weekend?'

'Possibly,' says Claudia.

He feels like giving her a shake. Or striking her. But if he did she would very likely strike back, and this is a public place and both of them have recognisable faces. Instead he puts a placatory hand on her arm and says that he must catch his train.

'Incidentally,' says Claudia, staring still at the glass case, 'I'm pregnant.'

He is seized, suddenly, with intense amusement. He no longer wants to strike her. Trust Claudia, he thinks, to come up with something new.

Lisa spent most of her childhood with one grandmother or the other. A London flat is no place for a child and I was frequently travelling. Lady Branscombe and my mother had much in common, not least the tribulations of offspring beyond their comprehension. They faced up to the illegitimacy bravely, sighed to one another over the telephone and tried to do what they could for Lisa, arranging for Scandinavian *au pair* girls and boarding schools.

Jasper never dominated my life. He was significant, but that is another matter. He was central to the structure, but that is all. Most lives have their core, their kernel, the vital centre. We will get to mine in due course, when I'm ready. At the moment I'm dealing with strata.

One of my favourite Victorians is William Smith, the civil engineer whose labours as a canal constructor enabled him to examine the rocks through which his cuttings were driven and their fossil contents, and draw seminal conclusions. William Smith shall have honoured treatment in my history of the world. And John Aubrey too. It is not generally realised that Aubrey, the supreme gossip, the chatterer about Hobbes and Milton and Shakespeare, was also the first competent field archaeologist and that, moreover, his simple but astute perception in the matter of church windows that one style precedes another and thus can we form a chronology of buildings makes him a seventeenth-century William Smith. And Perp. and Dec. the ammonites of architecture. I can see Aubrey swishing through the grass of a Dorset churchyard, notes in hand, anticipating Schliemann, Gordon Childe and the Cambridge Tripos with the same eye that I see William Smith in a stove-pipe hat squatting absorbed over the debris of a slice of Warwickshire.

I have a print – you can buy them at the Victoria and Albert Museum – of a photograph of the village street of Thetford, taken in 1868, in which William Smith is not. The street is empty. There is a grocer's shop and a blacksmith's and a stationary cart and a great spreading tree, but not a single human figure. In fact William Smith – or someone, or several people, dogs too, geese, a man on a horse – passed beneath the tree, went into the grocer's shop, loitered for a moment talking to a friend while the photograph was taken but he is invisible, all of them are invisible. The exposure of the photograph – sixty minutes – was so long that William Smith and everyone else passed through it and away leaving no trace. Not even so much of a mark as those primordial worms that passed through the Cambrian mud of northern Scotland and left the empty tube of their passage in the rock.

I like that. I like that very much. A neat image for the relation of man to the physical world. Gone, passed through and away. Suppose though that William Smith – or whoever did walk down that street that morning – had in his progress moved the cart from point A to point B. What would we see then? A smudge? Two carts? Or suppose he had cut down the tree? Tampering with the physical world is what we do supremely well – in the end, perhaps, we shall achieve it definitively. *Finis*. And history will indeed come to an end.

William Smith was inspired by stratification. My strata are less easily perceived than those of Warwickshire rock, and in the head they are not even sequential but a whirl of words and images. Dragons and Moon Tigers and Crusaders and Honeys.

The Chinese dragon dish is still in the Ashmolean. I saw it last month.

I was thirty-eight when Lisa was born, and doing nicely. Two books under my belt, some controversial journalism, a reputation for contentious provocative attention-seizing writing. I had something of a name. If feminism had been around then I'd have taken it up, I suppose; it would have needed me. As it was, I never felt its absence; being a woman seemed to me a valuable extra asset. My gender was never an impediment. And I must also reflect, now, that it perhaps saved my life. If I had been a man I might well have died in the war.

I know quite well why I became a historian. Quasi-historian, as one of my enemies put it, some desiccated don too frightened of the water to put a toe out of his Oxford college. It was because dissension was frowned upon when I was a child: 'Don't argue, Claudia', 'Claudia, you must not answer back like that.' Argument, of course, is the whole point of history. Disagreement; my word against yours; this evidence against that. If there were such a thing as absolute truth the debate would lose its lustre. I, for one, would no longer be interested. I well remember the moment at which I discovered that history was not a matter of received opinion.

I was thirteen. At Miss Lavenham's Academy for Girls. In Lower Four B. Doing the Tudor Monarchs with Miss Lavenham herself. Miss Lavenham wrote names and dates on the board and we copied them down. We also, to her dictation, noted the principal characteristics of each reign. Henry VIII was condemned by his marital excesses, but was also no good as king. Queen Elizabeth was good; she fended off the Spaniards and ruled firmly. She also cut off the head of Mary Queen of Scots, who was a Catholic. Our pens scratched in the long summer afternoon. I put up my hand: 'Please Miss Lavenham, did the Catholics think she was right to cut off

14

Mary's head?' 'No, Claudia, I don't expect they did.' 'Please, do Catholic people think so now?' Miss Lavenham took a breath: 'Well, Claudia,' she said kindly, 'I suppose some of them might not. People do sometimes disagree. But there is no need for you to worry about that. Just put down what is on the board. Make your headings nice and clear in red ink . . .'

And suddenly for me the uniform grey pond of history is rent; it is fractured into a thousand contending waves; I hear the babble of voices. I put my pen down and ponder; my headings are not nice and clear in red ink; I get 38% (Fail) in the end of term exams.

2

'From the wrath of the Northmen, O Lord deliver us ...' Doesn't that give you a twinge, reading there on your sofa, the light on, the door locked, the twentieth century tucked cosily around you? And of course He didn't, or not always. He never does, but they weren't to know. He delivered, merely, the words; the poor monk who wrote them probably got a chunk of Viking iron through the throat, or went up in flames with his church.

When I was about nine I asked God to eliminate my brother Gordon. Painlessly but irreversibly. At Lindisfarne, as it happens, to which we had been taken not to reflect upon the Viking raids of which probably Mother had never heard but to walk out to the island along the causeway and have a picnic thereon. And Gordon and I raced across that spit of land, and Gordon being one year older and quite a bit faster was all set to win, of course. And I gasped up this prayer, in fury and passion, meaning it – oh, quite meaning it. Never again, I said, will I ask You for anything. Anything at all. Just grant this. Now. Instantly. It is interesting to note that I had to demand Gordon's extinction, not that I should be made a faster runner. And of course God did nothing of the kind and I sulked throughout a glorious windswept sea-smelling afternoon and became an agnostic.

Years later we went there again, Gordon and I. Not racing

this time. Soberly walking; discussing, I recall, the Third Reich and the coming war. And I remembered that monastic prayer and said that it was as though the Vikings were here again, the blood-red sails on the horizon, the tread of men heavy with weapons. And the sea-birds called and the turf on the cliffs was sponge-springy under our feet and full of wild flowers, as no doubt it was in the ninth century. We ate sandwiches and drank ginger beer amid the ruins and afterwards lay in the sun in a hollow. Jasper was unknown to us, and Lisa. Sylvia. Laszlo. Egypt. India. Strata as yet unformed.

We talked about what we wanted to do, in the war and after, if there was an after. Gordon was trying to wangle himself into the Intelligence (everyone wangled in those days – wangled and pulled strings). I knew what I intended. I was going to be a war correspondent. Gordon laughed. He said he didn't give much for my chances. Have a go, he said, and good luck to you, but frankly . . . And I strode on ahead. You'll see, I said. You'll see. And he had to catch up with me and propitiate. We were still rivals. Among other things. Alongside other things. Then, and later.

The doctor pauses and glances through the glass port-hole in the door. 'Who's she talking to? Has she got a visitor?' The nurse shakes her head; for a moment they watch the patient, whose lips move, whose expression is . . . intent. There does not appear to be anything clinically amiss; they scrunch and squeak away on down the corridor.

Claudia confronts Gordon, not on the sea-blown Lindis-farne shore but in the pink alcoholic atmosphere of The Gargoyle in 1946. She feels incandescent, aflame with private triumphs.

Gordon is scowling. 'He's a creep,' he says.

'Shut up.'

'He can't hear. He's busy furthering his career.'

Jasper, a couple of yards away, stands at another table, talking to its occupants. His tanned face is lit by the candle below it: expressive, handsome. He gestures, delivers a punch-line, laughter rings out.

'You always did have dubious taste in men,' Gordon continues.

'Really?' says Claudia. 'Now that's an interesting remark.'

They stare at one another.

'Oh, stop it, you two,' says Sylvia. 'This is supposed to be a celebration.'

'So it is,' says Gordon. 'So it is. Come on, Claudia, celebrate.' He upends the bottle into her glass.

'It really is terrific,' says Sylvia. 'An Oxford fellowship! I still can't quite believe it.' Her eyes never leave Gordon, who does not look at her. She twitches a thread from the sleeve of his jacket, touches his hand, gets out a packet of cigarettes, drops them, retrieves them from the floor.

Claudia continues to observe Gordon. Out of the corner of an eye, from time to time, she takes stock of Jasper. Others also note Jasper; he is a person people see. She raises her glass: 'Congrats! Again. Remind me to come and dine at your High Table.'

'You can't,' says Gordon. 'No ladies.'

'Oh, what a shame,' says Claudia.

'Where did you find him?'

'Find who?'

'You know damn well who I mean.'

'Oh – Jasper. Um, now . . . where was it? I went to interview him for a book.'

'Ah,' says Sylvia brightly. 'How's the book going?'

They ignore her. And Jasper returns to the table. He sits down, puts his hand on Claudia's. 'I've told them to bring a bottle of champers. So drink up.'

Sylvia tries to get out a cigarette, drops the packet, grovels for it on the floor and feels her expensive hairdo falling to pieces. And the dress is not a success, too pink and pretty and girlish. Claudia is in black, very low-cut, with a turquoise belt.

'How *is* the book going?' she asks. And Claudia does not

answer, so Sylvia must fill the gap lighting her cigarette, puffing, looking round the room as though she hadn't expected a reply anyway.

It has been like that all evening. Like it always is when Claudia is there. That electric feeling, whether they are fighting or not (and goodness knows *she* never fought with *her* brother like that), as though no one else existed. Making you feel intrusive, as though you should leave the room. And Gordon hasn't touched her once.

Jasper returns and she exclaims in relief, 'Where did you get that marvellous tan?'

'Swanning around the South of France?' says Gordon. 'I thought you people were kept so busy?' I know your type, he thinks: cavalry twill trousers and an eye to the main chance.

The champagne arrives. Explodes. Is poured. Jasper raises his glass. 'Here's to you, Gordon! I popped down to the South of France for a few days to see my father.'

'I suppose you'll be posted to some glamorous place soon?' says Sylvia.

Jasper spreads his hands, pulls a face. 'My dear girl, the FO will probably dump me in Addis Ababa, who knows?'

Gordon drinks his champagne in two gulps. 'Surely a career diplomat expects to take a bit of the rough with the smooth? Or don't you see yourself as that? Incidentally how did you get into the FO at your age?' He eyes Jasper's hand, which lies on Claudia's.

'Gordon . . .' murmurs Sylvia. 'That sounds awfully *rude*.'

'Not rude at all,' says Jasper, smiling. 'Astute. You may well ask. Late entry, it's called. A word or two from the right people helped.'

'No doubt,' says Gordon. The hands, now, are lightly entwined. 'And this is for keeps, is it? I understand you've had quite a varied career hitherto.'

Jasper shrugs. 'I believe in being flexible, don't you? The world's much too interesting a place to let oneself get stuck with one aspect of it.'

Gordon cannot, for the moment, think of anything to say that is sufficiently biting; the champagne is having its effect. Sylvia nuzzles a knee against his. He cannot quite account for the scale of his dislike for this man; Claudia has produced men before, often enough. One has resented them all, naturally. Jasper, for some reason, is of a different order. He helps himself to some more champagne, drinks, glowers at Jasper: 'Very adroit of you to have a father living in the south of France.'

Claudia laughs. 'You're plastered, Gordon,' she says.

The strata of faces. Mine, now, is an appalling caricature of what it once was. I can see, just, that firm jaw-line and those handsome eyes and a hint of the pale smooth complexion that so nicely set off my hair. But the whole thing is crumpled and sagged and folded, like an expensive garment ruined by the laundry. The eyes have sunk almost to vanishing point, the skin is webbed, reptilian pouches hang from the jaw; the hair is so thin that the pink scalp shines through it.

Gordon's face always mirrored, eerily, mine. We were not considered alike, but I could see myself in him and him in me. A look of the eye, a turn of the mouth, a shadow. Genes declaring themselves. It is an odd sensation. I have it occasionally with Lisa, who also resembles me not at all (nor her father, for that matter – she might be a changeling, poor thing; has, indeed, all the classic changeling pallor and physical sparsity). But I look at her and for an instant my own face flickers back. Gordon's hair was thick and fair, not red; his eyes grey not green; at eighteen he was six feet tall, and had that lank, casual, attenuated look of those who go through life with their hands in their pockets, whistling. A golden lad, Gordon. Winning prizes and making friends.

A handsome pair, they used to say, to Mother. Who murmured, deprecatingly. Not at all the thing, to admire your own children. And anyway Mother had reservations.

By the time we were both at university Mother was well into her retirement from history. She had drawn south Dorset

20

around her like a shawl and blocked out as many aspects of our times as she could. The war, of course, was tiresome. It called for stoicism, though, and stoicism was one thing she was quite good at. She didn't mind going without petrol and putting up blackout curtains and bathing in two inches of hot water. The departure of cooks and gardeners was endurable, too. What she was retreating from was any profundity of feeling and therefore any commitment more intense than light church attendance and an interest in roses. She had no opinions and she loved no one, was merely fond of a few people, including I suppose Gordon and myself. She acquired a Highland terrier which had been trained to roll over on its back at the command 'Die for your country!'; apparently Mother did not find this disturbing.

History is of course crammed with people like Mother, who are just sitting it out. It is the front-liners who are the exception – those who find themselves thus placed whether they like it or not and those who seek involvement. Gordon and I were front-liners, in our different ways. Jasper eminently so. Sylvia would have sat it out if she could and up to a point did, except that she had hitched herself to Gordon and therefore was towed, from time to time, into the front line. To America, of which she would happily have remained in ignorance.

Sylvia came to see me last week. Or yesterday. I pretended I wasn't here.

'Oh dear,' says the nurse. 'I'm afraid it's one of her bad days. You never know, with her . . .' She leans over the bed. 'Here's your sister-in-law, dear, aren't you going to say hello? Wake up, dear.' She shakes her head, regretfully. 'Well, why don't you sit with her for a bit anyway, Mrs Hampton, she'll appreciate it, I'm sure. I'll bring you a cup of tea.'

And Sylvia, gingerly, sits. She watches the high bed with its apparatus of hoists and wires and tubes, and the figure marooned upon it. The closed eyes, the thin beaky face. She is reminded of those figures on stone tombs in country churches.

There are flowers in a vase beside the bed, and others on the windowsill. Sylvia rises with an effort (the chair is low and she is stouter than she would like, alas) and goes across to have a peek at the card alongside. She glances, nervously, over her shoulder; 'Claudia? It's me – Sylvia.' But the figure on the bed is silent. Sylvia sniffs the flowers, picks up the card. 'Best wishes from . . .' She cannot read the squiggle, and puts on her glasses. There is a twitch from the bed. Sylvia drops the card and scuttles back to her chair. Claudia's eyes are still closed, but there comes the sound, unmistakably, of a fart. Sylvia, red in the face, busies herself with her handbag, hunting for a comb, a hankie . . .

'Please, Miss Lavenham,' I said, when I was fourteen, all guile and innocence. 'Why is it a good thing to learn about history?' We have got to the Indian Mutiny now, and the Black Hole of Calcutta, and are suitably appalled. Miss Lavenham, as I well know, does not welcome questions unless they are matters of dates or how to spell a name, and this one, I surmise though I do not quite know why, verges on the heretical. Miss Lavenham pauses for a moment, and looks at me with dislike. But she is equal to the occasion, surprisingly. 'Because that is how you can understand why England became a great nation.' Well done, Miss Lavenham. I'm sure you never heard of the Whig interpretation of history, and wouldn't have known what it meant, but breeding will out.

The teachers all disliked me. 'I'm afraid,' wrote someone on a school report, 'that Claudia's intelligence may well prove a stumbling-block unless she learns how to control her enthusiasms and channel her talents.' Of course, intelligence is always a disadvantage. Parental hearts should sink at the first signs of it. It was an immense relief to me to observe that Lisa's was merely average. Her life has been the more comfortable. Neither her father nor I have had comfortable lives, though whether we would have wished them different is another matter. Gordon's life has also been intermittently uncomfortable, but then so, come to that, has Sylvia's, which would

22

appear to destroy my theory about intelligence and happiness. Sylvia is profoundly stupid.

Gordon met her after the war. She was someone's sister (naturally – just as she is now someone's wife). He met her at a dance, found her pretty (she was), made a pass at her, took her home, started sleeping with her and, in the fullness of time, announced his engagement to her.

I said 'Why?'

He shrugged. 'Why not?'

'Why that one, for heaven's sake?'

'I love her,' he said.

I laughed.

She has given little trouble. She has devoted herself to children and houses. A nice old-fashioned girl, Mother called her, at their third meeting, seeing quite correctly through the superficial disguise of pink fingernails, swirling New Look skirts and a cloud of Mitsouko cologne spray. There was a proper wedding, which Mother loved, with arum lilies, little bridesmaids and a marquee on the lawn of Sylvia's parents' home at Farnham. I declined to be matron of honour and Gordon got rather drunk at the reception. They spent their honeymoon in Spain and Sylvia settled down to live, as she thought, happily ever after in north Oxford.

The unfortunate thing, from her point of view, was that Gordon's academic discipline is frontline stuff, from the point of view of history. Economists are in the thick of things. Sylvia would have been better off with a classicist, rooting around in Greece and Rome. Gordon is concerned not only with here and now but with tomorrow, which is what governments are interested in. They need people like Gordon at their beck and call, to confirm their worst fears, to bolster their confidence. Gordon began to leave north Oxford, for longer and longer periods; he was 'loaned' to emergent African states, to New Zealand, to Washington. Sylvia stopped saying how exciting it was Gordon being so much in demand and began to wonder how good it was for the children being moved around to different schools so often. She tried remaining in north Oxford, where she worried about what she might be missing, or what Gordon might be doing. She started eating too much, and got fat. She put a good face on things, which was the best she could do, and wiser than I would have given her credit for.

Presumably I am not the only one to find the marriage curious. There is Gordon, who has mutated from a golden lad to a successful man, shrewd, respected and handsome with it. Women fall for him from Singapore to Stanford. And there is Sylvia, whose girlish prettiness has given way to a plump and nondescript maturity, and whose conversation is of climate, the price of things and children's schooling. I have watched others watching Sylvia trail in Gordon's wake like some stumpy dinghy towed by a yacht, have observed hostesses tuck her safely away at the end of the table, seen the yawn in the eyes of Gordon's high-flying friends. But I may well be the only one to know that Gordon has a deep seminal laziness. Oh, he works . . . he will work himself into the ground, when it is a matter of the intellect. His laziness is more subtle than that, it is a laziness of the soul, and Sylvia is its manifestation. Gordon needs Sylvia like some people need to spend an hour or two every day simply staring out of the window, or twiddling their fingers. Gordon's intellectual energy is prodigious; his emotional energy is minimal. Those sharp clever women with whom, from time to time, he is seen, would never do as permanencies. Sylvia has always been more secure than perhaps she realises.

Long ago, when we were thirteen and fourteen and rivals in everything, we competed for the attention of a young man Mother hired one summer as tutor. He was supposed to coach Gordon in Greek and Latin. He was an undergraduate, nineteen or twenty, I suppose, a stocky dark young man called Malcolm whose skin turned a rich coffee brown during that interminable languid Dorset summer. At first we resented his presence and the erosion of our idle days. We were dragged scowling to the schoolroom; outside it we ignored him. And then something interesting happened. I came into the room one day when Gordon was alone with Malcolm, construing

24

Virgil, and I noticed two things: that Gordon was enjoying what he was doing and that there was an affinity between them. Malcolm's hand rested on Gordon's shoulder as he bent to look at an exercise book. I looked at the hand – a lean brown hand – and then at Malcolm's face with its thick dark eyebrows and brown eyes intent upon Gordon and what Gordon was saying. And I was filled with hot jealousy; I wanted the hand on my shoulder; I wanted that adult, male, and suddenly infinitely attractive look trained upon me.

I went to find Mother, among her roses, and announced that I wanted to learn Latin.

You could say, I suppose, that the ease with which, several years later, I sailed through Matriculation, is due to the first stirrings of sexual desire. For the rest of that summer I laboured over Kennedy's *Latin Primer*. I swept from nominatives and accusatives to the subjunctive, to conditional clauses, to Caesar and Gaul. There was no stopping me. I leaned against Malcolm's warm sturdy thigh with my grammar in my hand, seeking explanations; I allowed my arm to brush against his as he corrected my exercises; I primped and posed and curried favour. Gordon, driven frantic, flew through *The Aeneid* and embarked on *The Iliad*. We goaded each other to more furious efforts. Poor Malcolm, who had thought to spend an undemanding summer earning a bit of pocket money, found himself devoured by relentless adolescent obsession. I was powered by nascent sexuality and the need to do better than Gordon; Gordon was powered by rivalry with me and the outrage of seeing Malcolm's interest in him distracted and diluted. Malcolm, a decent conventional public schoolboy, probably had his fair share of homosexual leanings. He probably had decent conventional itchings after Gordon – until I started laying my pubescent paws on him – rubbing my newly swollen bosom against him in puppyish play, making eyes at him. I confused and alarmed him. By the end of the summer the wretched young man was as overheated as we were.

Mother, impervious, entered for both the Floribunda and Hybrid Tea classes of the Royal Horticultural Society's south-west summer show and won a Reserve.

I didn't, of course, at thirteen, know the mechanics of sex. Mother, poor thing, was putting off the evil day of explanation. All I knew was that clearly there was something very underhand that went on or it would not be so shrouded in mystery. I had my suspicions, too; not for nothing had I studied Gordon's anatomy over the years, whenever I got the chance. And the feelings aroused in me by Malcolm's chunky, golden, male-smelling body compounded my curiosity.

The summer ended, Malcolm left. I went back to Miss Lavenham's and Gordon to Winchester where his house-master, delicately approached by Mother with murmurings about his fatherless condition, had him into his study one evening for a chat.

He has hugged to himself, for the whole of the first week of the Christmas holidays, his superiority. And eventually, as he has always known he would, he can resist gloating no longer and out it comes, at a point where he is fed up with her, when she has been swanking insufferably.

'Anyway,' he says, 'I know how babies are made.'

'So do I,' Claudia says. But there has been an infinitesimal, a fatally betraying pause.

'Bet you don't.'

'Bet I do.'

'How, then?'

'I'm not going to say,' says Claudia.

'Because you don't know.'

She hesitates, trapped. He watches her. Which way will she jump? She shrugs, at last, wonderfully casual. 'It's obvious. The man puts his – thing – into the lady's tummy button and the baby goes inside her tummy until it's big enough.'

Gordon collapses in glee. He rolls about on the sofa, howling. 'In her tummy button! What an absolute ass you are, Claudia! In her tummy button . . .!'

She stands over him, scarlet not with embarrassment but with chagrin and rage. 'He does! I know he does!'

Gordon stops laughing. He sits up. 'Don't be such a cretin. You don't know *anything*. He puts his thing – and it's called a penis, you didn't know that either, did you? – *there* . . .' And he stabs with a finger at Claudia's crotch, pushing the stuff of her dress between her thighs. Her eyes widen – in surprise? In outrage? They stare at each other. Somewhere downstairs, out of sight, in her own world, they can hear the tranquil hum of their mother's sewing-machine.

'I'm not going to tell you,' she says.

'Because you don't know.'

She could gladly hit him, lolling there complacent on the sofa. And anyway she does know – she's almost sure she does. She says defiantly, 'I do know. He puts his thing in the lady's tummy button.' She does not add that the inadequacy of her own navel for such a performance bothers her – she assumes that it must be going to expand when she is older.

He hurls himself around in laughter. He is speechless. Then he leans forward. 'I knew you didn't know,' he says. 'Listen. He puts his penis – it's called a penis incidentally – *there* . . .' And he stabs with his finger against her dress, between her legs.

And her anger, strangely, evaporates; eclipsed by something different, equally forceful, baffling. Something mysterious is present, something she cannot nail or name. She stares in wonder at her grey-flannelled brother.

▲▲▲▲▲▲▲▲▲▲▲▲▲▲

3

▼▼▼▼▼▼▼▼▼▼▼▼▼▼

The cast is assembling; the plot thickens. Mother, Gordon, Sylvia. Jasper. Lisa. Mother will drop out before long, retiring gracefully and with minimum fuss after an illness in 1962. Others, as yet unnamed, will come and go. Some more than others; one above all. In life as in history the unexpected lies waiting, grinning from around corners. Only with hindsight are we wise about cause and effect.

For a moment we are still concerned with structures, with the setting of the stage. I have always been interested in beginnings. We all scrutinise our childhoods, go about the interesting business of apportioning blame. I am addicted to arrivals, to those innocent dawn moments from which history accelerates. I like to contemplate their unknowing inhabitants, busy with prosaic matters of hunger, thirst, tides, keeping the ship on course, quarrels and wet feet, their minds on anything but destiny. Those quaint figures of the Bayeux tapestry, far from quaint within their proper context, rough tough efficient fellows wrestling with ropes and sails and frenzied horses and the bawling of ill-tempered superiors. Caesar, contemplating the Sussex coast. Marco Polo, Vasco da Gama, Captain Cook . . . all those mundane travellers preoccupied with personal gain or seized by congenital restlessness, studying compasses and dealing with the natives while they make themselves immortal.

And that most interesting arrival of all, a creaking top-heavy vessel named from an English hedgerow, crammed with pots and pans, fish-hooks, muskets, butter, meal and pig-headed, idealistic, ambitious, foolhardy people nosing its way into the embracing arm of Cape Cod. Little did you know what you were setting in motion – William Bradford, Edward Winslow, William Brewster, Myles Standish, Steven Hopkins, Elizabeth his wife and all the rest of you. How could you envisage slavery and secession, the Gold Rush, the Alamo, Transcendentalism, Hollywood, the Model T Ford, Sacco and Vanzetti, Joe McCarthy? Vietnam. Ronald Reagan, for heaven's sake. You were worried about God, the climate, the Indians, and those querulous speculators back in London. But I like to think about you all the same, searching out a place for habitation, chopping, building, planting, praying. Marrying and dying. Stomping around the wilderness noting sorrel, yarrow, liver-wort, watercresses and an excellent strong kind of flax and hemp. Unimaginative folk, probably, and just as well. The sixteen-twenties in Massachusetts were no time for airy exer-cise of the imagination – that's a luxury for the likes of me, thinking of you.

You are public property – the received past. But you are also private; my view of you is my own, your relevance to me is personal. I like to reflect on the wavering tenuous line that runs from you to me, that leads from your shacks at Plymouth Plantation to me, Claudia, hopping the Atlantic courtesy of PanAm and TWA and BA to visit my brother in Harvard. This, you see, is the point of all this. Egocentric Claudia is once again subordinating history to her own puny existence. Well – don't we all? And in any case what I am doing is to slot myself into the historical process, hitch myself to its coat-tails, see where I come in. The axes and muskets of Plymouth in 1620 reverber-ate dimly in my own slice of time; they have conditioned my life, in general and in particular.

I like to pick out the shards of opinion that link your minds to mine – a few sturdy views about the rule of law, distribution of property, decent behaviour and regard for one's fellow men.

But the shards are few; I am peering for the most part into a mysterious impenetrable fog in which what I would call intolerance is sanctified as belief, in which you can cheerfully spike the head of a slaughtered Indian outside your fort, in which you endure privations that would kill me off in a week or so but in which also you believe in witchcraft, in which you do not merely believe but *know* that there is a life hereafter.

In one sense, of course, you were right, though not in the way you had in mind. I am the life hereafter. I, Claudia. Squinting backwards; recording and assessing. Not that you would care for me at all – ungodly foulmouthed old woman with a bloodcurdling record of adultery and blasphemy. No, you wouldn't like me one little bit; I'd confirm all your worst fears of the way things might go.

But you deserve and shall have a considerable space in my history of the world. I shall wander among you, indulgently, pointing out your orderliness, your sense of justice, your capacity for hard work. Your courage. The Indians, you had been told, 'delight to torment men in the most bloody manner that may be, flaying men alive with the shells of fishes, cutting off the joints and members of others by piecemeals, and broiling them on the coals, and causing men to eat the collops of their flesh in their sight whilst they live . . .' And still you set sail. It is the Indians, of course, who bite the dust in the end, poor sods. And you might equally well have had your ears or noses sliced off in the home counties, given the prevailing climate of opinion. In a raw world maybe courage has to be differently assessed. Nevertheless, you command respect.

It seems like a fantasy world, yours. A malevolent Garden of Eden with oaks, pines, walnuts and beech among which howl wolves and lions. You never even mention the poison ivy, which did for me once on a picnic in Connecticut. The environment dominates: no nonsense then about conserving it; the all-important question is whether it will be so kind as to conserve you. Indirectly, it picks off a good many of you from malnutrition and disease. Those who struggle through that fearful first winter do their best to interfere with nature.

You fell trees by the thousand; you manure your fields with herrings, improbably, arranging them heads up in little mounds of earth like Cornish stargazy pies; you are as historically calamitous for the beaver and the otter as for the Wampanaug and the Narragansett. You affected the lives of the periwinkle and the quahaug, quiet clean-living sea-creatures who found themselves turned into money, polished and drilled to become wampum, Indian hard currency in the fur trade. The price of beaver on the London market determined the value of wampum; an agreeably bizarre economic circumstance – that a hat worn under a rainy Middlesex sky should be a matter of life and death for sea-shells creeping in the shallows of Cape Cod.

There was a spaniel on board the *Mayflower*. This little dog, once, was chased by wolves not far from the plantation and ran to crouch between its master's legs 'for succour'. Smart dog – it knew that muskets are sharper than teeth. What I find remarkable about this animal is that I should know of its existence at all, that its unimportant passage through time should be recorded. It becomes one of those vital inessentials that convince one that history is true.

I know about the little spaniel. I know what the weather was like in Massachusetts on Wednesday March 7th 1620 (cold but fair, with the wind in the east). I know the names of those who died that winter and of those who did not. I know what you ate and drank, how you furnished your houses, which of you were men of conscience and application and which were not. And I know, also, nothing. Because I cannot shed my skin and put on yours, cannot strip my mind of its knowledge and its prejudices, cannot look cleanly at the world with the eyes of a child, am as imprisoned by my time as you were by yours.

Well, that can't be helped. Even so, I get a *frisson* from contemplating you, innocents at large in that Garden of Eden (well, as innocent as any product of seventeenth-century Europe). It doesn't do, though, to push the analogy much further. What I relish is to set you against what is to come, against the unthinkable, against the teeming continent I know

31

– marriage of all that is admirable with all that is appalling.

I like America. Gordon likes America. Sylvia does not like America. Poor Sylvia. She floundered there, flapping and lumbering like a turtle out of its element. She never learned the language, the style, the customs. There are those who have chameleon qualities (I have them, so does Gordon, so – naturally – does Jasper) and there are those who were set hard sometime in youth. Sylvia's response to circumstances froze when she was about sixteen; she aspired to a nice time, children, a nice home, nice friends. She achieved all those things and expected then to live happily ever after. She had not reckoned with external factors. Gordon's career prospered. In middle age Sylvia found herself living for half of every year on the other side of the Atlantic while Gordon carried out his Harvard duties.

Sylvia, of course, is consigned to the back of the car. She brings it upon herself, laying her hand on the door and saying 'I'll get in back, Claudia', the Americanism rising to her lips and rapidly corrected – faucet and apartment and sidewalk and so forth one has come to willy-nilly but there are limits. Only sometimes, when she is flustered, as of course she is flustered now, she no longer it seems can control her speech and what slithers out is some horrid hybrid, neither the language that is hers nor the language of America. She has become disoriented, and knows it. Neither her feet nor her tongue are any longer firmly anywhere. She never gets things right over here – is always out of kilter, shaking hands when she should have embraced, embracing when she should have shaken hands, saying too much or too little, unable to gauge status, relationships, implications. Unlike Gordon, who slides from Oxford to Harvard without modification of speech, dress or approach and is equally at home in either, equally welcomed, equally regarded.

Claudia does not say 'Oh no – I will, Sylvia.' She simply gets in the front with Gordon while Sylvia, puffing a little, squeezes herself into the back of the compact, wishing you still had those lovely big squashy cars in the States.

She settles, resignedly, for the long drive. 'Don't come, you don't have to,' Gordon has said, but of course she must, even on this appalling steaming midsummer Massachusetts day, the temperature sign beside the freeway flashing 98°, her dress sticking to her, sweat trickling between her shoulder-blades. If she had not come she would have sat in the cool house all day feeling left out, unwanted, thinking of them laughing and enjoying without her, feeling them walking away from her, disregarding her. And already she is compelled to make her presence felt, leaning uncomfortably forward to ask Gordon if they can't have the windows shut and put the air-conditioning on, trying to hear what it is Claudia is saying.

'Shut?' says Claudia. 'We need some fresh air, for heaven's sake!'

So the fresh hot air roars through the car and green scorching Massachusetts flows past and Sylvia presently gives up and slumps back. Claudia's hair, she notes, is now three colours – grey and white and swatches of the old dark red. It is clipped short and carelessly combed but contrives to look (of course) smart. Sylvia's own, skilfully set and highlighted every month, is still ash-blonde and is currently taking wicked punishment from the howling gale of freeway wind. She rummages for a scarf. Claudia is wearing denim trousers and matching jacket with a skimpy French-looking striped top. How, at her age, she can get away with this Sylvia cannot imagine – it looks (of course) not mutton dressed as lamb but merely dashing.

'All right?' says Gordon, over his shoulder.

'It's frightfully windy,' says Sylvia. Gordon winds up his window a foot and Claudia hers two inches.

Sylvia thinks about food. At least there will be a lovely air-conditioned restaurant at this place and she will have, um, well she will sort of half stick to her diet and resist ice-cream or club sandwiches but she will definitely have an absolutely enormous tuna salad with loads of dressing. One thing about America is the food. That has been one compensation in the ten years of their schizophrenic life, to and fro, six months at Oxford and six months at Cambridge, Mass. Always packing up and putting away and unpacking and readjusting. What a marvellous way to live! people say and Sylvia gamely agrees. She resolutely contemplates her two nice houses and thinks what lots of interesting and well-known people she knows, on either side of the Atlantic, though somehow not a lot of them are her close friends, not people you sit down and have a natter with, just people who come to dinner or drinks or invite you to dinner or drinks, always greeting Gordon first and then saying hello Sylvia afterwards. Gordon, she has been told, is one of the highest paid academics in the business. The size of her housekeeping account still startles her; she can no longer think of anything more to spend it on. Gordon, of course, is frequently away; that is the price of fame. She sometimes wonders, in the watches of the night, if he still has, from time to time, other women. Possibly. Probably. But if he does she does not want to know. He will not, now, leave her for them because it would be a nuisance and interfere with his work. And she learned, long ago, at the time of the Indian woman statistician, that to make a fuss was not expedient. If you sat it out it would pass.

'How much longer?' she enquires, plaintively. Claudia, glancing at the road-map, says another half hour or so. She flings this over her shoulder, a mite impatiently. She is arguing (of course) with Gordon and then suddenly the argument ends and they both explode in laughter. 'What's the joke?' cries Sylvia. 'Tell you later,' says Gordon, still laughing.

And, at last, they arrive. They park the car. Sylvia stares around. 'I can't see any log cabins,' she says. 'Or all these people in fancy dress.' She doesn't see either why Claudia has insisted on this trip – a place where people dress up and pretend to be living in history sounds too silly for words and not Claudia's sort of thing at all. Or Gordon's. Claudia and Gordon are already heading across the tarmac of the car park to something called the Orientation Center; Sylvia gratefully plunges into the air-conditioned cool and makes for the

Ladies'. She does her hair and her face and glances at the information sheet she has been given. Plimoth Plantation, she reads, is a re-creation of the Pilgrim Village in 1627. You are about to leave your own time and step back into the seventh year of colonial settlement. The people you will meet portray through dress, speech, manner and attitudes known residents of the colony. They are always eager for conversation. Feel free to ask questions; and remember, the answers you receive will reflect each individual's seventeenth-century identity.

Sylvia giggles. She feels a bit better now, powdered and relieved. She rejoins the others. 'This place sounds quite mad,' she says.

'Another half hour,' says Claudia. Sylvia, throughout the drive, has been wanting windows put up or put down, interrupting and asking how much further. Like a child, for God's sake, thinks Claudia, just like having Lisa or one of Gordon's brats in the back. But Sylvia is best dealt with by ignoring her, as one usually has. And it is months since she and Gordon have seen one another. She disposes of Sylvia and goes on talking to Gordon. They are disagreeing, vehemently and enjoyably, about the politics of Malawi, where Gordon has recently been. Gordon advises the ministers of such places on how to manage their economies. 'Rubbish, Claudia,' he says. 'You don't know what you're talking about. You've never been to the damn place.' 'Since when,' says Claudia, 'did I depend on personal experience for an informed opinion?' And they both laugh. Sylvia, behind, is bleating away.

They arrive. They watch, in a cool and darkened auditorium, slides; a commentary gives a brief, simplified but lucid account of the colonisation of the eastern seaboard. Not bad, Claudia thinks, not bad at all.

They emerge into the glare and into, evidently, 1627. They enter the stockaded settlement and tour the little fort. They pass out and into the long sloping village street with log cabins at either side. Chickens and geese scratch in the dirt. A figure in a leather jerkin and large-brimmed hat sits mending a hurdle, surrounded by bare-limbed T-shirted onlookers. A sun-bonneted woman chivvies fowls with a broom; someone takes her photograph.

Claudia walks into the first of the log cabins. Within is a fire on which a black cookpot bubbles, elementary furniture, dried plants hung upside-down from beams, a rag-covered bed curtained off by a hanging. And a young man, in breeches and white shirt, who is contemplated in silence by a cluster of visitors. Claudia asks him if he came over in the *Mayflower*. No, he says, in the *Anne*, a couple of years later. Why did you come? enquires Claudia. The young man explains his religious convictions and consequent difficulties in England. Claudia asks if he hopes to get rich in the New World. The young man replies that many of the colonists have expectations of ultimate reward, after the struggles of these early years. You stick it out, advises Claudia, I'll tell you one thing – it works out very interestingly in the end. The young man gives her a quizzical look and says that they have faith in the Lord. You'll need it, says Claudia. He starts spreading His patronage around in a while, I'll tell you that too. Ask him if that dried stuff is marjoram, says Sylvia, I've never seen it growing over here. Ask him yourself, says Claudia, he speaks English. Oh I can't, says Sylvia, it feels so silly. The young man is busy mending a fishing-line and ignores her. Well, says Claudia, good luck in the Indian Wars. She leaves the cabin, followed by Sylvia, and stalks down the street and into the next, where Gordon is talking to a burly fellow with an Irish accent. The Irishman is explaining that he was headed for Virginia and fetched up here accidentally. He intends, in the fullness of time, to go south where, he hears, there are good prospects growing this crop tobacco. Gordon sagely nods; you might well be on to something there, he says. Take my advice though, adds Claudia, don't start importing labour, you'll avoid a whole lot of trouble later on that way. You're spoiling the story, says Gordon. Perhaps there's an alternative story, says Claudia. And what about the theory of manifest destiny? enquires Gordon. Claudia shrugs; I've always thought that was dangerous stuff. Pardon, ma'am? says the Irishman. Destiny, says Claudia, overrated, to my mind. I don't imagine you're giving it a thought, right now? Well . . . says the Irishman. Exactly, Claudia continues, any more than I am. It's only later on that people start preaching about destiny. Oh dear, complains Sylvia, I'm getting out of my depth. Now you people, says Claudia to the Irishman, live in stirring times. Ideologically speaking. Mind, you may feel that sort of thing is passing you by rather, right now, but believe me the consequences are far-reaching. Some might feel it's downhill all the way thereafter. The Irishman, at this point, is beginning to look slightly alarmed. Other bystanders shift awkwardly. Oh come now, says Gordon, there's the Enlightenment to follow. And look what that led to, says Claudia. 'A tide in the affairs of men . . .' says Gordon. Another overworked idea, says Claudia. It's awfully hot in here, murmurs Sylvia. Anyway, it's a thought, says Claudia to the Irishman, stay with subsistence agriculture and see what happens. Yes Ma'am, says the Irishman, a touch wearily. He turns, with some relief, to a woman who wants to know how he lights his fire without matches.

They emerge from the cabin. Sylvia takes a Kleenex from her bag and wipes her face. Claudia bears down upon the man mending a hurdle under a tree and asks him his name. Winslow, he replies, Edward Winslow. I know one of your descendants, says Claudia. Stop name-dropping, says Gordon. The young man inclines his head graciously. They're extremely rich, says Claudia. The young man looks disapproving. He's no more interested in prosperity than you or I, says Gordon. On the contrary, retorts Claudia, he's very interested. *Après moi le déluge* is a corrupt and relatively modern notion – you were always short on historical sensitivity. And you, says Gordon, have never been interested in ideas, merely addicted to sweeping and inaccurate opinions. You have always dismissed anything that does not interest you. Ideology. Industrial history. Economics.

Economists, says Claudia to the Massachusetts sky, are academic accountants. And polemical so-called historians, begins Gordon . . . For goodness sake! snaps Sylvia, people are listening! No they're not, says Claudia, our friend Mr Winslow here is safely tucked up in 1627 so a twentieth-century family discussion is outside his experience. Oh! cries Sylvia, you're being ridiculous both of you. Her face puckers. She is, they see, about to burst into tears. I've had enough of this place, Sylvia cries, I'm going to have some lunch. And she hastens away up the dusty road between the log cabins, tripping once, a dark patch of sweat across the back of her dress, her hair in a mess.

Oh dear, says Claudia.

Gordon says, Well, you were pushing it a bit, weren't you? He watches the stumbling figure of his wife, thinks of going after her, decides that she will pull herself together better on her own, knows that is not what he should have decided. Sorry about that, says Claudia to Mr Winslow, genially. You're welcome, ma'am, says Mr Winslow. Claudia frowns; I'm not sure about that for contemporary speech – I think you may be anticipating a bit. The young man, at this point, betrays a trace of irritation. Excuse me, he begins, but we all take an intensive course in . . . Claudia, says Gordon, taking her arm, enough is enough.

I'm just getting into my stride, says Claudia, allowing herself, nevertheless, to be led away. I know, says Gordon, that's the trouble. I said this place sounded promising, says Claudia, and it is. All the same, says Gordon, I think perhaps we'd better come down to earth.

Claudia hangs over a fenced enclosure to inspect a torpid pig, asleep in a patch of shade. Don't you find the idea of alternative history even faintly intriguing? she asks. No, says Gordon, it's a waste of time. I thought you were supposed to be a theorist? says Claudia, prodding the pig with a piece of stick. My kind of theory, says Gordon, deals in possibilities, not fantasies. Leave that wretched animal alone. How incredibly boring, says Claudia. And it's a fact universally admitted that pigs like having their backs scratched. By the way I saw Jasper last month. We took our grandsons to an appalling musical.

What a charming domestic outing, says Gordon. How is he enjoying being a lord? Inordinately, says Claudia. Destiny, says Gordon, has certainly been Jasper's line – his own. Himself as man of. True, says Claudia. And yours, continues Gordon, would have been a damn sight less fraught if it had never got mixed up with his. Oh, I don't know, says Claudia – I should think I was doomed to Jasper, or if not him then to someone similar. And I always gave as good as I got, you must admit. Of course, says Gordon. Is he married these days? In a manner of speaking, I believe, says Claudia, even at his age.

The pig gets up and lumbers to the far end of the pen. The stupid thing doesn't understand tradition, says Claudia. I suppose we ought to go and find Sylvia. Yes, says Gordon, I suppose we ought. They remain where they are. How inconsistent you are, says Claudia, you're prepared to consider alternative fates within a personal context. I consider that people make choices, says Gordon, though I would concede that some do it better than others. But it is only the irredeemably lumpen who exercise no control at all over their lives. Like this unfortunate twentieth-century pig, says Claudia, condemned to live in seventeenth-century conditions in the interests of tourism and the American national heritage.

They begin to walk, slowly, towards the Reception Center, the present day, and Sylvia. I've thought of a new game, says Gordon, only to be played with each other. It's like Consequences. We each admit Bad Choices and then the other invents an alternative. You concede Jasper and I deal you instead . . . um, let me see . . . I deal you Adlai Stevenson whom I remember you did briefly meet once and took a shine to. By whom you became the mother of a fine son presently running for Governor of Massachusetts. And what do you admit? enquires Claudia. I admit my occupation, says Gordon, I should have stayed with cricket, I'd be retired Captain of England now and command respect where it matters. Don't be silly, says Claudia, I see this game has one set of rules for me and another for you, I'm not playing. Anyway, I want a drink.

They enter the restaurant. Sylvia sits alone at a table before a glass of iced tea and a very large plateful of salad. Her face is blotched. She greets them with pained dignity. I had no idea when you were going to turn up, she says, so I started. Gordon lays a hand on her shoulder. Sorry, love, he says, we really are. We were dawdling. I hope you feel revived. Can I get you anything else? Sylvia replies, injured and distant, that perhaps she'll have some ice-cream.

Car parks, reception centres, lavatories and restaurants are superimposed upon the wilderness. And for me that place is several places – real and unreal, experienced and imagined. It becomes a part of my own sequence of references; the collective past becomes private territory. Gordon and Sylvia, on an afternoon a few years ago, move alongside the Plymouth settlers and a bunch of museum officials in fancy dress.

4

'What's that?' she whispers, pointing.

'What's what, Miss Hampton?' says the nurse. 'There's nothing – just the window.'

'There!' – she stabs the air – 'Thing moving ... What's it called? Name!'

'Nothing that I can see,' says the nurse briskly. 'Don't fuss, dear. You're a bit muzzy today, that's all. Have a sleep. I'll draw the curtains.'

The face, suddenly, relaxes. 'Curtain,' she mutters. 'Curtain.'

'Yes, dear,' says the nurse. 'I'll draw the curtains.'

Today language abandoned me. I could not find the word for a simple object – a commonplace familiar furnishing. For an instant, I stared into a void. Language tethers us to the world; without it we spin like atoms. Later, I made an inventory of the room – a naming of parts: bed, chair, table, picture, vase, cupboard, window, curtain. Curtain. And I breathed again.

We open our mouths and out flow words whose ancestries we do not even know. We are walking lexicons. In a single sentence of idle chatter we preserve Latin, Anglo-Saxon, Norse; we carry a museum inside our heads, each day we commemorate peoples of whom we have never heard. More than that, we speak volumes – our language is the language of everything we have not read. Shakespeare and the Authorised Version surface in supermarkets, on buses, chatter on radio and television. I find this miraculous. I never cease to wonder at it. That words are more durable than anything, that they blow with the wind, hibernate and reawaken, shelter parasitic on the most unlikely hosts, survive and survive and survive.

I can remember the lush spring excitement of language in childhood. Sitting in church, rolling it around my mouth like marbles – tabernacle and pharisee and parable, trespasses and Babylon and covenant. Learning by heart, chanting at the top of my voice – 'Lars Porsena of Clusium, By the Nine Gods he swore, That the great House of Tarquin, Should suffer wrong no more ...' Gloating over Gordon who could not spell ANTIDISESTABLISHMENTARIANISM, the longest word in the dictionary. Rhyming and blaspheming and marvelling. I collected the names of stars and of plants: Arcturus and Orion and Betelgeuse, melilot and fumitory and toadflax. There was no end to it, apparently – it was like the grains of sand on the shore, the leaves on the great ash outside my bedroom window, immeasurable and unconquerable. 'Does anyone know all the words in the world?' I ask Mother. '*Anyone?*' 'I expect very clever men do,' says Mother vaguely.

Lisa, as a child, most interested me when I watched her struggling with language. I was not a good mother, in any conventional sense. Babies I find faintly repellent; young children are boring and distracting. When Lisa began to talk I listened to her. I corrected the inanities encouraged by her grandmothers. 'Dog,' I said. 'Horse. Cat. There are no such things as bow-wows and gee-gees.' 'Horse,' said Lisa, thoughtfully, tasting the word. For the first time we communicated. 'Gee-gee gone?' enquired Lisa. 'That's right,' I said. 'Gone. Clever girl.' And Lisa took a step towards maturity.

Children are not like us. They are beings apart: impenetrable, unapproachable. They inhabit not our world but a world we have lost and can never recover. We do not remember childhood – we imagine it. We search for it, in vain, through layers of obscuring dust, and recover some bedraggled shreds of what we think it was. And all the while the inhabitants of this world are among us, like aborigines, like Minoans, people from elsewhere safe in their own time-capsule.

I used to take Lisa for walks in the woods near Sotleigh when she was five and six, shedding Jasper's mother and the bovine Swiss au pair girl. She amused and intrigued me – this small unreachable alien creature locked in her amoral pre-literate condition with no knowledge of past or future, free of everything, in a state of grace. I wanted to know how it felt. I would question her, craftily, with adult sophistry, with the backing of Freud and Jung and centuries of perception and opinion. And she would slip away from me, impervious, equipped with her own powers of evasion, with Indian lore, with techniques of camouflage.

Claudia and Lisa, five foot eight inches tall and three foot seven, forty-four years old and six, wade through bluebells, wood anemones and leaf mould. The trees resound with bird-song. An old labrador shuffles ahead, nosing toadstools. Coins of sunlight fall down through the trees and lie on feet, on branches, on arms and legs, on the dog's back. Claudia hums. Lisa squats, from time to time, to extract minute objects from the undergrowth with tiny, meticulous fingers.

'What have you got?' enquires Claudia.

'A thing,' says Lisa.

Claudia bends to inspect. 'That's a wood-louse.'

'It's got legs,' says Lisa.

'Yes,' says Claudia, with a faint shudder. 'Lots of legs. Don't squash it like that. You'll hurt it.'

'Why doesn't it want me to hurt it?'

'Well ...' Claudia struggles, frowning. 'You don't like people hurting you, do you?'

Lisa stares at Claudia expressionless. She drops the wood-louse. 'You've got funny eyes.'

Claudia, whose eyes have attracted much favourable comment, loses her expression of benign interest.

43

'They've got black holes in them,' Lisa continues.

'Ah,' says Claudia. 'Those are called pupils. You've got them too.'

'No I haven't,' says Lisa, laughing lightly. She walks on, immediately in front of Claudia, who has to modulate her step so as not to fall over her. Claudia feels oddly disadvantaged, both because of the inconveniently short paces she is having to take and for another, less identifiable, reason. She stops humming and thinks about this. Presently she says, 'Do you remember when I took you to the beach and you went swimming?'

'No,' replies Lisa, at once.

'Of course you do,' says Claudia sharply. 'I bought you a yellow rubber ring. And a spade. It was last month.'

'It was a long time ago not as long as all that,' says Lisa.

'There! You do remember.'

Lisa is silent. She turns to look at Claudia, who sees that her eyes are hideously crossed.

'Don't do that – you'll get a squint.'

'I'm making a face.'

'So I see. It isn't a very nice one.'

A robin sings, piercingly. The wood shivers and quivers and sways around them. Warm summer Devon breezes stroke their faces and their limbs. The dog defecates on to a cushion of moss. Lisa observes, without comment. Claudia sits down on a fallen branch. 'Why are you sitting down?' asks Lisa.

'My legs get tired.'

Lisa rubs her calf. 'Mine aren't.'

'They're shorter,' says Claudia. 'Perhaps that's why.'

Lisa stretches out a leg and contemplates it. Claudia watches. The dog lies on a patch of grass, nose between paws. Lisa says, 'Rex has got short legs too. More legs.'

'If he's got more legs,' says Claudia, 'do you think he's more tired?'

'I don't know,' replies Lisa promptly. 'Is he?'

'I don't know either. What do you think?'

Lisa is now picking the heads from a clump of buttercups

and assembling them in a heap. She ignore~~s~~

out a cigarette and lights it. The smoke th~~at~~

mingles with the yellow shafts of sunlight a

soupy churning density in the clear air of the w

her feet and wades through this to reach the d

the buttercup heads on to his back. The dog d

Lisa kneels beside him and mutters something.

Claudia says, 'What are you talking to Rex ab~~out?~~

'Nothing,' replies Lisa, distantly.

The trees are singing. They also make whooshing and hissing noises and eyes stare from their trunks, shapes of big cruel eyes at which you must not look or creatures might pounce out and get you – ghosts and witches and old men like the old man who sweeps the street outside Claudia's house in London. If she can count to ten before she gets to the tree, that one whooshing and shushing and watching her, if she can count to ten without going wrong nothing will get her, the horrid eyes will vanish; she does, and they do.

Claudia is really Mummy, but she does not like being Mummy so you have to say Claudia. Granny Hampton and Granny Branscombe both like being grannies so it is all right to say Granny. Mummy is a silly word, whereas Claudia is my name. Whereas is a funny word; you do not say it, you blow it. Whereas, whereas. Whereas Claudia is my name.

Lisa is a better name. Claudia bangs, like the gong in the hall at Sotleigh. Bang – whoom! Lisa makes a nice silky noise, like streams or rain. Lisa. Lisa. If you say it over and over again it is not you any more, not me Lisa, I, me, but a word you never heard before. Lisa. Lisa.

The thing with legs, the wood thing, it suddenly occurs to her, will probably bite. She drops it quickly. She would stamp on it to make sure, horrid thing, but Claudia is watching. Claudia's eyes have black holes just like the eye in the tree, and inside Claudia there are little fierce animals that might come peeping out of those eyes, little biting animals, little animals with sharp teeth.

...s on tiptoes to see Claudia's eyes better and
...face turns cross.

...e upon a time a long time ago not as long ago as all that
...went to the beach with Claudia. She went to the beach in
...laudia's car. The trees beside the road went past the car
sha-sha-sha-sha and the hedges slid about and then there was
the beach and the sea rushing at you, too wet too deep too
rough. Claudia made you get inside a yellow rubber ring and
go out of your depth. It's all right, said Claudia, you're
perfectly all right, I've got you, I won't let you go. And
underneath you there is nothing but water deep deep water
with fishes in it and if Claudia lets you go you will sink to the
bottom. All that was a long time ago. Quite a long time ago.

She will spread butter on Rex's back and make him into a
sandwich. A dog sandwich. First butter and then jam. The
berries on that bush can be the jam. But first the butter . . . lots
and lots of butter. If she does not listen to Claudia, if she does
not answer, Claudia will stop asking things and disappear.
Whoosh! Whoosh into the air she will disappear like magic,
like the smoke from her cigarette melting melting going away
into nothingness, emptiness. You can walk through the smoke,
the yellow sunny smoke, you can push it away with your
hands, walk through it like through water.

She will magic Claudia away like the smoke. She tells Rex
that she is magicking Claudia.

That Lisa – that Lisa fettered by ignorance but also freed by
it – is as dead now as ammonites and belemnites, as the figures
in Victorian photographs, as the Plymouth settlers. Irretrievable also for the Lisa of today, who must grope with the rest of
us for that distant self, that other self, that ephemeral teasing
creature. The Lisa of today is an anxious busy woman going on
for forty trying to cope with two truculent adolescent sons and
a husband generally referred to as a prominent local estate
agent and in my view a ripe example of British degeneracy
between the Age of Macmillan and the Age of Thatcher. To
these have we sunk. Harry Jamieson has a damp handshake,

damp opinions steeped in the brine of the local Rotary Association and the *Daily Telegraph*, an appalling homestead on the outskirts of Henley with tennis court, swimming-pool and sweep of gravel that apes the country estate to which he aspires. I have not spent more than half a dozen hours in his company since the wedding. This, let me say, out of charity as much as self-preservation: the poor man is terrified of me. At the very sight of me his vowels falter, his forehead glistens, his hands dispensing gin and tonic or Pimms No. 1 fumble with ice-cubes, send glasses flying, cut themselves with the lemon knife. When I want to see Lisa I take her out to lunch in London, leaving Harry Jamieson to the tranquillity of Rotarian dinners, the golf club and the local Bench.

Why did she marry him? Ah, why indeed. Here I go again – pondering the curious forces that weld two people together, send them clamped to one another down the years. I should imagine that in this instance the fault is mine as much as anyone's. Had I not been as I am, Lisa would not have felt impelled, at nineteen, to grab at the status of marriage, at a world of her own, at the first likely young man to come along.

Naturally, I attended the wedding. So did her father.

Claudia stands face to face with Jasper, in the centre of a discreet vacuum; they are pruriently eyed by the other guests.

'Well,' she says. 'So here you are.'

'Here I am. And here are you. You're looking very well, Claudia.'

There are touches of grey to his hair. He has still that slightly rumpled look – expensive suit in need of a press, tie askew, ash on his sleeve. She takes a deep whiff of him. 'I hear you've got a new girl friend. And that they're getting younger all the time. That's a bad sign – you used to be more stylish.'

This he ignores. He waves his glasses at the room. 'Who are all these people?'

'The *jeunesse dorée* of Henley,' says Claudia.

'We should circulate, I suppose.'

'Circulate away.'

He smiles, his sexual confiding smile, and she feels herself curdle with irritation and desire.

Jasper sees, across this roomful of dowdy strangers, Claudia. Claudia in a red dress, unhatted amid the veils and feathers, wonderfully inappropriate. They advance upon each other. He stands considering her, remembering her, savouring her. 'I see your last book all over the place, Claudia.'

'So I should hope.'

'Are you well?'

'Fine.'

'Is this young man . . . adequate?'

'He seems,' says Claudia, 'reasonable enough.'

'Lisa looks splendid.'

'No she doesn't. She's washed out, as usual, and that dress is a disaster. Your mother's doing.'

He glances over her shoulder and sees his mother, valiantly smiling and greeting. 'We should circulate.'

'Circulate away,' says Claudia. She looks at him, and he decides suddenly that he will not go back to London tonight after all.

'Have dinner with me?'

'Not on your life,' snaps Claudia.

He shrugs. 'Someone expecting you?'

'Mind your own business, Jasper.'

At which point what had been a whim becomes a necessity; he puts his hand on hers, to take her glass. 'Let me get you another drink, Claudia.'

And Lisa, so clenched that she feels she might well burst – out of her own thin body, out of the heavenly tussore silk dress Granny Branscombe ordered from Harrods – sees *them* standing together in the middle of the room (people furtively staring . . .) and her stomach churns. Are they having a row? If they are not having a row that is possibly even worse. She chews her lip and her heart thumps and the glory of the day is dimmed. She wishes they had not come, that they would go away, that they

48

did not exist. Her mother hasn't bothered to get a hat, and her father is not wearing morning dress like Harry's father, just an ordinary suit. But even so they look more glamorous than everyone else, larger and brighter and more interesting.

Jasper and I spent the night together in a hotel in Maidenhead, quarrelled over breakfast and did not see one another again for two years. Just like old times. The sex was prolonged and memorable; the quarrel also. It centred on Jasper's current activities as a television mogul. He was the power behind the lavish series recently screened which presented a dramatised history of the last war. A fictional figure, a young officer, was followed in his progress through various theatres of war, from the Balkans to the Far East, against a background of enacted scenes of history – Churchill's War Cabinet, D-Day, Yalta . . . The enterprise was much praised and discussed; it was to be the forerunner of many such glossy, expensive productions, meticulously reconstructing the recent past. Jasper was purring with satisfaction. He sought a tribute from me. I said 'I detested it.' He asked why. I told him: because it diminished the past, turned history into entertainment. Opinionated and dogmatic as ever, said Jasper, the trouble with you is you have no flexibility of mind; this is a new medium. The emotional temperature rose. I said that it was indeed, and it enabled people like him to make a lot of money out of the suffering of others. You, snapped Jasper, take royalties on your books, which deal with similar matters. I held forth about the difference between history as reasoned analysis and history as spectacle. He said my books were overblown flashy stuff; he said I was jealous. He dragged in that film about Cortez. Different, I said, I was merely an onlooker. We slammed at each other to and fro across the starched white tablecloth of some flowery riverside pub while waitresses cowered against the walls. And eventually he said, 'You're absurdly overheated about this, Claudia. You seem to take the series as a personal affront. Why, one asks oneself.' I got up and walked out. Stupid thing to do.

Claudia, alone, sits before the television. The room is warm and quiet; the curtains are drawn, shutting out rain and traffic; she has a glass of wine to hand and her feet up, the day's work is done. The titles roll, the story begins. It is both a public story and a private one; the young hero, called up in 1939, is seen saying farewell to his fiancée and his mother, the German army rolls into France, Churchill confers with his advisers. And the telling, too, has two dimensions. There is the expensive fiction, with its accomplished actors, its considered production, its attention to every detail from the precise sheen of the hair oil on the young hero's head to the dents in the NAAFI tea-urns and the background rattle of a Jeep engine. And slotted into this are clips of film, looking in contrast somehow amateurish, quaint and not quite real – shots of bucking guns, silent running soldiers, lines of tanks or lorries trooping in at one side of the picture and out at the other. Fiction is in full warm colour, the actors have pink faces, there is green grass and blue sky; reality is black and white, the young soldiers grinning and waving on the deck of a ship have white faces, the sea is black and desert grey. Claudia sips her wine and watches intently – she notes the pack of Players cigarettes that the hero takes from his battle-dress pocket and the tilt of his fiancée's saucer hat; the sticky scent of nostalgia is trapped there behind the glass screen. She observes a black file of Italian prisoners trudging through the grey desert, black smoke streaming from a crashed plane, white smoke puffing from the gun of a tank.

The story that she is watching has, now, a third dimension, that is both more indistinct and yet clearer by far. This dimension has smell and feel and touch. It smells of Moon Tiger, kerosene, dung and dust. Its feelings are so sharp that Claudia gets up, slams the television into silence and sits staring at the blank pane of glass, where the story rolls on.

'History,' Jasper spat across the breakfast table in Maidenhead, 'is after all in the public domain.'

Oh, it is indeed. That's just the trouble, as the wretched public has been finding out, century after century. And of course he has a point – historians reap their royalties so why not Jasper and his like? It is only opinionated dogmatic bitches like me who are going to argue that there are certain sanctities, that by the time we have reduced everything to entertainment we shall find that it was no joke after all.

Jasper got rich. He had been comfortable enough before; now he was wealthy. On the boards of film companies and merchant banks, adviser to this and that, in demand everywhere; admired, disliked, fawned upon, mistrusted.

I published my Tito book, five years' work, and received much attention. Jasper wrote. 'Congratulations, my dear. "People in glasshouses . . ."'

Enough of Jasper. It should be clear by now how he fits into the scheme of things. Lover to begin with, sparring partner always, father of my child; our lives sometimes fusing, sometimes straying apart, always connected. I loved him once, but cannot remember how that felt.

I was talking earlier about language. I have put my faith in language – hence the panic when a simple word eludes me, when I stare at a piece of flowered material in front of a window and do not know what name to give it. Curtain. Thank God. I control the world so long as I can name it. Which is why children must chase language before they do anything else, tame the wilderness by describing it, challenge God by learning His hundred names. 'What's that called?' Lisa used to ask me. 'And that? And that?'

What I could offer Lisa was not the conventional haven of maternal love and concern but my mind and my energy. If she had not acquired these genetically then I was quite prepared to show her how to think and act. I was no good at kissing away tears or telling bedtime stories – any mother can do that: my uses were potentially far more significant.

She was a disappointment to me. And I, presumably, to her. I looked for my own *alter ego*, the querying rebellious maverick child I had been myself; Lisa looked for a reassuring clothes-shopping sherry-drinking figure like the mothers of her school friends. As she grew older I felt more and more her silent stare, each time I visited her at Sotleigh, took her over to Beaminster to stay with my mother, or had her in the flat in London for a couple of days. There, she would wander around, a skimpy pallid little figure standing in doorways or perching on a sofa. I bought her books. I took her to museums and art galleries; I tried to encourage opinion and curiosity. Lisa, growing longer of limb and less flexible of mind, became ordinary. She began to bore me. And I sensed her disapproval. I have attracted disapproval all my life. Usually it leaves me indifferent, occasionally it delights me. But the disapproval of a child is oddly unsettling. I would look up from my desk and see Lisa hanging on a curtain, chewing a fingernail, eyeing me. She is frozen thus in the mind's eye, many times over, preserved in those hours that both our lives contain. Recollections that we barely share. My hours and Lisa's are different; as different as I am different from Lisa.

'Go and read the book I gave you,' says Claudia, her pen working to and fro across the paper.

'I've been reading it.'

'Then ...' Claudia pauses, scans what she has written, ponders. She looks up. At Lisa – intrusive distracting little shadow at the window. 'Don't bite your fingernails like that, darling. And don't pull the curtain.'

Lisa is silent. Her finger falls from her mouth, her hand from the curtain. Otherwise she does not move.

Claudia reaches for another sheet of paper, writes. 'Please, Lisa, go and find something to do. I'm busy. I have to deal with these letters. Later we'll go out.'

'I don't know what to do,' says Lisa, after a minute ... two minutes.

No more of this, thinks Claudia, next time I'll get a girl from an agency to take her to the park, the Zoo, anything ... You need a certain mentality to cope with children. I don't have it. Thank God.

Claudia's fingernails are pink. Bright pink like sugar mice. If you had fingernails like that you would be like Claudia; you could do what you liked and say what you like and go where you liked. You would be busy busy all the time talking to your friends on the telephone, coming in going out back later tell the porter to get us a taxi darling, put your coat on hurry hurry.

If you bite your fingernails no one will want to marry you, Granny says. No one has ever married Claudia. Jasper and Claudia did not get married because they didn't love each other enough, Claudia says. You have to love someone very much before you marry them. If they had bitten fingernails you wouldn't want to marry them even if you loved them. You cannot paint your fingernails pink until you are grown-up, which is never. On Claudia's dressing-table there are little bottles with different kinds of pink – Pink Clover and Blush Pink and Hot Pink and Hawaiian Red. On Granny's dressing-table there is Eau de Cologne and Pond's Cold Cream and the Maison Pearson hairbrush and the mirror with the silver handle.

'Find something to do,' says Claudia. I can't, shouts Lisa, I can't I can't I can't I don't know where to find it I don't know where to look I want pink fingernails like yours I want to be you not me I want to make you look at me I want you to say Lisa how pretty you are.

▲▲▲▲▲▲▲▲▲▲▲▲▲▲

5

▼▼▼▼▼▼▼▼▼▼▼▼▼▼

'God,' she says, 'is an unprincipled bastard, wouldn't you agree?'

And the nurses, who are aged twenty-one and twenty-four, freeze for an instant amid their deft tucking and folding and heaving. They exchange quick knowing glances. 'Goodness,' says the fair nurse. 'That's a funny thing to say. Do you want tea or coffee, Miss Hampton?'

'Come,' says Claudia. 'You can't work in a place like this and never have given the matter a thought. Is He or isn't He?'

'Oh, I'm not religious,' says the dark nurse. 'Not a bit. My mum is, though, she goes to church. Tea or coffee, dear?'

'Well, I hope she knows what she's about,' says Claudia. 'Tea. No sugar.'

I would never have agreed to Lisa being christened. Jasper wouldn't have cared one way or the other. The grandmothers, in cunning collusion, had it done without mentioning the matter, smuggling her along to the vicar at Sotleigh (and a nice little tea-party for a few old friends after, I don't doubt). I found out by accident, months later, and rounded on them both. 'What's this?' I said. 'Spiritual vaccination? A bit of crafty life insurance? And who asked me?' They defended themselves according to their lights. 'We didn't ask you because you were so busy,' said Mother. 'And we knew you

54

wouldn't want to come.' Lady Branscombe sighed, 'Claudia dear . . . We just thought it would be nice. The poor little pet – one wants to do everything one can for her. And the vicar would have been so hurt not to be asked.' Lisa was enrolled in the Church of England in order not to give offence and so that Lady Branscombe could get out the family christening robe and the Crown Derby tea service. 'Well,' said Jasper, 'it does no positive harm, I daresay.' Oh no, none at all; just as well to belong to several clubs, you never know which may come in useful.

'Incidentally,' says Claudia, 'have you ever resigned from the Church?'

Lisa jumps, and lowers the book she has been reading; her mother's eyes are still closed, her sharp thin nose points still at the ceiling, but she is not, evidently, asleep.

'You're awake . . . I hadn't realised.'

'Ah,' says Claudia. 'Is that what I am? I sometimes wonder.'

Lisa closes the book. She rises, smooths her dress, and goes to stand looking down on Claudia. It occurs to her that she has not often before looked on Claudia from above. She asks if there is anything Claudia needs. Should she call the nurse?

'No,' says Claudia. 'I see quite enough nurses. You haven't answered my question.'

'I don't often go to church,' says Lisa, 'if that's what you mean. Just occasionally – Christmas, special services at the boys' school, that sort of thing.'

'It isn't what I meant,' says Claudia.

Lisa considers Claudia's face, which is the colour of yellowed ivory, in which the eyes lie within deep violet sockets; beneath the puckered skin she can see the bones of Claudia's skull. 'I'm not sure that I believe in God.'

'Oh I do,' says Claudia. 'Who else could bugger things up so effectively?'

A nurse puts her head round the door – the fair nurse, aged twenty-one. 'Everything all right?'

'Fine,' says Lisa. 'Thank you.'

'She's having one of her good days. Nice and chatty.'

The door closes. Claudia opens one eye, checks the nurse's departure, stares up at the ceiling. 'Tell me what you've been doing.'

'Well,' says Lisa. 'It was the boys' half-term last weekend so Harry took them to a rugger match. And on the Saturday evening we all went to the theatre – the RSC *King Lear*. Very good. And dinner after at Rules – a treat for Tim's birthday. And . . . um . . . let's see . . .'

And on Monday afternoon I visited the man who has been my lover for four years now and of whom you know nothing nor ever will. Not because you would disapprove but because you would not. And because since I was a small child I have hidden things from you: a silver button found on a path, a lipstick pilfered from your handbag, thoughts, feelings, opinions, intentions, my lover. You are not, as you think, omniscient. You do not know everything; you certainly do not know me. You judge and pronounce; you are never wrong. I do not argue with you; I simply watch you, knowing what I know. Knowing what you do not know.

My lover is called Paul. I have told him about you, and about Jasper; up to a point, insofar as it is possible for another person to do so, he understands. He would like to meet you, out of interest. Perhaps one day I will bring him here, just to look – through that round glass porthole in the door. You would not see him.

' "Let us pray . . ." ' says Claudia. 'Huh! Twice in my life have I prayed, and a fat lot of good it did me. Or anyone.'

God shall have a starring role in my history of the world. How could it be otherwise? If He exists, then He is responsible for the whole marvellous appalling narrative. If He does not, then the very proposition that He might has killed more people and exercised more minds than anything else. He dominates the stage. In His name have been devised the rack, the thumbscrew, the Iron Maiden, the stake; for Him have people been crucified, flayed alive, fried, boiled, flattened; He has generated the Crusades, the pogroms, the Inquisition and more wars than I can number. But for Him there would not be the *St Matthew Passion*, the works of Michelangelo and Chartres Cathedral.

So how am I to present Him – this invisible all-pervasive catalyst? How am I to suggest to my reader (no informed enlightened reader – a visitor from outer space, let us say) the extraordinary fact that for much of recorded time most people have been prepared to believe in the presidency over all things of an indefinable unassuageable Power?

I shall take a building. A building shaped like a cross, furnished neither for habitation nor defence. I shall multiply this building by a thousand, by ten thousand, by a hundred thousand. It may be as small as a single room; it may soar into the sky. It may be old or it may be new; it may be plain or it may be rich; it may be of stone or it may be of wood or it may be of brick or of mud. This building is in the heart of cities and it is in the wild places of the earth. It is on islands and in deserts and upon mountains. It is in Provence and Suffolk and Tuscany and Alsace and in Vermont and Bolivia and the Lebanon. The walls and furnishings of this building tell stories; they talk of kings and queens and angels and devils; they instruct and they threaten. They are intended to uplift and to terrify. They are an argument made manifest.

The argument is another matter. What I am trying to demonstrate at this point is the amazing legacy of God – or the possibility of God – by way not of ideas but of manipulation of the landscape. Churches have always seemed to me almost irrefutable evidence. They make me wonder if – just possibly – I might be wrong.

Which is how I came once to pray. To kneel down in St George's Pro-Cathedral, Cairo and ask a putative God for forgiveness and help. I was thirty-one.

She comes in from the glare and disorder outside – the heat, the rattle of trams and gharries, the people and carts and animals, the Cairo smell of dung and kerosene – into the calm and relative cool of the cathedral. Women in silk and crêpe-de-chine, gloved and hatted, smile discreetly at one another. Army officers – big bold moustached buccaneers crackling with khaki and leather – lay their caps on adjoining seats and bend for a moment with knee to ground and hand before eyes. Claudia, alone, furtive, reluctant and wretched, takes a place at the back, in the shadow of a pillar. She keeps on her sunglasses – defiant disguise.

The rituals of the Church of England are observed. The Lord is praised and besought and worshipped. Chairs scrape, dresses rustle, shoes squeak on the stone floor. Flies crawl upon sweating skin and are surreptitiously slapped. The Bishop seeks God's protection for British soldiers, sailors and airmen and a speedy victory in the Western Desert. 'Amen . . .' murmur the bowed heads – firm male voices, clear genteel female ones.

And Claudia makes her own silent isolated squirming intercession. O God, she says, or Whoever or Whatever, to this have I come, in my misery. I do not know what You are or if You are, but I am no longer sufficient unto myself and someone has got to do something for me. I can bear it no longer. Let him not be dead. Let him not be lying blown apart in the desert. Let him not be rotting out there in the sun. Above all let him not be dying slowly of thirst and wounds, unable to call out, overlooked by the ambulance units. If necessary, let him be taken prisoner. That I will tolerate. But please, O please, let him no longer be missing believed killed.

'Forgive us our trespasses . . .'

Claudia's silent voice hesitates. All right then, even that. Forgive me my trespasses. If such they are.

'I believe in God the Father, God the Son, God the Holy Ghost . . .'

Even that. All that. If You do Your part.

And a collection is taken for the children of the Coptic Orphanage in Heliopolis and the congregation prays once more ('Grant us Victory, O Lord, and enlighten our enemies . . .') and rises to its feet. They pass out of the cathedral, the silk and cotton dresses, the uniforms, the tropical suits, and into the tree-lined boulevard by the Nile. Claudia walks quickly through them, looking at no one, and crosses the road to be alone. She walks towards the bridge. She stands for a few moments staring across the river towards Gezira, at the grey-green feathering of palms and casuarinas, the glittering water, the white curve of a felucca sail. This is a land ridden by gods, she thinks. A god for every need. She adds, now, some further prayers. She casts prayers to the dry desert wind, indiscriminately.

Lisa sits watching Claudia, who may or may not be asleep. There is no telling; Claudia's eyes are closed but once or twice her lips twitch. When before has Claudia ever been thus? Lisa cannot remember illness, incapacity; it is as though you saw a familiar tree felled. Lisa does not think about possible outcomes because a world in which Claudia is not cannot be imagined. Claudia simply is, ever has been and always will be.

Lisa thinks about love. She loves her sons. She loves her lover. She loves in an eery way her husband. Does she love Claudia? Does Claudia love her, come to that?

These are questions she cannot answer, or does not wish to answer. What is between her and Claudia is, after all, inevitable. There is nothing to be done about it, nor ever has been. She knew that long ago, with the relentless vision of a child.

Lisa has read Claudia's books; Claudia would be surprised to learn this. Lisa has, tucked away somewhere, a brown envelope with two or three newspaper pictures of Claudia. There is also a long article about Claudia. 'Profile' it is headed, and yes, there is Claudia's profile, not pared down and yellow as it is today but delicate against a velvet hanging, elegantly posed and lit by some smart photographer. The text below is less carefully flattering: 'Claudia Hampton attracts controversy. As a non-professional historian – a "populariser" – she has been loftily disdained by some academics, angrily refuted by others. The disdain enrages her – "Just because I've had the nerve to go it alone instead of settling for the comfortable insurance policy of an academic stipend they think they can patronise" – the refutations she enjoys, they give her the chance to fight back. "I love a good swashbuckle in print. Anyway, I usually win." She cites her sales figures – "And who persuades the general public to read history? People like me – not the Eltons and the Trevor-Ropers." Nevertheless, for all her defiance, Claudia Hampton has some literary scars to show. Reviewers have frequently condemned her out of her own lush and – it must be said – frequently imprecise and contradictory prose. "Technicolor history", "the Elinor Glyn of historical biography", "the preaching of an autodidact"; this is the language her critics have used.'

Lisa's view of all this is an impartial one. She has in fact found the books more readable than she expected; that they are flawed she is quite prepared to believe. She knows Claudia, after all; she knows Claudia can be wrong about simple basic things. Claudia has always been wrong about Lisa.

For Claudia has never seen Lisa detached from Claudia. Lisa is extinguished by Claudia, always has been; even now, in the alien dispassionate hospital room she sits warily, awaiting Claudia's next move. Claudia snuffs Lisa out – drains the colour from her cheeks, deprives her of speech or at least all speech to which anyone might pay attention, makes her shrink an inch or two, puts her in her place. The other Lisa is not like that. The other Lisa, the Lisa unknown to Claudia, is positive while not assertive, is prettier, sharper, a good cook, a competent mother, an adequate if not exemplary wife. She knows now that she married too young too quickly the wrong man, but has found ways of making the best of the situation. She has also discovered that she is good at deft unruffled organization; for the last five years she has been indispensable secretary to the private practice of a top-flight surgeon, which is how she met her lover, who is also a doctor. Eventually, one day, when the boys are older, Lisa and her lover may marry, if she can persuade herself that Harry would be all right, would get over it, would find himself someone else.

It is getting dark in the hospital room; the winter afternoon is lapping at the windows. Lisa gets up, puts the light on, wonders about drawing the curtains, starts to gather her belongings. As she puts an arm into her coat Claudia opens her eyes.

'Don't get me wrong,' says Claudia. 'A preoccupation with God doesn't mean I consider myself about to meet Him. It's entirely abstract.'

Her face, suddenly, contorts. The lips pinch and tighten. A hand crawls across the sheet. Lisa says, 'Are you all right?'

'No,' says Claudia. 'But who is?'

Lisa is halted, one arm into her coat, the other out. She is seized by the oddest feeling. For a moment or two she cannot even identify it. She stands looking at Claudia. She recognises, now, the emotion. She is feeling sorry for Claudia; pity grabs her, like hunger, or illness. She has felt sorry for people before, naturally. But never for Claudia. She lays a hand, for a moment, on Claudia's arm. 'I'll have to go,' she says. 'I'll come in again on Friday.'

When I look at Lisa now I see the shadow of middle age on her face. This is disconcerting. One's child, after all, is forever young. A girl, perhaps, a young woman even – but that hardening of the features, that softening of the body, that hint that time past is levelling up with time ahead . . . dear me, no. I look with surprise at this home counties matron, wondering who she is – and then from the eyes round which spread little vulnerable fans of wrinkles there stares at me the eight-year-old, and the sixteen-year-old, and the one-year-wedded Lisa with red shrieking baby.

It becomes more and more difficult to credit Lisa with being a quarter Russian. Somewhere within and behind this quintessentially middle-class middle-England figure in her Jaeger suit and floppy-bowed silk shirt and her neat polished shoes lies the most tormented people in the history of the world. Somewhere in Lisa's soul, though she knows little of it and cares less, are whispers of St Petersburg, of the Crimea, of Pushkin, of Turgenev, of million upon million enduring peasants, of relentless winters and parched summers, of the most glorious language ever spoken, of samovars and droshkys and the sad sloe-eyed faces of a thousand icons. Blood will out – I believe that as profoundly though not as fearfully as poor Lady Branscombe, doing her best to forget her granddaughter's unfortunate ancestry (and all her fault, too, poor Isabel, bearing for ever after the guilt of that youthful Parisian infatuation). Lisa carries in her spirit matters she knows not of. I find that interesting. I find that enthralling, indeed. I look at Lisa and wolves howl across the steppe, the blood flows at Borodino, Irina sighs for Moscow. All derivative, all in the mind – the confection of fact and fantasy that is how we know the world. Nevertheless, Lisa had a Russian grandfather, and that signifies.

Jasper's father appears to have been an excellent reason for the Russians to have a revolution: a man of total moral fecklessness who never did a day's work in his life and disposed of the family fortunes – as much of them as had been left by his own father – before he was thirty. He spent the early part of his life in Paris, Baden Baden and Venice, with occasional sorties to Russia to sell off a few more versts or the St Petersburg mansion; after the divorce he lived in somewhat reduced circumstances on the Riviera, augmenting his funds as best he could by gambling or attaching himself to rich women. Jasper's late adolescent fascination with him soon declined: Jasper meant to be a success; Sasha, a glamorously bohemian figure to a sixteen-year-old schoolboy, was seen differently by the twenty-year-old undergraduate – as a seedy sponger impressive only to naïve American heiresses and minor French society hostesses. After 1925 Jasper rarely saw his father. I met him only once. It was in 1946. Sasha had turned up in London, having spent as comfortable a war as he could manage in Menton, somehow avoiding internment, and now in search of funds and useful contacts of which his mildly celebrated son seemed the most promising. Jasper gave him lunch at his club and asked me to join them. Sasha was seventy, and beginning to look it: a face crumpling into folds, ravaged hooded eyes, the foxy smile of the professional charmer. He kissed my hand

and said the things he had been saying to every woman he met for fifty years. And I, maliciously, insisted he take the most comfortable chair and asked with concern if the cold weather was bothering him. Sasha, no fool, adjusted his approach to that of gallant father-figure – called me 'my dear', applauded Jasper's successes with sycophantic gusto, invited us both to the villa on the Riviera. We never went, needless to say. Jasper found his father an embarrassment; I thought him creepy. But I can see him still, in his carefully preserved pre-war cashmere overcoat and his Hermès scarf, a down-at-heel survivor, the ashes of a class and of an age. And after that lunch Jasper and I had a disagreement: an interesting skirmish, a preliminary to our later more full-blooded engagements.

'So . . .' says Jasper. 'That's him, the old fraud. What you expected?' Claudia, brilliant in emerald green, sails along Pall Mall, attracting discreet glances; he takes her arm, parrying the glances.

'Up to a point.'

'I slipped him a cheque for a hundred quid,' says Jasper. 'Let's hope he'll take himself off quietly now, at least for a year or two.'

'Hm,' says Claudia.

'What?'

'I said – hm.' She looks ahead blandly. Not at Jasper, who feels that tingle of exasperation that only Claudia can induce. A *frisson* that is inextricably mixed with the creep of sexual desire.

They pause at the corner of St James's. 'You have his hands,' says Claudia. 'And something about the mouth.'

'I hardly think so.'

Claudia shrugs. 'You can't dismiss ancestry.'

'I am what I make myself,' says Jasper, stepping into the road. 'Come on, we can cross.' Claudia has dropped his arm to take something from her bag. He walks ahead. Claudia remains. Cars and taxis divide them. Jasper halts on the opposite pavement. Claudia, blowing her nose, strolls across.

'Plus,' she says, 'what you have been endowed with. Sasha has endowed you with a rather dramatic past. Don't you find that interesting?'

'Not particularly.'

'You're not interested in a thousand turbulent years of history?'

Claudia's voice – clear, carrying – rings out. One or two bowler-hatted heads turn.

'It has nothing to do with me,' says Jasper. 'And you're being portentous.'

'I do not see,' says Claudia, forging now up St James's a step or two ahead, 'how you can be so majestically egotistical as to place yourself in total detachment from your antecedents just because you find your father inadequate.'

Jasper is now suddenly glowing hot, although the day is chill December. He catches her up. 'You're talking rather loudly, if you don't mind me saying so, Claudia. And if I have to take on the whole of Russia, then you presumably bear the cross of generations of torpid Dorset farmers. Hardly your style, darling.'

'Oh, I don't know,' says Claudia. 'They probably account for certain qualities of endurance.' She smiles sweetly at Jasper, who is scowling.

'And what have you ever endured?'

'More than you'll ever know.'

And Jasper, who has known Claudia now eight months and nine days, struggles furiously with his feelings. She maddens him; she is the most interesting woman he has ever met; he would gladly be without her; he cannot wait to be in bed with her again.

'Thank you for my nice lunch,' says Claudia.

Why have the winds of all the Russias blown into the brown leather brown curtained brown floored dining-room of Jasper's club? How is it that this spurious devious old tramp from Monte Carlo bears with him a whiff of genuine incense, an eery echo of another time another place? Of things the old sham

64

knows nothing about, thinks Claudia. What does he know of history? And I bet he's never read Tolstoy.

The point is, of course, that I have. What he brings is in my head, not his. But isn't that interesting? Time and the universe lie around in our minds. We are sleeping histories of the world.

'One of these days,' she says, 'I'm going to write a vastly pretentious book. I'm going to write a history of the world.'

But Jasper is already half way across St James's, striding imperiously ahead. She pauses on the traffic island, blowing her nose, considering Jasper's arrogance, Jasper's obstinacy, Jasper's potent body. She joins Jasper on the pavement and continues the discussion, which is amusing because Jasper is getting annoyed. Jasper will have none of either nature or nurture because Jasper is sublimely egotistical, and the egotist of course sees himself as self-propagated, he can afford no debts or attributions. His achievements are his own.

'Thank you for my nice lunch,' she says.

'Don't mention it.'

'I must be off,' she says. 'Lots to do . . .'

'When will I see you?'

'Mm . . .' says Claudia. 'Give me a ring . . .' She is tempting providence; Jasper if sufficiently irritated may not ring for a day, two days, three four days, and that would be bad – oh very bad. But *amour-propre* is more central than anxiety; never will Claudia allow Jasper to have her at a disadvantage.

'Dinner tomorrow,' says Jasper. It is a statement, not a question.

'Maybe . . .' says Claudia.

▲▲▲▲▲▲▲▲▲▲▲▲▲▲

6

▼▼▼▼▼▼▼▼▼▼▼▼▼▼

I've grown old with the century; there's not much left of either of us. The century of war. All history, of course, is the history of wars, but this hundred years has excelled itself. How many million shot, maimed, burned, frozen, starved, drowned? God only knows. I trust He does; He should have kept a record, if only for His own purposes. I've been on the fringes of two wars; I shan't see the next. The first preoccupied me not at all; this thing called War summoned Father and took him away for ever. I saw it as some inevitable climatic effect: thunderstorm or blizzard. The second lapped me up but spat me out intact. Technically intact. I have seen war; in that sense I have been present at wars, I have heard bombs and guns and observed their effects. And yet what I know of war seems most vivid in the head; when I lie awake at night and shudder it is not experience but knowledge that churns in the mind. There, but for the whim of God, went I – along with all those other millions casually wiped out: on the Somme, in France, Germany, Spain, the Balkans, Libya, Russia. In Russia . . . above all in Russia. That is where Sasha should have died respectably amid history, instead of coughing himself away with bronchitis and emphysema in a Monte Carlo nursing home. He should have been a statistic, and then one could have responded to him. He should have been a part of those figures that freeze the blood: the million dead of Leningrad, the three million labour slaves from Belorussia and the Ukraine, the two million prisoners of Kiev, the quarter million maimed by frostbite, the twenty million give or take the odd man, woman or child who were simply no longer citizens of Russia or indeed of anywhere by 1945. Sasha should have been an old man in Smolensk or Minsk or Viazma or Gzhatsk or Rzhev, dying slowly in the frozen landscape while his home lay in rubble and the German hordes swept onwards. He should have been that bent rag-clad figure with a box on its back that shuffles through the lunar landscape of blitzed Murmansk in 1942, in a photograph I once saw; he should have been that other eternally surviving anonymous grey face, crouched over the shot bodies of wife and daughter in Smolensk or Minsk or Viazma or Gzhatsk or Rzhev.

It is in these words that reality survives. The snow, the twenty degrees below zero temperatures of the winter of 1941; the Russian prisoners herded into open-air pens and left till they died of either cold or starvation; the furnace of Stalingrad; the thirty destroyed cities, the seven million slaughtered horses, the seventeen million cattle, the twenty million pigs. And beyond the words the images: the skeletal buildings pared by fire to chimney stacks and naked walls; the bodies chewed by frost; the screaming faces of wounded men. This is the record; this is what history comes down to in the end; this is the language of war.

Not that other language – that lunatic language that lays a smokescreen of fantasy – that crazy language of generals and politicians: Plan Barbarossa, with its Wagnerian invocations; Operations Snowdrop, Hyacinth, Daffodil and Tulip dancing feyly towards Tobruk. That was the language I used to hear in Cairo, on the lips of the Eighth Army buccaneers – the laconic chat about Matildas and Honeys, coy disguise for several tons of mobile death-dealing metal, and the amiable euphemism whereby such things when hit did not explode (roasting alive their crew) but 'brewed up'. And it was a picnic, too, of course, and men did not die but bought it, were not shot but stopped one. The eccentricity of it occurs only with hindsight; at the time it seemed normal, even acceptable. Words were my business, but it wasn't the moment for close analysis of their implications – or at least not that kind of analysis. Communiqués from GHQ . . . briefings from the Press Officer . . . my own reports banged out on the portable Imperial that I still have. Those were the words I dealt in – a language that seems fossilised now, superseded by new jargons, new camouflages. I have lived since in the world of overkill and second strike and negative capability; the scenarios of future wars or probably the final war are preceded by their distracting code-words. Speech regenerates itself like the landscape; words die and others are born, just as buildings melt away and others take their place, as the sand blew over the carcasses of the Matildas and the Honeys and the Crusaders.

I have seen Cairo since the war years and that time seemed to shimmer as a mirage over the present. The Hiltons and the Sheratons were real enough, the teeming jerry-built dun-coloured traffic-ridden deafening city, but in my head was that other potent place, conjured up by the smell of dung and paraffin, the felt-shod tittuping sound of a donkey's hooves, kites floating in a Wedgwood blue sky, the baroque gaiety of Arabic script.

The place didn't look the same but it felt the same; sensations clutched and transformed me. I stood outside some concrete and plate-glass tower-block, picked a handful of eucalyptus leaves from a branch, crushed them in my hand, smelt, and tears came to my eyes. Sixty-seven-year-old Claudia, on a pavement awash with packaged American matrons, crying not in grief but in wonder that nothing is ever lost, that everything can be retrieved, that a lifetime is not linear but instant. That, inside the head, everything happens at once.

The terrace at Shepheard's is packed. There is not a table free, and round each table crowd three, four, five chairs, each its own society; the noise is an orchestration of languages. The suffragis with their trays of drinks weave their way between the tables and Claudia stalks among them. Taking her time, ignoring the blandishments of a pair of tipsy South Africans, the stare of a Free French officer, invitations to join a friend here, a group of acquaintances there. She knows many of these people; the rest are defined for her by dress and speech. Each one wears the regalia of occupation, race and creed.

This is medieval, she thinks – why did I never think of that before? She notes the gold insignia encrusting the sleeve of a naval officer, the red-banded hat dumped by a brigadier on his knee, the conferring red fezzes at another table. This is a bang-up-to-date nineteen-forty-one medieval urban scene; a structured world in which you can see who everyone is. Those are two Sephardic Jewish ladies and that is a Sikh officer and there is a tribe of three from the home counties. That man knows how to fly an aeroplane and that one is trained to command tanks and that girl knows how to dress a wound. And over there if I am not mistaken is this chap who might wangle me a ride up to the front if I play it right.

She smiles – the glossy lipsticked smile of the times. She approaches his table – a neat figure in white linen, bright coppery hair, high-heeled red sandals, bare sunburned legs – and he rises, pulls out a chair, clicks his fingers at the suffragi.

And looks appreciatively at the legs, the hair, the outfit which is not the get-up of the average woman press correspondent.

At least it is to be assumed that that is what he was doing since he tried later to get me into bed, as the price for a place in a transport plane going up to the desert next day. I didn't pay the price – or not quite – but I got the seat. I've no idea now what his name was; I see, vaguely, a ginger moustache and that dark brown leathery face they all had. He is neither here nor there – just some Ordnance chap who had clout when it came to transport – except that he is one of those vital hinges, the factor without which I would not have gone to Cyrenaica, would not have been in a truck that broke down, would not have been rescued from the middle of nowhere by two officers in a jeep one of whom . . .

Would not have sat in transcendent happiness on the terrace of the Winter Palace at Luxor, nor lain in misery in a hospital bed in Gezira, would not in short have become what I am. Not even the most maverick historian – myself, perhaps – would deny that the past rests upon certain central and indisputable facts. So does life; it has its core, its centre.

We reach, now, this core.

I arrived in Egypt alone in 1940; I was alone when I left in 1944. When I look at those years I look at them alone. What happened there happens now only inside my head – no one else sees the same landscape, hears the same sounds, knows the sequence of events. There is another voice, but it is one that only I hear. Mine – ours – is the only evidence.

The only private evidence, that is. So far as public matters go – history – there is plenty. Most of it is in print now; all those accounts of which general comes out of it best, who had how many tanks, who advanced where at which point and why. I've read them all; they seem to have little to do with anything I remember. From time to time I quarrel with a fact – a name or a date; mostly they just don't seem relevant. Which of course is an odd comment from one who has written that kind of book herself. I was interested enough in relevance at the time – I had to get a story to file. If I didn't pursue events and find out what was going on and get myself in a position to witness what was going on if possible I had no story to file. A tart cable from London would have ended my justification for being in the Middle East. But none of that seems important; it has melted away like the language of then or like the baroque balconied buildings of old Cairo supplanted by office blocks and sky-scrapers for tourists.

Gordon had said I would never make it as a war correspondent. All the more reason, of course, why I had to. As he pointed out, I was not, on the face of it, qualified. I had to push as I'd never pushed before. I pulled every string I knew of, trailed around to see everyone I'd ever known who might be able to help, and eventually got myself taken on as stringer for a Sunday newspaper and correspondent for one of the weeklies. I had to fight for it, and neither of them would pay me enough. I dipped into capital – the nest-egg I had from a grandmother – to have enough to live on in Cairo. And I was always on sufferance – both with the editors back in London and with my male colleagues in the Press Corps. I was as good as my last despatch. But the despatches were good. Of course, I made a point of sending them to Gordon; to say – see, I told you so . . . They used to reach him months late, training on some Scottish moor and then afterwards out in India and he used to write back, also months later, as though one were carrying on a conversation with a time-lag, correcting what he considered infelicities of style. We continued to quarrel – amiably enough – across continents. I didn't see him for over four years and by the time I did we had both been jolted into another incarnation of ourselves. We met on a platform at Victoria and he said, 'Christ! You've had your hair dyed! I had no idea it was so red. I'd been thinking of it as a sort of brown colour.' We didn't kiss; we stood there staring at each other. I said, 'Why have you got that mark on your cheek?' 'I had some disgusting skin disease in Delhi. My war wound. Where are yours?' I didn't answer.

Gordon was in Intelligence. Naturally. He spent most of his war in an office with occasional sorties to more insalubrious places. We both told each other what we saw fit about those years. Once Gordon said, 'I ran across a bloke who knew you in Egypt. He remembers meeting you in a hotel in Luxor. He had a drink with you and some uniformed boyfriend of yours.' I said, 'That would have been the Winter Palace, I imagine.' 'Who was the boyfriend?' 'There were two or three hundred thousand members of the armed forces stationed in and around Cairo at that point,' I said. 'You can take your pick.'

It certainly was the Winter Palace. I don't think there were any other hotels. We arrived off the night train from Cairo in which all the sleepers had been booked so we had to sit up through the hot trundling night squashed thigh to thigh sharing a compartment with a bunch of nurses on leave from the military hospital in Heliopolis and a padre who kept trying to

71

get up a game of whist. Eventually they all went to sleep and when the dawn came up – that translucent glowing desert dawn – we were the only ones awake and we watched the line of hills on the far side of the Nile go from pink to amber and the water turn sapphire blue. There were flights of white egrets and herons sitting hunched on the trees that overhung the bank and a black ibis posed like a sculpture on a sandbank. The fields in the cultivated mile or so between the river and the desert were bright with green clover or tall thick sugar-cane and they hummed with life – bare-legged fellaheen with their galabiehs looped up between their thighs, little figures of children in brilliant dresses – vermilion and crimson and lime – strings of camels and donkeys and buffalo. And the whole place seemed to be gently shifting – the grey-green feathery palms with their curving snakeskin trunks swaying and waving in the light desert wind. We sat holding hands and staring out of the window and it was like looking at a picture. A Breughel perhaps – one of those busy informative paintings full of detail, of people doing particular things, of a dog cocking a leg, a cat sitting in the sun, a child playing, those pictures where you feel you look into a frozen moment of time. I said that one of the things one never did was notice this place. See it for itself. For us it was nothing but a backdrop. 'It's a beautiful country,' I said. 'And we don't see it.'

And he said, 'We shall always see it.'

We got to Luxor and fought our way out of the station through the dragomen and the sellers of scarabs and black basilisk heads of Rameses the Second and flywhisks and each other's sisters and got a room at the Winter Palace. We went to bed and stayed there till the late afternoon. We lay naked on the bed with the midday sun slicing in stripes through the shutters; we made love more times than I would have thought possible. He had five days' leave. The first I had known of it was his voice on the phone asking if I could get away for a long weekend. He had been up at the front and he'd be going back there next week. Or to wherever the front by then was – that indeterminate confusion of minefields and dispositions of vehicles in the empty neutral sand. He once described it to me as more like a war fought at sea than on land, a sequence of advances and retreats in which the participants related only to each other and barely at all to the landscape across which they moved. A war in which there was nothing to get in the way – no towns, no villages, no people – and nothing tangible to gain or lose. In which you fought for possession of a barely detectable rocky ridge, or a map position. In which there were suddenly hundreds of thousands of men where there had been nothing, but still the place remained empty. He spoke of the desert as being like the board in some game in which opposing sides manoeuvred from square to square; I used the image in a despatch and got a pat on the back from London office and told him I should have given him a credit. He said he'd wait for that till after the war.

Eventually, at dusk, we got up and dressed and went down for a drink on the terrace overlooking the Nile. Maybe that was the point when I spoke to Gordon's acquaintance. If so, he is gone now; all that remains is the long low fawn shoulder of the hill above the Valley of the Kings with the sun going down behind it in a smoulder of gold and pink and turquoise. And the bland Egyptian evening sounds of ice chinking in glasses, the slap of the suffragis' slippers on the stone of the hotel terrace, the buzz of voices, laughter – the sounds of a hundred other evenings, at Gezira Sporting Club, the Turf Club, Shepheard's. But that evening – or the next or the next – is isolated in my head. I know that I sat on a cane chair, the pattern of the cane printing my flesh through my cotton dress, looking at the river, the white swooping sails of feluccas, the sunset sky in which presently glittered the brilliant enhanced stars of the desert. I know how I felt – richer, happier, more alive than ever before or ever since. It is feeling that survives; feeling and the place. There is no sequence now for those days, no chronology – I couldn't say at which point we went to Karnak, to the Colossus, to the tombs – they are simultaneous. It is a time that is both instant and frozen, like a village scene in a Breughel painting, like the walls of the tombs on which fly, swim and walk the same geese, ducks, fish, cattle that live in, on and beside the Nile today.

'The Pharaoh . . .' says the guide, indicating. 'See the pharaoh making sacrifice to the gods and godses. See the sacred *ankh*. See the wife of pharaoh. The wife of pharaoh is also sister of pharaoh. He is loving his sister.'

There is a faint stir of interest. The heat is appalling and the tomb stifling. 'Incest,' says the army padre. 'Quite acceptable in those days, apparently.' The two ATS girls announce that they will die if they stay in here much longer. 'Right then, Mustapha, let's push on, shall we?' says the padre. The small group shuffles through the sandy torch-lit gloom.

Claudia lingers. She looks at the handsome boyish figure of the pharaoh and his slim, sloe-eyed high-breasted consort.

'Fine couple,' says Tom.

'Yes.'

The beam of Tom's torch slides over a team of oxen, slaves carrying dead gazelles, a flight of duck erupting from a reed bed.

'Let's see them again,' says Claudia. The torch beam swoops and hovers. 'She's lovely. Is your sister pretty?'

'Jennifer? Good Lord – I've never thought about it. Yes, I suppose she is.' He laughs. 'But I shouldn't feel *that* way inclined.'

He puts his arm round her. 'Please be coming,' cries the guide from further along the dark corridor of the tomb. 'Lady and gentleman . . . please be coming now.'

Claudia continues to stare at the brilliant impervious figures, forever young, forever coupled.

'What are you thinking about?' he asks.

'Mm . . . nothing.' His arm is round her shoulders, the heat of him against her breast. She is so erotically possessed that she feels she may quite possibly take all her clothes off and lie down in the dust. He turns and kisses her, his tongue searching her mouth.

It had seemed, for the year or so in which I had been there, merely a backcloth, that country. I had been dropped into its heat and dust and smells and they became a fortuitous appendage to the more urgent matter of the war. You learned to cope with it – the discomforts and obstructions and hazards – and got on with what mattered. The British army superimposed itself on the landscape and the society: its lorries jammed the roads, its depots littered the delta from Cairo to Alexandria, its personnel filled the streets and cafés of Cairo with English voices. The speech of Lancashire, of Dorset, of the East End, of Eton and Winchester, rang around the mosques and bazaars, the Pyramids and the Citadel. Cairo, polyglot and multi-racial, both absorbed and ignored what had happened. At one level the place exploited and manipulated the situation, at another it simply went on doing what it had always done. The rich got richer; the poor continued to wade in the mud of the canals, make fuel out of buffalo dung and beg in the streets.

Perhaps I saw it for the first time that weekend in Luxor. It seems to me now that I did. I saw suddenly that it was beautiful. I saw the cluttered intense life of the fields and villages – a world of dust and water, straw and leaves, people and animals – and I saw the stark textural immensity of the desert, the sand carved by the wind, the glittering mirages. It had the delicacy of a water-colour – all soft grey-greens and pale blues and fawns and bright browns. Beautiful and indifferent; when you began to see it you saw also the sores round the mouths of children, the flies crawling on the sightless eyes of a baby, the bare ulcerated flesh on a donkey's back.

I saw it through him and with him. Now, he and that place are one, fused in the head to a single presence of his voice and his touch, those sights and those smells.

She lies awake in the small hours. On the bedside table is a Moon Tiger. The Moon Tiger is a green coil that slowly burns all night, repelling mosquitoes, dropping away into lengths of grey ash, its glowing red eye a companion of the hot insect-rasping darkness. She lies there thinking of nothing, simply being, her whole body content. Another inch of the Moon Tiger feathers down into the saucer.

Tom stirs. Claudia murmurs, 'Are you awake?'

'I'm awake.'

'You should have said. We could be talking.'

He lays a hand on her thigh. 'What should we talk about?'

'All the things there's never been time for. Practically everything.'

'We've spent about fifty hours together now. Since we met.'

'Forty-two,' says Claudia.

'You've counted?'

'Of course.'

There is a silence. 'I love you,' he says.

'Well, good,' says Claudia. 'So do I. Love you, I mean. Talk to me. Tell me things.'

'Very well. What sort of thing do you want me to tell you? Do you want my opinion of Aldous Huxley? My views on the League of Nations? We could find an area of disagreement – I know you enjoy a good dust-up.'

'Not right now. Let's talk about each other, that's all I'm interested in at the moment.'

'Me too,' says Tom. He takes her hand. They lie, side by side. Like, thinks Claudia, figures on tombs, or the bundled shapes of sarcophagi. The Moon Tiger gently fumes and glows; beyond the shuttered window is the hot black velvet night – the river, the desert.

Tom lights a cigarette. Two red eyes glow now in the dark room – the Moon Tiger and the Camel. 'People in our situation always think themselves unique. All the same . . . That we should both have fetched up out here . . .'

'Hostages to fortune,' says Claudia. 'Orphans of the storm.'

'Quite so. But what luck. I owe Hitler for you. What a thought.'

'Let's not think it,' says Claudia. 'Give it a more respectable name. Fate. Life. That sort of stuff.'

They lie, for a while, in silence. 'You tell me things,' says Tom. 'What a lot I don't know . . . Can you play the piano?

When did you learn to speak French? Why is there a scar on your knee?'

'Those are boring things. I don't want to. I want to be pampered. I want to lie here – for ever – listening to *you* talking. I want to fall asleep with you talking. You could tell me a story.'

'I don't know any stories,' says Tom. 'I'm a profoundly unimaginative fellow. I only know my own.'

'That'll do nicely,' says Claudia.

'If you insist. It's an unexceptional story, at that. Born in the home counties to parents of moderate but sufficient means. Father a schoolmaster, mother a . . . mother. Childhood marred only by unconfessed fear of large dogs and the patronage of my sister. Schooldays distinguished for inability to construe Latin and ineptitude with a cricket bat. Youth . . . Well, youth becomes perhaps marginally more interesting, our hero is seen to become somewhat less torpid, egocentric, introverted etc. – in fact to start paying a bit of attention to other people and indeed to show vaguely idealistic tendencies, desire to reform the world and so forth.' 'Ah,' sighs Claudia. 'One of those . . .' 'One of those. Do you disapprove?' 'Certainly not. Go on. What did you do about it?' 'All the usual innocent enthusiastic things. Joining worthy organisations. Attending political meetings. Reading books. Talking late into the night with like-minded cronies.' 'Innocent?' says Claudia. 'What's innocent about that? Practical, I'd call it.' 'Hush – this is my story, and I'll tell it my way. Autobiographers are entitled to editorial comment. So . . . Period of youthful social indignation culminating in a stint as reporter on a northern provincial paper – did you ever visit the north-east during the Depression?' Claudia ponders. 'If you have to think about it,' says Tom, 'then you didn't. It wonderfully concentrated the mind, I'll tell you that. Hampshire was never the same again. So anyway, fired by the dole queues I decided politics was the only career – I mean, it was obvious, at twenty-three, one would be able to set the world to rights in a trice, given the opportunity, quite simple, I had it all tied up, my personal manifesto –

education, opportunity, social welfare, re-distribution of income.' 'So . . .' says Claudia. 'Why . . .?' 'Why didn't it work out like that? Because as you and I both know now that is not how things are. Our feckless hero bites the dust as aspiring politician and looks around to see what comes next. Having grown older by a year or two and learned a little wisdom if not a lot. In fact, having realised that he is by and large an ignorant so-and-so and there is no prospect of confounding your enemies until you have the arguments with which to do it. So I thought I'd better keep my mouth shut and my eyes and ears open for a bit. An aunt left me a small legacy and I blew it on the fare to America. Have a look at the land of the free, I thought. Learn a thing or two. Look and listen. Earn a few bob writing the odd article. So I did. And came back older and wiser still.' 'Look here,' says Claudia. 'You're missing out great chunks of this story.' 'I know. We haven't got time for all of it. Not now. We're sticking to essentials. America. The mid-west. The south. Social outrage again, but more reflective now. Journalism. Sober, considered journalism. A few small successes in that line.' 'You should be doing what I'm doing,' says Claudia. 'In fact why didn't you . . .?' 'I wish you wouldn't anticipate. We haven't got to that bit yet. The Nazis are nothing more than a disagreeable noise across the Channel at the moment. And our hero rather fancies himself now as a traveller.' 'Stop saying our hero,' says Claudia. 'It sounds like the *Boy's Own Paper*.' 'What a well-read girl you are. I thought the reference might escape you. As I say, I fancied myself as a traveller. I sold pieces on the plight of the Greek peasantry or chicanery among Italian politicians and when I couldn't do that I hawked myself around travel agencies as a courier. Got around most of Europe that way. Went once to Russia. Was thinking it was about time to turn my attention to Africa, see how one's dreams come true? And then the disagreeable noises from across the Channel began to get louder. To become distinctly disturbing.' 'Yes,' says Claudia, 'I want to say something.' 'I thought you wanted me to do the talking?' 'I do. It's just that you leave out the interesting part.'

'I thought all this might be reasonably interesting.' 'It is,' says Claudia. 'But it's not very personal. I don't know much about how you're feeling. And,' she adds lightly, 'I don't know if you're doing all this on your own or with someone else.'

'Oh,' says Tom. 'Aha. I see. Well, I'll try to do better. I think I can tell you why it doesn't sound all that personal. All this time our hero ... sorry, sorry. All this time I had these grandiose ideas about public life and being hitched to one's times and so forth. I tended to think impersonally – a luxury of comfortable circumstances, as I'm well aware. But let me assure you' – and he slides a hand down her bare body – '... let me assure you all that has utterly changed. There's nothing like being hitched to one's times in a way one never anticipated to make one think very personally indeed. I think I've had enough of all this. Look, it's beginning to get light. There – you've had your story.' He turns towards her.

'Not quite,' says Claudia. 'You didn't say if ...'

'Entirely on my own,' says Tom. 'So far. Not for much longer, I rather hope.' He puts out a hand, traces the outline of her face with one finger. Claudia can just see, now, in the dawn glimmer, his eyes, his nose, his lips. 'I like this part of the story best,' she says.

'Me too,' says Tom. 'Oh, me too.'

And oh God, thinks Claudia, may it have a happy ending. Please may it have a happy ending. The Moon Tiger is almost entirely burned away now; its green spiral is mirrored by a grey ash spiral in the saucer. The shutters are striped with light; the world has turned again.

▲▲▲▲▲▲▲▲▲▲▲▲▲▲

7

▼▼▼▼▼▼▼▼▼▼▼▼▼▼

I cannot write chronologically of Egypt. Ancient Egypt. So-called ancient Egypt. In my history of the world – this realistic kaleidoscopic history – Egypt will have its proper place as the complacent indestructible force that has perpetuated itself in the form of enough carved stone, painted plaster, papyri, granite, gold leaf, lapis lazuli, bits of pot and fragments of wood to fill the museums of the world. Egypt is not then but now, conditioning the way we look at things. The image of the Sphinx is familiar to those who have never heard of pharaohs or dynasties; the new brutalism of Karnak is homely to anyone who grew up with 'thirties architecture.

Like anyone else, I knew Egypt before ever I went there. And when I think of it now – when I think of how I am going to invoke Egypt within the story of the world – I have to think of it as a continuous phenomenon, the kilted pharaonic population spilling out into the Nile valley of the twentieth century, the chariots and lotuses, Horus and Ra and Isis alongside the Mameluke mosques, the babbling streets of Cairo, Nasser's High Dam, the khaki convoys of 1942, the Edwardian opulence of Turkish mansions. Past and present do not so much co-exist in the Nile valley as cease to have any meaning. What is buried under the sand is reflected above, not just in the souvenirs hawked by the descendants of the tomb robbers but in the eternal, deliberate cycle of the landscape – the sun rising from the desert of the east to sink into the desert of the west, the spring surge of the river, the regeneration of creatures – the egrets and herons and wildfowl, the beasts of burden, the enduring peasantry.

In the Rameses Hilton a few years ago I met a man who was the biggest world-wide distributor of lavatory cisterns. Or so he claimed. A mid-westerner on the brink of retirement and a member of one of those groups of footloose geriatric Americans who stream through hotels from Dublin to Singapore. This man, unattached, picked me up in the bar, taking me for a bird of the same feather. 'What I don't get about these guys,' he said, easing his polyester-clad bum on to the stool next to mine, 'is the motivation. Lemme buy you a drink. Never mind the engineering, and believe me that's quite sumpin', it's the motivation gets me. All that, to get yourself buried.' I let him buy me a whisky and asked him if he was afraid of death. 'Sure I'm afraid of death. Everyone's afraid of death, aren't they?' 'The Egyptians weren't. They were concerned with the survival of the spirit. Or the soul – call it what you like. Not that that makes them unique, but it's a thing we've rather lost interest in nowadays.' He gave me a suspicious look – regretting the whisky; no doubt wondering what he'd landed himself with. 'You some kind of professor?' 'No,' I said. 'I'm a tourist, like you. What do you do?' And so he told me about the lavatory cisterns and we struck up something that while it could not be called a friendship was a sort of eery alliance because he was a robust, honest, not incurious man who liked someone to talk to and I was – not lonely, I have never been lonely – but alone. And thus it was in his incongruous company that I went for the second time and forty years later to Luxor, to the Valley of the Kings, to Esna and Edfu. And to the Pyramids and to the Citadel and to the bank of the Nile beside Kasr el Nil bridge where St George's Pro-Cathedral in which I once prayed no longer exists, replaced by a roaring flyover system for Cairo's unquenchable traffic. He is neither here nor there now, the American – I don't even remember his name – like that Ordnance officer on the terrace of Shepheard's, but like him he is forever tethered to a certain place, a certain time. His story – whatever his story is – was twined briefly with mine. In both our stories there is a temple wall before which we stand, screwing up our eyes against the hard brilliance of the sky above as the complex scenes carved in relief upon the stone resolve themselves into what they are – a chronicle of bloodshed. Half-naked soldiers are being decapitated, run through with spears, flattened by chariots. These scenes are repeated on the other three walls, to a height of twenty or thirty feet. The guide explains that this is both a record and a celebration of the pharaoh's various triumphs over his enemies. And there indeed is the pharaoh, several times over, bigger than everyone else, driving his chariot with casual ease, reins in one hand, weapon in the other. Bodies lie around. 'Tough guy,' comments my companion. 'I thought he was supposed to be the god as well as the king? So how come it's all right for him to go around wiping people out?' 'Would it be incompatible?' I ask. The guide explains that the decapitated figures we see probably represent units – thousands or tens of thousands – it's a system of recording the slaughtered enemies. 'Jesus,' says the American. 'That's one hell of a massacre. You'd think things would have been rough enough on them back then anyway without carving each other up on top of it.' We stand there in contemplation of this silent carnage. 'I was in France in 'forty-four,' says the American. 'I never saw combat, but I saw what it leaves behind. It's not pretty, let me tell you.' I do not bother to say that he has no need to.

It is an infinite sandy rubbish-tip, as though some careless giant hand has showered down on to it the debris of a thousand junk yards – the burned-out carcasses of vehicles, heaps of old tyres, empty petrol cans, rusted tins, sheets of corrugated iron, tangles of barbed wire, used shell-cases. All this litter lies amid the desert's natural untidiness, the endless scatter of bony apparently lifeless scrub that speckles it from horizon to horizon. The only clear spaces are the tracks along which wind the occasional line of trucks or armoured cars, the 'Tin-Pan Alleys' defined by petrol cans.

They have been following just such a road for two hours now. It is easy, though, to lose the track in the confusion of tyre-marks and rough sign-posts, and when this happens the driver, a small wiry Londoner baked to the colour of burned custard, navigates by a combination of map-reading and guesswork. He drove a taxi before the war, it emerges, and treats the desert with contemptuous familiarity, as though it were some Alice-in-Wonderland inversion of London topography. When they meet up with other vehicles he bawls queries and information into the wind. Everyone is looking for someone else or somewhere else. This area was at the centre of the last action, during which units were scattered; the landscape is full of thousands of men trying to sort themselves back into some kind of order.

Claudia sits beside the driver. Jim Chambers of Associated News is in the back with a New Zealand correspondent. Conversation has to be shouted above the din of the truck's engine. Claudia feels as though all the bones in her body have been rattled loose and her eyes are red-rimmed and smarting from the dust. The driver, who is protective and amused about this exceptional passenger, warns her to tuck a scarf between her neck and shirt or she will have desert sores like everyone else.

They are heading for Seventh Armoured Division HQ, and the driver is worried about getting there before sunset. They have already taken the wrong track once and got stuck in soft sand three times through leaving the track altogether. When that happens the driver swears, jumps down, hauls out the sacks and they all set about the gruelling sweating process of digging out.

He points out a tank. 'One of Jerry's. Brewed up in the first push. Want to take a look, miss?'

They climb out of the truck and walk across to the tank. It is a blackened hulk and it stinks. It lies lurching on one side, beached in a sand-dune, and around it is strewn more debris, small-scale intimate debris – a mess tin, a tattered airletter that flutters in the wind, a packet of biscuits from which a neat black stream of ants pours away towards a rock. Jim Chambers takes some photographs.

There is continuous noise. When planes pass overhead – transport planes, fighters – the whole sky roars. From beyond the horizon come dull thumps and every now and then a silver glitter of tracer fire rises from its rim, or a jewelled explosion of Very lights. And the entire landscape smokes. Burned-out vehicles stream grey in the wind, the sky-line erupts with white puffs, a black column towers away to their right where captured enemy ammunition has been blown up. Smoke and dust fume upwards together, each truck, car or motor-cycle trailing its own buff-coloured wake. In the distance, there is a column of lorries, so blotted out by dust that only their shapes can be seen creeping across the waste and evoking another wilderness and another time – covered waggons on the prairie. And when another cloud of dust comes near enough to disgorge the outlines of tanks they too seem to be something quite else – the high complex turrets of ships riding an ocean, complete with bright pennants.

'We'll stop for a brew,' shouts the driver. 'I want to take a shufti at the map.' They are climbing a slight ridge at the top of which is the hollow of a gun-emplacement with camouflage net and scattered leaking sand-bags. This makes a useful shelter from the wind which is getting up. A fire is made in a can of petrol-soaked sand and tea is brewed in a mess tin. 'Cuppa, miss?' Claudia sits drinking the tea and staring over the top of the sand-bags down into the shallow valley from which they have come; she wonders who lay here a few days before, trying to kill someone else. A little earlier they passed three crosses erected in a line near the burned shell of a truck. One of them had a tin helmet beside it and an inscription pencilled on the rough plank of wood: 'Corporal John Wilson, killed in action.'

The driver thinks they are in for a fucking sandstorm – 'Pardon my French, miss.' They climb back into the lorry and rattle down the other side of the ridge where the landscape of the last hour, and the one before, repeats itself. The track is badly marked but the driver heads for the distant black smudges of other vehicles which resolve themselves, as they get closer, into a couple of Red Cross trucks, stationary near the carcass of a tank. A bundle lies nearby on a stretcher. Men are clambering on the tank. The driver stops and jumps out, as do Jim Chambers and the New Zealander. 'I'd stay put, old girl, if I were you,' says Jim Chambers to Claudia, who disregards him. They walk towards the tank and she sees now that the figures on the tank are dragging from it what has been a man, a reddened, blackened thing with smashed head and a shining splintered white bone for an arm. There is a reek of burning and decay. Two more bundles on stretchers lie in the back of the ambulance truck, whose driver is giving directions to their driver. They are all, it seems, off the track. This is the scene of one of last week's tank battles and yes, the ground is criss-crossed all over with the crenellated plough-marks of their tracks, reaching away on all sides, a silent mayhem in testimony of what has happened here.

They get once more into the truck. The sand is blowing hard now; the sharp clarity of vision has gone, the horizon can no longer be seen. The driver puts on goggles and finds a pair for Claudia. They crash on into the murk, the driver stopping every now and then to jump down and examine a marker, but presently the petrol cans and posts give out altogether and they are forging into emptiness with occasional tyre-marks roving off in all directions. The sand rises in clouds. The whole world turns a lurid pinkish orange; it is impossible to see more than ten or fifteen yards ahead.

They creep on through the sandstorm. The firm going gives way to softer sand from which jut treacherous boulders that grate against the underneath of the truck. Twice they flounder to a halt and have to dig out. And the second time no sooner are they going once more than there is a grinding smash from somewhere beneath and the truck judders to a stop. The driver jumps down and vanishes beneath. He comes up to announce that the fucking back axle is done for.

Everyone, now, is cursing. The New Zealander has an

interview lined up that he sees evaporating if they do not reach HQ by nightfall. The driver, who clearly regards Claudia as his special responsibility, says, 'Don't worry, miss, we'll get you there.' 'I'm not worried,' says Claudia, who is not. She takes the cover off her typewriter and sits in the cab of the truck, typing, while the desert roars around, now white, now sulphur, now rose-coloured. Jim Chambers produces a flask of whisky. The driver says this may not be blinking Piccadilly but there'll be someone by sooner or later, they can't be far from the fucking track and once the sandstorm dies down they can get their bearings again. 'How do you spell "incandescent"?' enquires Claudia. 'Don't show off, Claudia,' says Jim. The driver, now besotted with her, offers yet another cigarette.

Claudia types. She has to pause from time to time to shake sand from the typewriter. She types partly from expediency and partly to exorcise what is now printed on her eyeballs. She tries to reduce to words what she has seen and thought. She types also because she is dog-tired, thirsty, aching and bad-tempered and if she does not occupy herself she might give away some of this, and be ashamed.

And now out in the howling sand there is another sound, and something solid moving in the murk that presently forms itself into the outline of a jeep in which are two figures. Shouts are exchanged. The jeep approaches. The figures jump out. They are a tank officer called Tom Southern and another officer. Their reaction to Claudia's presence is one of amused concern. They are making for HQ and can give a lift to two. The driver will stop with the truck until the breakdown blokes can be reached. Jim Chambers volunteers to stay also. So, grimly, does the New Zealander. So, naturally, does Claudia. In the end it is decided that Jim will stay and the rest continue.

Claudia climbs into the passenger seat of the jeep. Tom Southern drives. The sandstorm is dying down and it is again possible to see the contours of the desert and to pick up the track. She is so tired that she is unable to respond to anything said by the others and at one point she dozes off, slides against Southern's arm and feels him gently but firmly prop her upright again. She sits there half-asleep, seeing little, just his hand on the driving-wheel, a brown hand with a scatter of black hairs between wrist and knuckles; forty years on, she will still see that hand.

My cushioned and carpeted return to Egypt, courtesy of Pharaohtours and the Hilton, included a brief trip into the desert, seen this time through tinted windows from within an air-conditioned coach. The driver stopped so that his passengers might descend and taste for themselves the authentic desert air; there was also a fine view of the Pyramids of Dashur. 'Don't you want to get out?' said my American friend. I shook my head. 'You sure you're OK?' he enquired solicitously. 'You've not spoken a word this trip.' 'I'm fine,' I said. 'I was thinking, that's all. And I've already seen the desert. You get out and have a look around. I'll stay here.' He heaved himself up. 'OK then. How come you've seen the desert, though – you been here before or something?' 'Not here exactly,' I said, evasively. He did not pursue the matter; his attention span was short and camel touts had appeared from nowhere, camera fodder not to be missed. He got out and I was left alone with the tinted glass through which I saw my own images, the distant but vivid shapes and colours of another time, the tanks hunched into the sand, the surrealist sepia swirls and blots of camouflage.

I wasn't thinking of Tom but of myself. And of a self who seemed to be not 'me' but 'she'. An innocent, moving fecklessly through the days, knowing nothing, whom I saw now with awful wisdom. This is how I have felt – how surely anyone must feel – contemplating those poised moments of the past: the night before the storming of the Bastille, the summer of 1914 in the valley of the Somme, the autumn days in Warwickshire before Edgehill. Nothing to be done; no halting or diverting the foreordained. This is the story; these are the things that must happen.

My Texan got back into the coach again, stowing his photographic equipment away, having preserved for posterity some *mafioso* on camel-back who brandished a Lawrence of Arabia rifle in one hand and a string of plastic lapis lazuli beads in the other. 'One helluva place to call home,' he observed. 'That fellow,' I said, 'probably lives in an apartment in Cairo and commutes out here on the bus.' 'You think so?' He looked regretfully at the departing huckster. 'I daresay you're right. I'm a sucker for local colour. Never could spot a phoney. But you're one sharp lady, aren't you, Claudia?'

And I suppose I used his name too. Ed? Chuck? I don't remember, though I do recall that easy incongruous companionship, the peculiar temporary alliance of strangers in transitory circumstances. In an odd way I was glad of him; his impervious presence was a shield. I had hesitated to make this journey, had put it off year after year but had known always that eventually it must be undertaken. And, confronted at last with the mirage – with the shining phantom of that other time – I was surprised to find that it was myself that was the poignant presence. Not him – not Tom. It was in other ways that Tom was there.

I shared a flat in Zamalek with another girl. Camilla was a frothy secretary from the Embassy, one of those silk-clad scented camp-followers who do well out of wars. Camilla, under other circumstances, would have had to spend her youth in the shires, breeding dogs, hunting and going up to town for a show occasionally. As it was, she was having the time of her life, doing a bit of typing in the mornings for someone Daddy was at school with and taking her pick of the officers of the 8th Hussars in the evening.

Teeming polyglot Cairo of the nineteen-forties seems now an apt manifestation of that strange country. The landscape, fusion of antiquity and the present, had its counterpart in the brimming life of the city, where all races met, all languages were spoken, where Greeks and Turks, Copts and Jews, British, French, rich, poor, exploiters and oppressed all brushed past each other on the dusty pavements. The pavements were all they had in common, though. I once saw an old woman sit down on the steps of a mosque and die; across the *maidan* ice-creams and confectionery were being eaten on the terrace of a café. We Europeans rode the streets in cars or in horse-drawn gharries; alongside and among us moved the donkey-carts, the bicycles, the barefoot thousands, the trams so loaded with humanity that they looked like a bee-swarm. For some of us a war was being fought; there must have been many who had no idea what this war was, whose it was or why it was. Like some theatrical lion it roared off-stage while the actors got on with their business. And all the while the extraordinary backcloth eerily reflected the juxtapositions – that scenery in which the lush vegetable borders of the Nile ended so abruptly that you stepped from fields to desert in one pace; in which a crumbling monument might be Greek, Roman, pharaonic, medieval, Christian, Muslim; in which illiterate peasants with a life expectancy of thirty lived in shanty houses set up between the soaring columns of temples inscribed with the complex mythologies of three thousand years before. There was no chronology to the place, and no logic.

'See the picture of Rameses the Second,' says the guide. 'See the king is making a sacrifice to the gods and godses. See up there the lotus. See the magnificent carved pillar. Is three thousand two hundred year old. Is twenty-three metres high. See at the top the carving of Victoria.'

'See *what*, Mustapha?' says the padre.

'Please be using your binoculars, sir. See up there.'

'Oh, I get you. Victorian, he means. Graffiti by Victorian travellers. Extraordinary thing, eh?'

'How did they get up there?' exclaims one of the ATS girls, and the others collapse with laughter. 'The temple wasn't dug out then, you ass. It was full of sand. They were walking about at the tops of the pillars.' And they drift out into the blinding sun again, towards the gharries that will take them back to Luxor, while Tom and Claudia linger in the hot dark shade, with Rameses the Second and the Rev. John Fawcett of Amersham in the county of Buckingham 1859.

'Let's go back to the hotel,' says Tom. 'There are only six more hours till the train.'

'We may never be here again,' says Claudia, staring upwards. 'Think of the Reverend John Fawcett, stumping about over our heads, back then.'

'To hell with the Reverend John Fawcett,' says Tom. 'I want to go.'

'I love you,' says Claudia, not moving.

'I know. Come back to the hotel.'

'On Wednesday morning you'll be in the desert again.'

'You aren't supposed to think of that.'

'I have to,' says Claudia. 'In order to keep a grip on things.'

For there are moments, out here in this place and at this time, when she feels that she is untethered, no longer hitched to past or future or to a known universe but adrift in the cosmos. At night she looks at the sizzling stars, which cannot be the same stars that glimmer in English skies, and she feels eternal, which, far from being tranquil, is like some hideous fever – a psychological version of the malaria, typhoid, dysentery and jaundice that smite each and all at some point in this continent.

You lived from day to day. That of course is a banality but it had a prosaic truth to it then. Death was unmentionable and kept at bay with code-words and the careless understated style of the playing fields. Women whose husbands had bought it during the last push were seen a few weeks later being terribly plucky beside the swimming-pool at Gezira Sporting Club. I remember laughing immoderately. Dancing. Drinking. People flowed into my life and out of it again, people I have never seen since, people I knew intimately: cronies in the Press Corps, men on leave from the desert, attachés at the Embassy, *éminences grises* at GHQ, and the flotsam of Cairo itself, the long-term residents, professional Middle Easterners running banks and businesses, peddling culture with the British Council or the English language to schools and universities. The heroes of the hour – the swashbuckling brigadiers and colonels and majors of the Eighth Army – flitted like medieval barons between the battlefield and the sybaritic excesses of the city. They left their tanks to come back for a few days' polo or some snipe shooting down at the Fayoum. I knew a whiskered colonel who kept a string of ten polo ponies and a couple of Egyptian grooms, a laconic Hussar who set up a pack of hounds at Heliopolis to harry the jackals. The very form of the war itself seemed to stress the analogy – sieges, tented armies, raids and skirmishes, a seasonal ebb and flow as the desert itself dictated advance and retrenchment. And, as the myth of Rommel grew, it was as though Saladin himself lived again – the cunning but gentlemanly enemy, giving no quarter but essentially chivalrous. I wrote a piece about the modern Crusaders and sent it to a leftish London weekly – and got a tart response from an editor who did not see an analogy between the conscripted British working class and feudal retinues. Well, he had a point, of course, but at the same time you had to be stubbornly literal-minded not to perceive in this war an echo of that other European descent into the desert, that other pouring of men and weaponry into an alien landscape. I sent the piece to Gordon, tongue in cheek, and had his answer flung back at me months later – 'Typical Claudia romanticism.' I didn't notice or care; by then I was thinking of other things.

In the Press Corps war was our business, of course. We hung around waiting for communiqués, press releases, rumours. We pursued those close to the moguls of GHQ, curried favour with crisp young attachés who might get us an interview here, some off-the-cuff remarks there. We sat grumbling at the Censors' Office, waiting our turn in the labyrinthine processes of getting our copy to London. Or to New York or Canberra or Cape Town, for we were as international a bunch in our small way as the Cairo crowds. And I have to admit that like that chicken-brained Camilla with whom I shared a flat I too had a sexual field-day. I was one of very few women in what was predominantly a male occupation, and I was by far the best

91

looking. As well as the most resourceful, the most astute, the least deceivable.

And the most immodest.

'And how did you wangle yourself out here?' he enquires.

'Natural talent,' replies Claudia crisply. And immediately wishes she hadn't. It is the wrong note to strike – slick café society talk and they are not in Cairo now but somewhere in Cyrenaica and they are sitting on petrol cans eating a meal of bully beef, tinned rice pudding and marmalade. Tom Southern looks at her and then down at his map. Someone puts a tin mug of tea into Claudia's hands. 'Thank you,' she says, humbly; she has learned, in these brief twelve hours out here, the value of such an offering.

It is perhaps midnight, and very cold. They sit outside the Press Tent. Within, the New Zealander is clattering out his account of the interview with the C.-in-C. All around, figures move darkly against the silver sand, going to and fro between the just defined shapes of vehicles and tents. The sky is an immense black dome spiced with brilliant stars; the long white fingers of searchlights wander across it; the horizon flames with orange tongues; Very lights fly up – red, white and green. Somewhere beyond it – where and how far no one is prepared to tell them – is The Front, that elusive shifting goal: a concept rather than a place. The men are hunched into greatcoats or tattered sheepskins. Claudia wears slacks, two sweaters and an overcoat and still shivers. Jim Chambers – who caught up with them again a couple of hours ago – yawns and says he will turn in now. Claudia and Tom Southern are left alone.

'Actually,' she says, 'I talked my way into it somehow.'

He folds the map and puts it back in his pocket.

'That's what I assumed,' he says. He smiles. He has the red-eyed, fixed look that they all have. A few hours earlier Claudia listened to a man talking in the deliberate, slurred tones of, as she thought (faintly incredulous), a drunk. Until she realised that what she was hearing was the voice of exhaustion. Many of these men have not slept for nights on end. The last push was only three days ago.

And they begin to talk not of pushes or of flaps or of the next show, but of another time and another place. 'When I was a child,' says Tom Southern, 'I was fascinated by the idea of deserts. Who wouldn't be, raised in deepest Sussex? It all stemmed from the notion of John the Baptist howling in the wilderness, and the illustrations in the Sunday School Bible – all those people in fancy dress with camels and donkeys. We once made a flour and water relief map of the Holy Land, I remember, with the Red Sea painted bright blue and Sinai a good hot yellow. Sometimes when I look at the maps in HQ I remember that.'

He has been here six months. Training in the Delta and now commands a troop of tanks. Was in last week's action.

'The nearest I've ever been to a desert,' says Claudia, 'is the beach at Charmouth. My brother and I used to collect fossils there. Fight over fossils.'

'There are fossils here,' says Tom Southern. 'I found one yesterday. Would you like it?' He rummages in the pocket of his battle-dress.

'Thank you,' says Claudia. 'It's a starfish, isn't it? Goodness. All this was sea, once, then.'

'Must've been. Which somehow puts one in one's place.'

'Yes,' says Claudia. 'It does.'

They sit, hands cupped round tea-mugs. Inside the tent the New Zealander's typewriter still clatters; the skyline still roars and sparkles; the shadowy figures plod to and fro across the sand.

'I keep a diary,' says Tom. 'Nicely cryptic, of course, in case I get put in the bag. But one of these days one may want to remember what all this was like.'

'What is it like?' asks Claudia after a moment.

He lights a cigarette. He stares at her. His face, in the moonlight, is not brown but a blackish colour. 'Hm . . . What is it like? Let's see . . .' But before he can go on the New Zealander appears, shuffling typescript and offering a hipflask of whisky. And it is decided that Claudia (who protests, of course) shall sleep in the Press Tent while the others will use the truck. Tom Southern is going to the coast tomorrow to bring up some tank replacements and has offered them a lift.

Claudia lies in a sleeping-bag in the tent. She does not sleep much. Once she raises the flap of the tent and looks out over the sand. There are other tents around, so small that she can see the booted feet of their occupants sticking out at one end. Elsewhere, bundled shapes lie up against trucks and jeeps. A petrol can cooking-stove quietly smoulders. She turns on her side and the starfish, which she has put in her pocket, grinds against her hip. She takes it out and lies with it in her hand, running her fingers from time to time over the gritty stone, the five symmetrical arms.

No, I don't still have it. I used it as a paperweight in the Cairo flat. It lay on the table in front of the mesh-covered window before which I was writing, looking out on to a garden brilliant with zinnias and bougainvillia and red canna lilies. A garden boy would sweep the paths, very slowly, all morning, or wander with a length of hose among the flower beds, chivvied by the French landlady. When I left I gave Madame Charlot the few bits and pieces I had accumulated – the brass tray from the Mouski, the leather pouffe, the primus stove. Perhaps the starfish is in that garden, edging a path.

Madame Charlot referred to herself as French. In fact her father was Lebanese and her mother one of those essentially Cairene figures of an ancestry as complex as the city – a tiny red-haired old lady whose native language certainly appeared to be French but who also spoke Arabic and Russian and a maverick form of English. She and her daughter festered their days away in an overfurnished under-aired room full of Empire chairs and sofas from which they emerged to harry the servants and cast inquisitive looks upon their tenants. Madame Charlot's sharp eyes would peer from beyond the latticed wood folding screen that shielded their private rooms as Camilla's admirers clattered up and down the stairs. When in the evenings we entertained friends on the balcony of our flat she would patrol the garden, watering the lurid lines of zinnias and glancing covertly upwards. She always wore shapeless black dresses, topped by a grey cardigan in winter, and with stockings throughout the stifling Cairo summer. I never once heard her refer either to the war or to her husband who was never seen or heard of. Both, presumably, were inconveniences kept at bay by ignoring their existence. When I returned from that trip to the desert I told her where I had been and she persisted in referring to '*votre petite vacance*'. Did she ever consider what would happen to her should the Germans reach Cairo? She and her mother would simply have melted into the cosmopolitan soup, I imagine – have become someone else, changed their skins to fit the background like those other old Cairenes, the chameleons that lurked in the garden trees, skew-eyed and spiral-tailed, creeping invisible along the branches with their three-fingered gloved hands.

When I came back I was ill. I typed with a rising temperature, bribed Camilla with a bottle of 'Evening in Paris' to take the stuff down to the Censors' Office and then lay rocking in bed for a week with malaria, wondering if it had not all been a figment of the fever.

The place is stirring long before sunrise; but it has never really slept. The orange glow of cooking fires lights up the pre-dawn darkness. Claudia shares with Jim Chambers and the New Zealander a half pint of water for washing. By the time it is light Tom Southern appears from the Command Tent with a sheaf of maps and papers saying they must get a move on. They get into the truck – Tom driving, Claudia alongside, the other two in the back. Jim and the New Zealander are in uniform – the ubiquitous perfunctory uniform of corduroy trousers, battle-dress jacket and overcoat. Tom tells Claudia to fix her green and gold War Correspondent badge more conspicuously to her person – 'or you'll raise even more eyebrows than you do already.' He thinks he may be able to wangle them a few minutes with the C.O. of the tank regiment that led last week's push. He will drop them off at the airstrip by the coast road whence they will get a lift back to Cairo. Jim and the New Zealander argue between themselves about their chances of commandeering a truck from somewhere and trying to get up to the front. 'Not you, old girl, I'm afraid,' says Jim to Claudia. 'You'll have to be satisfied with getting this far.' Claudia does not answer, distracted by what she now sees – a concourse of shabby men in blue-green ragged uniforms squatting in the sand, hundreds of them (she tries to make a quick count, sorting them into blocks of ten); the truck bumps past them, going fast on a belt of hard gravelly sand, and as it does so the men eye them apathetically, except for a few who discern Claudia's gender and gaze astonished. One rises to his feet and with elaborate pantomime blows a kiss. The New Zealander laughs: 'Trust a bloody wop!'

So that is the enemy, thinks Claudia. This is what the enemy looks like – a lot of down-and-out Italian waiters, average age about twenty-one. She says, 'They don't look particularly distressed.' 'They're not,' says Tom. 'They're damn glad to be out of it.'

They move, all day, through the smouldering debris of what has gone before. This is the area of last week's enemy advance and subsequent retreat. This thousand square miles of emptiness has been wrestled over for five days and nights; it has exacted the lives of several hundred men. And it is untouched, thinks Claudia. Already the sand is starting to digest the broken vehicles, the petrol cans, the tangles of wire; a few more storms and they will sink beneath it. In a few years' time they will have vanished. She watches Tom Southern pore over his maps; these scribblings too are arbitrary – the sand has no boundaries, no frontiers, no perimeters.

She talks, during the day, to innumerable men. Tom Southern stops to have a word here, exchange some information there; they lose themselves in this tract of sand that is both empty and populous. Scores of vehicles are on the move – solitary motor-cyclists bumping doggedly across the wastes, trucks, armoured cars, ten-ton lorries in long stately files, battered tanks being taken back to base workshops, ambulances, jeeps. And those who are not on the move have established themselves, hunched down into the landscape in makeshift arrangements of shacks, shelters, holes in the ground. Claudia squats above a trench and talks to two soldiers brewing tea within. They hand her up a mug. They are men of the 1st Argyll and Sutherland and have been at the front for two weeks. Spare and wiry, like a couple of fox terriers, they seem very much at home down there in the sand (thus, thinks Claudia, must their ancestors have come to terms with another kind of remorseless terrain); they advise Claudia, though, not to come in for a look – 'the bluddy Eyeties was in here, and they're not too fussy how they live.' And indeed the latrine smell billows upwards as Claudia returns the mug with thanks, makes some notes and rejoins the others.

She talks to an officer of the Black Watch, shaving meticulously beside his tent, who wonders if they haven't met sometime in town, do you know the Broke-Willoughbys, by any chance? She talks to a sapper who warns them away from a suspected minefield in the next *wadi* – in the distance she can see patient figures probing the ground, yard by yard, marking out the sand with intricate spider-webs of tapes and posts. She talks to men who speak in the accents of rural Gloucestershire, of Wapping, of Kensington. She meets both reticence and outpourings: this man's gun-emplacement was overrun and he was the only survivor – he describes what happened in the bleak unadorned language of a police report; another, his torso aflame with desert sores, has a girl friend in Cairo – will Claudia deliver a letter? She fills her notebook with scrawls. The sun has risen now and the flies crawl blackly over necks, arms, faces. The sand lodges in nose, eyes, ears.

They stop at a Company HQ. Tom Southern picks up Claudia's box Brownie and insists on snapping her with it, leaning up against the truck, laughing and protesting. They have lunch: bully beef and mugs of tea. The water in the flasks they carry is now itself as hot as tea. Claudia sits in the shade of the truck and types while Tom parleys with a brisk moustached major who peers warily at her – 'Press wallahs?' she hears him say. 'I've got enough on my plate just now, tell them. Sorry, old chap.' Presently, though, he relents and comes over to stand for a few minutes in embarrassed talk – ' 'Fraid we've got a bit of a flap on just now – lost radio contact with my CO. Otherwise we could have had a chat.' He eyes Claudia doubtfully. 'My chaps looking after you all right? I didn't know Cairo let you ladies up here.' 'They don't,' says Jim Chambers. 'Miss Hampton has a way with her.' Claudia beams. The major, shaking himself like a dog, turns and scuttles back to his tent.

They leave this centre of civilisation and plunge on. They are moving away now from the main concentration behind the lines, and from the more conspicuously marked tracks. Fewer vehicles come into sight. Tom Southern halts more often to consult his maps, to use his binoculars, to check his radio. They are heading for the coast road by way of a supply depot. The route takes them along a shallow *wadi*; at either side the sand rises in sculptured ridges to a height of thirty feet or so, blocking off the view; the occasional rocky overhang provides a slash of black shadow, the rest is a relentless glaring white. Small fleshy plants start up here and there; once, stopping to free the truck from a patch of soft sand, they see the paw-prints of a desert fox dancing away up the slope.

When Tom next halts to consult the map Claudia excuses herself and sets off up the ridge. 'Mind the rules, m'dear,' says Jim Chambers. She waves a hand – never go out of sight of your vehicle. At the top of the rise she selects a handy rock and squats behind it on the sand in lengthy relief. Rising, pulling up her slacks, she gives way to temptation and walks a quick few yards beyond the rise to where she can see down into the next *wadi* – wider, deeper and not empty. For a hundred yards or so away is the wreckage of an armoured car, lying on its side, one axle ripped off. And beside it is a body.

Claudia hesitates. She walks quickly down to the wreckage. The man is lying face down. His hair is fair, his tin hat lies beside him, part of his head is in black bloody shreds, the sand too is blackened, one leg has no foot. Flies crawl in glittery masses. And as she looks at all this she hears from the other side of the smashed car a noise. She steps round to see and there is another shattered body but this body moves. Its hand lifts from its chest and then falls back. Its mouth opens and makes a sound.

She stoops down. She says, 'I'm going to get help. There are three men with me – I'm coming straight back. Can you hear me? You'll be all right now.' She does not think that he can hear her at all. One of his eyes is a purple pulpy mess, the sand under him is dark black, his trousers have been ripped half from him and in the flesh of one thigh is a red hole into which you could put your fist. From it there crawls a line of ants.

She runs up to the top of the ridge. She waves and shouts. The others come. Tom Southern gets out his binoculars. 'You've been down there. You're a bloody fool. They hit a mine. There could be more.' 'I'm sorry,' says Claudia. 'There's a man still alive.' 'You're still a bloody fool,' says Tom. 'Stay there ... Chambers, get the field-dressings from the truck, would you.'

He walks down to the truck in Claudia's tracks, staring at the sand on either side. Once he stops, scrutinises something, stands again. Eventually he reaches the car and beckons to Jim Chambers. Claudia and the New Zealander watch from the ridge.

'You OK?' says the New Zealander.

'I'm OK,' says Claudia.

The two men return. 'He's been there a day or so, poor bugger,' says Tom. 'The search parties must have missed them.' He looks at Claudia. 'Lucky for him you picked that particular spot. I'm going back to the truck to radio the ambulance depot and we'll wait till they come. I've done what I can for him – he's not taking in much, poor sod.'

'I'm sorry I was a bloody fool,' says Claudia.

He considers her. 'Well, you're still in one piece. Don't do it again if you want to stay that way.'

ᛞ

'Lovely plant,' says the nurse. 'Your sister-in-law brought it, didn't she? Gorgeous colour. It'll be one of those hothouse species, I expect. I'll put it nearer the radiator.'

Claudia turns her head. 'That is a poinsettia,' she says. 'Indestructible things. They grow in sand. I should let it take its chance with the rest of us.'

The nurse sticks her finger in the pot and shakes her head. 'No, dear – some sort of peat this is in.' She moves it from the windowsill. 'There – we don't want it dying on us, do we? Mrs Hampton would be upset.'

No, she wouldn't. She'd accuse me of slaughtering it. To herself, of course – not out loud. I have heard many of Sylvia's silent accusations, over the years.

Typical of Sylvia to bring a poinsettia. As though she knew. The congenitally heavy-handed are capable even of unwitting brutalities.

This place has been a tiny seaside settlement. A line of rubble marks what were once small white stucco villas and a café. The café wall survives, with a Schweppes advertisement stuck to it, and the ruined houses are covered with swarming growth – trails of brilliant blue morning glory and a lace-work of scarlet poinsettia flowers. Claudia picks one and her fingers are at

100

once sticky with white sap; she drops it in the sand and wipes them on her slacks. The flowers amaze her. Just now they passed through a camp in which sheets of asphodels and night-scented stocks had sprung up amid the tents; the soldiers walked among them, the air was fragrant.

'It rained last week,' says Tom Southern. 'The seeds must lie dormant, I suppose.'

For months or years, thinks Claudia, what an extraordinary thing. And how even more extraordinary to stand here in this place at this time talking to someone about botany. The coast road is an endless rumbling jostling khaki stream of traffic, convoy upon convoy moving west, crawling at the slow remorseless army pace, tank and Bren-gun carriers, ten-tonners, ambulances, armoured cars. Beyond it the Mediterranean sparkles in a great blue curve with the grey outlines of ships perched upon the horizon. The sky echoes to the sound of aircraft.

'You asked,' he says, 'what it is like out here. For purposes of your article, I suppose?'

They are sitting, now, on the low wall that once marked the forecourt of the café. Jim Chambers and the New Zealander have departed for the front, having wangled a lift. Tom Southern will hand Claudia over to an RAF chap who is going to the air field and has offered to put her on to a transport plane going back to Cairo. The chap is just seeing someone at the Command Post and will be back shortly. And Tom will move on, to collect his tank, rejoin his squadron, move forward again.

'No,' she says. 'I wanted to know for myself.'

He hesitates. 'It's so many different things. Boring, uncomfortable, terrifying, exhilarating. In rapid succession. Pretty well impossible to convey.' He looks intently at her. 'Sorry — I'm not doing very well. It's like the whole of life in a single appalling concentration. It does lunatic things with time. An hour can seem like a day or a day like an hour. When you're flung from one state of mind to another with such speed the physical world takes on an extraordinary clarity. I have spent whole minutes gazing at the structure of a rock or the behaviour of an insect.' He is silent for a moment. 'My driver was killed in our first action. We'd trained together. It had been his birthday the week before. We celebrated with a tin of peaches and some whisky. He was twenty-three. And the same day he and I had seen a mirage in which there was an entire oasis village – palms, mud huts, camels, people walking about. I thought I was hallucinating until he said "Christ, sir – look at that!" You drive towards the things and as you do so they disappear, melt away before your eyes. But somewhere there is this mirror place going about its business in perfect impervious detachment. And now I think of my driver – Corporal Haycraft, from Nottingham – and when I'm dog-tired, moving around like a zombie, the one thing that bothers me is where has he gone? How can a man be sitting in a tank with you one day and nowhere at all the next? How?'

'I don't know,' murmurs Claudia. She looks at his feet; one of his sand-encrusted boots rests upon a huge brilliant poinsettia flower, a scarlet star with golden foam at the centre.

'We buried him that evening. The padre did his stuff. Maybe I should have asked the padre where Corporal Haycraft had gone. Nice embarrassing question. But perhaps you're a churchgoer?'

'No,' says Claudia, 'I'm not a churchgoer.'

'Then I haven't offended you. You can never be sure. An astonishing amount of piety goes out here, you'd be surprised. The Lord is frequently invoked. He's on our side, by the way, you'll be glad to hear – or at least it's taken for granted that he is.'

'Are we going to win the war?' asks Claudia.

'Yes. I assume so. Not because of the Lord's intervention or because justice will prevail but because in the last resort we have greater resources. Wars have little to do with justice. Or valour or sacrifice or the other things traditionally associated with them. That's one thing I hadn't quite realised. War has been much misrepresented, believe me. It's had a disgracefully good press. I hope you and your friends are doing something to put that right.'

'I hope we are too,' says Claudia.

'Though it's the chroniclers I'm thinking of rather than the reporters. I take it you don't regard yourself as a chronicler. The chroniclers, not having been in the thick of things, concentrate on justice and valour and all that. And statistics. When you find yourself in a position of a statistic it looks rather different.'

'Yes,' says Claudia, 'I'm beginning to see that.'

'What do you do,' enquires Tom Southern, '– when you're not globe-trotting in the service of the free press?'

Claudia considers several replies. She is surprised at herself. Considered response is not characteristic. She does not wish to sound brash, foolish, evasive, or pretentious. At last she says, 'I've written two books.'

'What sort of books?'

Claudia swallows. 'Well ... I suppose you'd call them history.'

Tom Southern contemplates her. 'History,' he says. 'I used to be rather keen on history myself. By which I mean I enjoyed reading it. Positively sought it out, indeed. I daresay I'll come back to it, in the fullness of time. Right now I feel rather differently. When the times are out of joint it is brought uncomfortably home to you that history is true and that unfortunately you are a part of it. One has this tendency to think oneself immune. This is one of the points when the immunity is shown up as fantasy. I'd rather like to go back to fantasising.'

Claudia can think of nothing to say. Nothing whatsoever. She sits on the battered wall of what was once a little seaside café; the convoys grind past and beyond them the sea glitters; grimy khaki figures plod to and fro. One of these, she sees out of the corner of one eye, is approaching them. Presumably this is the RAF chap who will take her to the airstrip. She looks at Tom Southern; forty-eight hours ago she had not set eyes on

103

this man. Now she finds herself quite disconcertingly anxious for his good opinion.

'I don't know what to say,' she says.

He laughs. 'Then keep quiet and take notes. Isn't that what you're here for?'

'Hello there,' cries the approaching figure.

Tom Southern rises. 'Your lift, I think.' He holds out his hand. 'Have a good trip back to Cairo.'

They shake hands. 'Thank you for all you've done,' says Claudia.

'All in the day's work,' says Tom. There is a silence.

'Perhaps . . .' Claudia begins.

But he interrupts. 'Maybe we could meet when I have some leave?'

Wars are fought by children. Conceived by their mad demonic elders and fought by boys. I say that now, caught out in surprise at how young people are, forgetting that it is not they who are young but I who am old. Nevertheless, the faces of the Russian front, the million upon million dead Germans, dead Ukrainians, Georgians, Tartars, Latvians, Siberians are the plump unlined faces of youths. As are the faces of the Somme and of Passchendaele. The rest of us grow old and tell each other what really happened; they, of course, will never know, just as they never knew at the time. The files of newspaper libraries are stuffed with these baby-faces, grinning cheerfully from the decks of troop-ships, from train windows, from stretchers. In pursuit of truth and facts, in the exercise of my craft, I have looked at them and thought of the slipperiness of whatever fact or truth it is that makes these faces change with the eyes that view them. It was not boys I saw in 1941.

Nor the grey of old newsprint. In the mind's eye is the blazing technicolour of a hot country, so that I seem to see it still squinting against the glare, dazzled by that relentless sun, moving in landscapes that shimmered in the heat haze. Mirages . . . Well, the mirror world, the vanishing oasis, is in my head now, not in his, and he is with it.

After I came back from the desert I was ill. I recovered and staggered out into Cairo again, half a stone lighter, pursued by complacent wailings from Madame Charlot and her mother who predicted death within a month if I did not observe the statutory convalescence. There was no time to be ill. In any case most Europeans were mildly ill a good deal of the time. I wrote up my desert experiences (three days, three paltry days – but it was still more than some of my male colleagues had achieved), pestered the Censors' Office and bombarded every editor I could think of. And in the meantime the weeks rolled past in the usual sequence of rumours, of talk of another push, another retreat, the arrival of this general or of that diplomat. I was always hanging around in corridors, waiting for the chance of a word with so-and-so, or sitting with ears pricked in cafés and restaurants, beside swimming-pools or in night clubs. I had an old Ford V8 in which I contended with the pot-holed dust-ridden roads, driving out to Heliopolis or to the Pyramids, to Maadi and to the airport to take down the banalities of incoming dignitaries. I was too busy to think about anything except what I was doing. So that I was almost taken unawares when Tom Southern telephoned.

The polar bear, its dark yellow flanks heaving, its coat tufted like a badly mown lawn, lies in a basin of dirty water.

'Wicked,' says Claudia. It is May; the temperature is ninety-eight.

'You can always tell how civilised a country is by its treatment of animals,' says Tom. 'The Middle East rates about as low as I've seen so far.'

'I can't stand it,' says Claudia. 'Let's find some lions.'

The Zoo is laid out like a French park; zinnias and petunias are trapped in geometrical beds, carefully raked gravel paths are edged with overlapping hoops of wire, little decorative kiosks provide shade and a seat for the gossiping, knitting attendants of the European children who rush hither and thither, shrieking in French or English. Prams are parked under palms and casuarinas. A small girl in blue frock, matching hair ribbon, white ankle socks, stares beadily at them as they pass. There are jungly cries and whoops from the birds and animals penned amid the trees and shrubs; everything is labelled in English, French and Arabic. An elephant perambulates the paths with its keeper; if you give it a five-piastre piece it will salaam and pass the coin to the keeper, who grins and salaams also. The hippos share a small lake with flamingos and assorted duck; a keeper stands alongside with a bucketful of potatoes – five piastres buys a couple of potatoes which you then hurl into the pink maw of the hippo. The adult hippos wallow with their mouths permanently agape while two young ones, who have not yet got the idea, cruise fretfully up and down, occasionally struck by inaccurate potatoes.

'Like an exotic form of hoop-la,' says Tom. 'Do you want a go?'

'Do you realise that potatoes are a luxury in this place?' says Claudia. 'I can't remember when I last ate a potato myself. We use yams. Mashed yam, roast yam, boiled yam. Ninety per cent of the population doesn't even have those.'

'Oh dear,' says Tom. 'Is indignation going to spoil your day? At least the hippos are happy, presumably.'

But Claudia knows that nothing can spoil her day – not the heat, the discomfort of an infected insect bite on her arm, the knowledge that today will give way to tomorrow. She is moving from minute to minute; she feels as though she were in a state of grace. Calm down, she tells herself. Just because this has never happened to you before. Because you have reached the ripe age of thirty-one without knowing this peculiar derangement. For derangement is what it surely is; only by stern physical effort can she keep herself from looking at him, touching him.

They wander past enclosures of gazelle and buck, cages of monkeys and birds, through the rank-smelling lion house. Grey shoebills stalk the paths or stand statuesque on one leg beside the knitting nannies. Gardeners with hoses patrol the flowerbeds; there is a rich smell of damp earth. 'Three days ago,' says Tom, 'I almost came to blows with a bloke over the last can of water from the first water-cart we'd seen in two days. But that was another time and another place. This is some sort of mad fairyland.'

From the Zoo they take a gharry to the Club. At the Club are more obsessively attended children, an acreage of grass that has cost a ransom in water and intensive labour, and, all around, bright confident English voices. They change into swimming costumes and sit beside the pool under a sun umbrella amid fumes of Nivea sun-cream; a suffragi brings them drinks in tall ice-chinking glasses. The swimming-pool is an intense turquoise, a mosaic of brilliant refracted light shattered every few minutes as someone dives from one of the high boards. Presently Tom and Claudia themselves plunge into the water, where the smell of Nivea is replaced by that of chlorine. Claudia floats on her back and watches Tom climb to the highest diving-board. He stands, a black outline against the piercing blue sky, the board dipping under his weight; he is unrecognisable at this distance, his outline is simply the outline of Man – head, torso, the fork beneath. 'Poor, bare, forked animal,' she mutters floating there, and giggles, a little wild with gin and tonic. 'Sorry?' says a passing swimmer, sleek seal-head turned sideways. 'Nothing,' says Claudia. 'Nothing at all.' And then Tom on the diving-board straightens, rises on his toes, raises his arms, and comes arching down; and surfaces a moment later beside her, spluttering, no longer universal, no longer symbolic, just another sunburned figure in the sparkling water.

And presently the long hot afternoon gives way to the long hot evening. 'Are you busy?' enquires Tom. 'I wondered if we might have dinner.' And Claudia is not busy (nor will be for the foreseeable future, for the three days or five days or whatever it is he has). They have dinner. They walk beside the Nile, where white felucca sails swim in the dusk and the egrets come floating in from the Delta to roost beside the English Bridge, so that the grey-green trees are speckled all over as though hung with decorations. The day is refracted, and the next and the one after that, all of them broken up into a hundred juggled

107

segments, each brilliant and self-contained so that the hours are no longer linear but assorted like bright sweets in a jar. At one moment they are leaning over the parapet of the Citadel, with the sprawling dun-coloured minareted city spread out below them and the Pyramids like grey cut-outs on the horizon. At another they are standing at the foot of the Great Pyramid, jostled by camels and donkeys hung about with tassels, beads, trappings of puce and orange; beside the medieval panoply of the animals the crowds of tourists are a drab lot – uniformed in khaki, navy and the prosaic European hot weather wear of white or buff. The Pyramids are doing good business; they preside over a humming centre of commerce – you can buy postcards, flywhisks, a ride on a donkey called Telephone, Chocolate or Whisky-Soda, a guided climb to the top of the Great Pyramid, which is studded all over with striving figures.

It is said to take forty minutes for those in good physical condition. Most of the climbers are presumably that, ripened by desert life. It seems curious to Claudia that men engaged in fighting the most extensive war of all time should spend their leisure hours scrambling up an antique artificial mountain.

'No thanks,' she says. 'I doubt if I'd make it, anyway. You go.'

'Not me,' says Tom. 'I should panic and fall off. A humiliating end. Whatever would the War Office tell my parents?'

So they walk to the Sphinx instead. 'Well,' says Tom. 'There it is. Not just a piece of literary self-indulgence after all. Solid rock. When the show's over here I'm going to apply for a posting to India. It wonderfully concentrates the mind at times like these – all this contemplation of the past.'

'When will the show be over here?' asks Claudia.

He shrugs. 'Who knows? Your guess is as good as mine.' And all of a sudden he takes both her hands. 'Not yet,' he says. 'Not yet.'

He is asleep. He lies beside her naked and asleep. In the twilight of the room she can only just make out the familiar shapes of wardrobe, dressing-table, chair and now this unfamiliar long shape in her bed. It is one in the morning. Beyond the shutters the gardens of Gezira chirrup with insect life; a cat yowls. Presently she must wake him and he must go to his hotel because the acute antennae of Madame Charlot would surely detect his presence in the morning; as it is, Tom and Claudia will have to creep down the stone stairs and open carefully the heavy front door. But in the meantime, for hoarded minutes, Claudia looks.

He is so sunburned that the parts that have not been exposed seem unnaturally pale – they glimmer in the darkness: his feet, an armpit, his buttocks and above all his crotch. The colour changes at his navel – above is brown, below is another man, as though like some crustacean a tough protective shell harboured a different creature, soft and vulnerable. White skin, curling black hair, and the wrinkled penis in the middle, with a knob like an acorn. She reaches out and lays a hand on it; he does not wake but his penis twitches a little at her touch.

An hour ago he kneeled above her. And, misinterpreting what he must have seen as panic in her eyes, said, 'You're not . . . Claudia, I'm not the first?' She could not speak – only hold out her arms. She could not say: 'It's not you I'm afraid of, it's how I feel.'

She takes her hand from his crotch and touches his arm. 'Tom?' she says. 'Tom?'

The main cinemas are showing *Snow White*, *Road to Rio* and a Sonja Henie film. There is a garden party in aid of the Army Benevolent Fund and a Choral Evensong at the Cathedral. Groppi's serves afternoon tea and Shepheard's an English Sunday lunch. The Club offers a race meeting or a polo match.

'No,' says Tom. 'None of those things. Today I want to see something of this place, if any of it is still visible beneath the trappings of war.'

And so they wander in the packed chattering streets of old Cairo, where the smell of animals, of humanity, of kerosene, coffee, drains, roast sweetcorn and frying oil is like some rich humus. 'Would you like a scarab ring?' says Tom. 'A khelim rug? A galabieh? A pouffe with profile of Queen Nefertiti? I want to give you something. Let's find you something to gaze at with dewy eyes when I've gone. Except that you're not that kind of girl, are you? I'm not at all sure what kind of girl you are. Self-contained, it seems. Self-sufficient?'

'Up to a point,' murmurs Claudia, peering into the small black cavern of a shop, from the depths of which the proprietor beckons, offering handfuls of leather slippers. 'But only up to a point.'

'Ah,' he says. 'Even if the dewy eyes are out of the question I might be able to insinuate myself somehow, then?' The slipper-seller has emerged from his lair and is scrabbling at Claudia's feet with a tape-measure. 'No,' she says. 'No, thank you.' 'Cheap. Very cheap. I make good price.' 'Yes, I'm sure – but no all the same.' Her ankle is clutched now. 'That's enough,' says Tom. 'We don't want them. *Imshi* . . .' And then, 'Christ – why does one talk to these people like this? The only words of Arabic I know are commands or insults.' 'People have been talking to them like that for centuries,' says Claudia. 'I suppose they're used to it.' 'All the same, it would be satisfying to depart from the norm.' 'We're conditioned too,' says Claudia. 'Some of us are less conditioned than others, or would like to be.'

'A brooch?' he says. 'A silver filigree brooch? A bottle of scent called "Mystery of the Orient"? A brass pyramid paper-weight? There must be something you need. Indulge me. Giving presents is one of the most possessive things we do, did you realise that? It's the way we keep a hold on other people. Plant ourselves in their lives.'

'I should like one of these,' says Claudia. And so he buys her a ring, a complex ring the front of which is a little compartment with a conical lid that opens on a hinge. It is called a poison ring, says the shopkeeper. For your enemies. 'Straight out of the Arabian Nights,' remarks Tom. 'Are you sure that's what you want? What enemies do you have?' But Claudia replies that yes, that is what she would like. The ring sits heavily on her finger. Later that day – or perhaps the next –

110

Tom fills the little box with sand from the Mokattam Hills, to which they have driven in the Ford V8. It is evening, the time when the Mokattams, seen from Cairo, are lilac-coloured. Claudia says that the sand should be blue, but it is not, it is the dull buff of sand everywhere.

The Nile, at night, is jewelled. The bridges wear necklaces of coloured lights; all along the banks the house-boats are ablaze, festooned with gold, glowing against the dark swirling patterned water. One of these house-boats is a nightclub; it throbs with music into the small hours.

'He insists they've no table,' says Tom.

'Give him fifty piastres,' says Claudia. 'Then miraculously there will be one.'

They sit squashed amid a group of 11th Hussar officers (other ranks not admitted) and nurses from the hospital at Heliopolis; the officers throw bread rolls at each other and at one point some of them roar out their old school song. The floor show is a raddled belly dancer; the nurses fall about with laughter. There is also a singer who fills the night with full-throated sobbing Arabic popular songs. One of the Hussars, reeling drunk, grabs the microphone when she has finished and gives a parody, clutching his stomach and rolling his eyes. The compère stands by grinning awkwardly and the other officers laugh themselves helpless.

'I think I may have had about enough of this,' says Tom. 'I'm evidently less acclimatised than you are.'

Camilla waves – one of the gay party now bargaining for entry.

'Who's that?'

'A girl I share a flat with,' says Claudia. 'Let's go, then. They can have our table.'

They pause on the bridge and lean on the railings to look down at the river. There is little traffic now, just the occasional clanging late tram, a few cars and clopping gharries. The houseboat, a couple of hundred yards downstream, continues to pulsate.

111

'There are moments,' says Tom, 'when this city seems to me more outlandish than the desert.'

'I don't think I've really taken it in yet. Perhaps that's something that happens much later.'

'I suppose you'll write a book about all this when it's over,' he says.

'No.'

'How can you be so sure? Most of your pals in the Press Corps are stashing stuff away right now, you can see it.'

Why is she so sure? She does not know – only that she is. 'If the war hadn't happened,' she says, 'I was going to do something hefty on Disraeli.'

'Ah. Instead of which you're getting a hefty dose of real life. Well, Disraeli will always be there when the war's over.'

Presently Claudia says, 'What will you do when the war's over?'

'That rather depends . . .' He looks at her, and then down into the water. '. . . on various things.' He takes her hand. 'Let's talk about them sometime. Not just now.'

9

You can no longer climb the Great Pyramid. There is an admonitory sign in English and Arabic: 'Don't climb the Pyramids'. 'Are they crazy?' demanded the Texan. 'Who'd think of a thing like that in this heat?' I shrugged and told him it used to be a popular sport in the nineteenth century. Gustave Flaubert, among others, made the ascent. 'No kidding? With the clothes they wore then?' A note of dissatisfaction had crept into his voice; he stared at the immense stepped cliff-face of the Pyramid. He felt, I knew, obscurely cheated: if Pyramid-climbing was once on offer then he should not be done out of it. He would have laboured up, just as he had, half an hour earlier, heaved himself gingerly on to the back of a camel. He was always game; I liked that about him.

Nor are there any house-boats moored on the Nile banks. The egrets no longer roost by the English Bridge and the polo grounds are gone. I felt quite dispassionate about all this. I do not think I would have wished to find them. Just as one's previous selves are unreachable, so should their surroundings be. In any case, I would have blenched at the thought of trying to explain polo to the Texan.

There was once a city in Egypt called Memphis. I shall devote a good deal of space to Memphis, in my history of the world; it is a salutary tale, the fate of Memphis, it nicely demonstrates the fragility of places. In pharaonic times Mem-

113

phis was a sprawling acreage of houses, temples, workshops – an administrative and religious centre, the seat of government, a magnet for artists and craftsmen: Washington, Paris and Rome all rolled together on the banks of the Nile. Dikes protected it from the inundations of the river. It sounds paradisial – a city of palms and greenery on the richest silt where Upper and Lower Egypt meet, with majestic temples and sphinx-lined boulevards; the hub of an intelligent complex society completely out of step with the rest of the world, constructing ashlar buildings when Europe was living in caves, recording itself in the most decorative script ever known, practising one of the most imaginative, impenetrable and perverse religions of all time.

And what is Memphis now? A series of barely discernible irregularities in the cultivation and an immense prone statue of Rameses the Second. How indeed are the mighty fallen. The political stability of ancient Egypt wavered, the dikes fell into disrepair, the Nile took care of the rest. Of the lives of the citizens of Memphis there remains no trace whatsoever, though of their deaths plenty. Pyramids, mastabas, tombs, sarcophagi, funerary monuments that litter the landscape – a people obsessed with mortality. All their beliefs are centred round the desperate flight from the idea of extinction. Well, they're not alone in that, merely more inventive in the pursuit of solutions. People die; bodies disintegrate. But death is intolerable. So you propose, ingeniously, that if the body is preserved either actually or symbolically, if it is hidden away and provided with the equipment of daily living, then death will not have happened. Something – soul, *ka*, memory, whatever you like to call it – will live for ever. You give this shadow-thing all it had in corporeal life, its furnishings, its jewellery, its servants, its food and drink, and from time to time it will come from whatever eternity it inhabits to take sustenance from its shell. A complicated interesting idea. You keep the dead with you for ever and deny the possibility of your own annihilation.

Nowadays, of course, we don't believe a word of it. Or at least we don't believe a word of our version of their beliefs. The difficulty though is not one of credulity but of experience. I cannot strip my mind of such concepts as the heliocentric universe, the circulation of the blood, the force of gravity, the circularity of the world and various other seminal matters. The vision of the Fourth Dynasty is as irretrievable as the vision of one's own childhood.

Christianity poses some of the same problems, of course. Science has done it a terrible disservice. Science and Reason. 'Where is God?' demanded Lisa, aged five. 'I want to see Him.' I took a deep breath, said *I* didn't think there was such a person as God, but others ... 'Granny Branscombe says He's in Heaven,' said Lisa coldly. 'And Heaven is in the sky.' Later, in her adolescence, she went through one of those phases of religiosity which are feverishly sexual and which the Catholic Church caters for so much better than the prosaic C. of E. In France or Spain Lisa could have had visions or thrown fits; as it was she had to settle for confirmation classes and Sunday Matins in Sotleigh parish church.

Muslims are forbidden to eat between dawn and dusk during Ramadan. They must also pray, facing Mecca, six times a day. The lawns of Gezira were littered with up-ended gardeners, studiously ignored by their English employers since it is impolite to display furtive interest in the religious practices of others. The French are less squeamish; Madame Charlot and her mother used to spend Ramadan harassing the cook and kitchen boy, who were made feckless by lack of nourishment, and grumbling loudly every time the gardener dropped to his knees. It was always mildly satisfying to see British racial complacency matched if not excelled by French xenophobia; the contempt with which Madame Charlot and her friends could invest the word '*arabe*' was more pungent even than the careless English 'Gyppo' or the curious pejorative use of 'native'. It made us seem positively liberal-minded. Madame Charlot was majestic in her stance of Gallic purity; the fact that she had been married to a Lebanese and that her entire life had been spent in Cairo made not the slightest difference: she represented all by herself the spirit of Charlemagne and the unimpeachable superiority of France. Other Europeans were to be tolerated, with polite disdain; Egyptians were in a category of their own.

In the world in which I moved there was no social intercourse between English and Egyptians. A few eccentrics in the British Council or university circles were known to consort occasionally with the middle-class Egyptian intelligentsia – a restricted group anyway in a country composed of millions of peasants, a rich merchant aristocracy and nothing much in between. The King was accorded a certain interest – he was after all a king – but considered a joke, an irresponsible playboy with his palaces and his red sports cars, though his beautiful wife, Queen Farida, was for some reason seen as saintly and put-upon, almost an honorary European. Egyptians could not belong to the Gezira Sporting Club or the Turf Club. Those of them with sufficient information, leisure and interest watched the progress of the desert war with detachment; when Rommel seemed unstoppable notices appeared in shop windows saying 'German officers welcome here'.

A revolution and the Assuan High Dam have changed all that. The fellaheen are still there but their mud huts have electricity now and infant mortality is no longer forty per cent. The King is gone and so are the English; that society is as distant as those of Memphis and Thebes. When Egyptians speak of the war they mean the Israeli war, not ours – which wasn't after all anything to do with them anyway.

'You should have been here yesterday evening,' says Camilla. 'Pip Leathers had this green smoke thing he'd pinched from the depot. A sort of signal. He let it off in the garden just behind Ahmed and Ahmed simply *howled*. It was absolutely killing. He thought it was an *afreet*, you see – the natives are so madly superstitious, they really believe in spirits and ghosts and things. We sat on the verandah and watched him rushing about wailing – honestly, I nearly died.' She is sitting on the edge of her bed painting her toenails. 'Do you want to try this, Claudia? It's rather heavenly – Elizabeth Arden Shocking Pink.

I say – is there something wrong? You're looking awfully browned off these days.'

'There's nothing wrong,' says Claudia.

'Gyppy tummy, I expect,' says Camilla blithely. 'I say – I'm going out with an Aussie tonight! Mummy would have a fit. Of course their accents *are* horrid but he's really awfully sweet and his people are something high up in Sydney. Will you be at the Club later on?'

Claudia wanders to the other room. She goes on to the verandah and stares out over Gezira, which begins to twinkle in the dusk. He has been gone three weeks now and she has heard nothing. There are rumours that the balloon will go up in the next month or two, that Rommel will break through, that there'll be a big show-down. Where is Tom? That rubbish-tip landscape of the aftermath of battle swims before her eyes: the shells of vehicles like animal carcasses, the intimate debris of people's lives – a tooth-brush, a tattered letter; the men plodding around in the sand. She conjures it up and mulls over it, and there is a dull grip in the pit of her stomach. Not Gyppy tummy, as Camilla suggests, unfortunately not. The war, she realises, has become something quite different. It is no longer prowling on the perimeter, like some large unpredictable animal that she is safely watching from afar, whose doings are of scientific interest. It has come right up close and is howling at her bedroom door; the shiver it provokes is the atavistic shiver of childhood. She is afraid, not for herself but with that indistinct cosmic fear of long ago. Thus she remembers persuading herself once in some dark night of infancy that the sun would never rise again.

Within the flat Camilla is shouting for the suffragi to bring the drinks tray. Down in the garden Madame Charlot harangues a neighbour about the price of meat.

There would be silence for weeks and then a letter. One of those inconsequential wartime letters bleached of information or intimacies by the shadow of the censor. And then suddenly he would be there, unheralded, a voice on the phone – three days' leave, five days' leave . . . We went to Luxor, to Alex. I have no idea how many days there were in all. They are distinguished now by their surroundings – the wide serenity of the Nile at Luxor, the barren silence of the Valley of the Kings, the crowds and chatter of hotels and bars, big lazy waves foaming in over the shallow beach at Sidi Bishr. And each time he went back again the lion snarled on the horizon, my scrutiny of communiqués and cultivating of press attachés took on an extra urgency. I tried again and again to get myself another trip to the desert – not because I would be anywhere near him but because I wanted to experience what it was he saw and heard and felt. I never again managed to get further than the training camps of Mersa Matruh – it was relatively easy for the men in the Press Corps, but I, and the occasional American or Commonwealth woman correspondent passing through, was frowned on by Eighth Army Battle HQ: the desert was no place for women.

'Why not?' demands Claudia.

'My dear girl, it's just not on, that's all. There'd be one hell of a stink. Randolph Churchill took some American lass up there and we got a lot of flak about it afterwards. They just aren't keen on females.'

'I am merely,' says Claudia, 'doing a job of work. Like the field hospital staff and the ATS drivers and various other women personnel who get to the desert.'

The new Press Officer at GHQ shrugs. 'Awfully sorry, m'dear, but there it is. I'll do what I can for you of course – if it was up to me we'd have you on a transport plane tomorrow. Incidentally, what about a drink this evening if you're at a loose end?'

Claudia smiles graciously, expediently.

There were weeks and months when nothing happened. All we knew was that out there the two armies were crouched motionless somewhere west of Tobruk, waiting to see what the other would do. There was little information because there was

118

none to give. It was then that the myth of Rommel took shape: the cunning, unpredictable foe, larger than life, a Napoleon of the sand, eclipsing the weathered homely legends of our own generals. Even Monty never had Rommel's mystique. There must have been realists in Cairo who expected the worst, yet never even later in the wilder moments of 'the flap', when the Panzer Army was poised at Alamein and the ashes of burning documents rained down from the sky do I remember the smell of fear. Crisis, yes; alarm, no. Those with wives and children sent them to Palestine; a few families got on boats for South Africa or India. There was plenty of the globe left into which to withdraw, and in any case it would only be a temporary measure, until things picked up again. I don't think anyone seriously envisaged Rommel's officers sitting around the pool at Gezira Sporting Club. Drinks were served at sundown, as they always had been; race meetings were on Saturdays; the amateur dramatics group did a production of *The Mikado*. Mother, writing from war-straitened Dorset, said she was so relieved I was somewhere safe, but thought the climate must be trying. Did she ever look at an atlas, I wonder? She had her own problems; patient endurance was the theme of her letters – shortages, the garden sadly neglected, her good saucepans nobly sacrificed to be rendered into war weapons. The flimsy aerograms with their neat script were eloquent with stoicism. Did she ever imagine German troops surging through Sturminster Newton?

But in those static months of early 1942 war seemed a permanent condition – a chronic disease that while not life-threatening impeded progress of any kind. I went to Jerusalem to try to get an interview with de Gaulle, who was rumoured to have turned up there, failed to get near him and did a piece on the Stern Gang instead. One or two of my colleagues, restless with the inactivity, took off altogether for more interesting centres and had to come belting back in a hurry when eventually the desert sprang into life again. It was a time that seemed even while it was in progress to go on for ever. The winter inched into spring; the temperature rose; at some point – when or for how long I do not know – he was there again.

'Let me tell you something extremely odd,' says Tom. 'I have never felt so good in my life.'

She considers him. He is lean; his muscles are like rope; his dark hair has a conflicting golden burnish from the sun. 'You look healthy, certainly.'

'Health is not really what I'm talking about. The spirit is what I had in mind. I'm quite remarkably happy. In the midst of all this. I think you are a sorceress, Claudia. A good sorceress, of course. A white witch.'

She cannot reply. No one, she thinks, has ever spoken to me like this before. I have never made anyone happy before. I have made people angry, restless, jealous, lecherous . . . never, I think, happy.

'And you?' asks Tom.

'Me too,' she says.

'*Après moi le déluge*,' says Tom. 'That is my unworthy sentiment these days.'

'Well,' she says. 'It may well be the case, I suppose. But even so there would be nothing we could do about it. I've always thought it a fairly reasonable sentiment.'

'Kiss me.'

'We're in a mosque,' she objects. 'We shall cause a riot.'

But even the mosque of Ibn Tulun has remote sequestered places.

'This is getting too much for me,' says Tom presently. 'We shall have to go back to your flat.'

'We haven't climbed the minaret.'

'I don't want to climb the minaret. I want to go back to your flat.'

'We may never come here again.'

'You are a remarkably obstinate woman,' he says. 'Or else you are putting me to some kind of test. All right – we'll climb the minaret and *then* we'll go back to your flat.'

And presently, looking down into the maze of humanity and

animals and balconies of washing Claudia says, 'What are you going to do after the war?'

'Ah. I wondered when we'd get to that.' He puts his arm around her. 'I'd thought of raising the matter myself. Well . . . First let me tell you what I *was* going to do after the war. I was going to go home full of fervour and high-minded notions and pronounced views on how society should be set to rights and stand for Parliament in some violently hostile constituency and retire beaten but unquenched. Or I might have settled for trenchant journalism in one of the better-class newspapers.'

'But you're not going to do this now?' murmurs Claudia – watching, far above her head, the kites that float in huge considered circles in the pale, pale blue sky.

'No. I feel less evangelical and more cynical and above all I've got other things in mind.'

'Such as?' asks Claudia. She tries to imagine the view from that kite's-eye height; can they see the curvature of the earth? The Red Sea? The Mediterranean?

'I want things I've never had much of a taste for hitherto. I want stability. I want to live in one place. I want to make plans for next year and the one after that and the one after that. I want' – he lays a hand on her arm – '. . . I want to get married. Are you listening to a word I'm saying?'

'I'm listening,' says Claudia.

'I want to get married. I want to marry you, in case I'm not making myself absolutely plain.'

'We could be evangelical together,' says Claudia, after a moment. 'I'm rather that way myself. You've no idea . . .'

'Well, all right then, if there's time. But I shall have to earn a living, which is something I've never bothered too much about up to now. I don't see why you should starve in garrets; I'm sure it's not what you're accustomed to.'

'Well, no. But I'm really quite good at fending for myself.'

'You can contribute,' says Tom, his arm now tightly around her. 'You can write these history books. For myself, I'm going to become a sober citizen. A son of toil. I want to get my hands dirty. Perhaps I'll be a farmer. I want to live somewhere where it rains a lot and things grow furiously. I want to see the fruits of the earth multiply and all that sort of thing. I want to make provision for the future. I want to lay up riches on earth since I don't believe in heaven. Not material riches – I want green fields and fat cows and oak trees. Oh, and there's one more thing I want. I want a child.'

'A child . . .' says Claudia. 'Goodness. A child . . .' She looks up again at the swirling kites; one is now much larger than the others, starting its slow descent upon some selected target.

'Ah,' says Sister, 'there you are, Mrs Jamieson. Well, we've had a bit of a crisis though I must say she's rallied marvellously this morning. But it was rather touch and go at one point. Anyway, Doctor doesn't think there'll be any more trouble for the moment. She's asleep now, if you want to sit with her for a bit. She was talking about you last night – not that she was compos mentis really, poor dear.'

Lisa looks through the porthole. Claudia is lying flat, eyes closed; one arm sprouts tubes and brightly coloured plastic pouches. 'What did she say?'

'She thought she was in childbirth again, bless her. She kept saying "Is it a boy or a girl?" ' Sister laughs gaily. 'Funny, isn't it – women often go back to that, towards the end. A lot of our old ladies harp on that. She was in a proper state – kept grabbing my arm: "Tell me if it's a boy or a girl . . ." So I said – you are her only one, aren't you, Mrs Jamieson? – I said, "It is a girl, Miss . . . Miss Hampton, but that was a long time ago." ' She clears her throat sharply: 'Of course the Miss is professional, I realise that, a lot of professional ladies keep Miss and I quite agree that Mizz business people use nowadays is awful. Well, there you are, Mrs Jamieson – you go on in, though I doubt if she's going to respond much today. But she may well know you're there.'

No she doesn't, thinks Lisa, she has no idea. Wherever she is it is not here, not in this room. She is somewhere a long way away.

Lisa sits. She opens the newspaper she has brought and reads. She will stay a quarter of an hour or so, in case. Occasionally she looks at Claudia. Once she gets up and crosses the room to prod the soil around the poinsettia by the radiator; the soil is correctly damp but the poinsettia looks sickly.

It's quite true, she thinks, you never forget having a baby. I remember every minute of each of the boys. She stands by the bed; Claudia's withered arms, her sunken face, the slack shape of her underneath the bedclothes fill Lisa with something that is both revulsion and a guilty pity. She thinks of her lover, whom she will see later that day. She savours, for a moment, her feelings about her lover. She thinks – and the thought is complacent – that Claudia has probably never known this feeling. She didn't love Jasper, certainly – at least not like that; very likely she has never loved anyone.

They have taken off her rings and her gold bracelet and put them on the bedside table. Lisa picks them up and looks at them – the big emerald that Jasper, presumably, gave her, the opal circlet and the diamond cluster (and where those came from, Claudia only knows). Then puts them down hastily; Claudia has always been funny about possessions – no, not funny, downright nasty.

'Can I have this?' asks Lisa.

'Can you have what?' says Claudia, continuing to type.

'This. This little box.'

Claudia turns her head. She looks at the ring in the palm of Lisa's hand, the ring with a little hinged compartment. Her eyes flicker. 'No,' she snaps. 'Put it back where you found it, Lisa. I've told you before not to touch the things in my jewellery box.'

'I want it,' mutters Lisa. And she does, she wants it more desperately than she has ever wanted anything, the fascinating ring-box with its crunchy silver-patterned lid, its tiny fastener. It is too big for her finger, far too big, but that does not matter.

She would keep things in it, very small and precious things.

'Put it back.'

Lisa opens the ring. 'It's dirty inside,' she reports. 'It's got little bits of dirt in it. I'm going to clean it.'

Claudia swings round in her chair. She reaches out and snatches the ring. 'Leave it alone,' she says. 'And don't touch it again, do you understand?'

Statistically, afterworlds – be they Christian, Greek, Pharaonic – must be populated almost entirely by children. Infants, toddlers. A terrible acreage of swaddled bundles, of little pot-bellied stick-limbed creatures, of wizened malformed dwarfs. With, prowling among them, a few bearded patriarchs, a scattering of old women, and a regiment of forty year olds. I see it as a scene by Hieronymus Bosch. There would be dragons, too, and devils with pitchforks and monstrous winged creatures. No angels; no heavenly choirs.

One can feel only relieved that one will not be going to such a place – merely to oblivion. And of course not even to that since we all survive in the heads of others. I shall survive – appallingly misrepresented – in Lisa's head and in Sylvia's and in Jasper's and in the heads of my grandsons (if there is room alongside football players and pop stars) and the heads of mine enemies. As a historian, I know only too well that there is nothing I can do about the depth and extent of the misrepresentation, so I don't care. Perhaps, for those who do, who struggle against it, this is the secular form of hell – to be preserved in forms that we do not like in the recollection of others.

Snide Claudia. Cynical Claudia. And fortunate Claudia, of course, to be granted the circumstances in which to reflect upon the way in which others will preserve her memory. Many would consider this a luxury. The other great proletariat of the afterworld, of course, is the soldiery – those myriads of boy-faces beneath their tin hats, helmets, turbans, bearskins . . .

'Hello,' says Camilla. 'I say, hasn't it been beastly hot today?

Our fan went kaput in the office and we nearly *died*. I must have a shower. By the way is it true there's been a big battle? You always hear everything – do tell. There are all sorts of rumours buzzing round the Embassy but no one's really saying. Go on . . . I won't utter, I swear.'

It is on the news. In the bleak clipped anonymous prose of the BBC – '. . . a number of engagements in the Western Desert in which severe losses were inflicted on the enemy.' Heavy fighting, says the impersonal voice, took place on several fronts.

'Isn't it exciting!' says Camilla. 'They're really at it in the desert again now, aren't they? Everyone's awfully keyed up at the Embassy. Apparently poor Bobby Fellowes is badly wounded – wretched for Sally, she's being terribly brave. But we're really bashing Rommel, everyone says.'

The phones and teleprinters at GHQ are busy twenty-four hours a day. Everyone is out of breath and impatient. No sorry not now my dear there's one hell of a flap on . . . see what I can do for you later . . . hang around there may be a communiqué at six . . . come back . . . wait . . . let you know as soon as we can.

Madame Charlot harangues the cook, in an unbroken monologue that lasts five minutes, a medley of French and kitchen Arabic in which certain words constantly recur – *baksheesh*, *piastres*, *méchant*, *mafeesh*, *mish kuwayyis*. The telephone rings. Her slippers slap across the stone floor of the hall. '*Mademoiselle Claudia . . . On vous téléphone . . .*' She returns to the kitchen; her voice – denouncing Lappas the grocer, questioning the absence of white flour, querying the change for a fifty-piastre note – runs parallel to that of someone with unconfirmed news of a tank battle in the Sidi Rezegh area, a withdrawal . . .

Claudia types, in the white heat of the day. In the next room Camilla sleeps, released from the Embassy for the essential afternoon rest. Down in the garden, the gardener also sleeps, in the shade of the banyan tree, hunched up into a bundle of old rags. Hoopoes pick delicately at the lawn; the petunias and marigolds blaze.

There is an advance. There is a retreat. We have lost this many tanks, that many aircraft, so many men have been taken prisoner. The Germans have lost this many, that many. Figures dance on bits of paper, tenuously related to machines, to flesh and blood. There is out there, where these things or something like them are supposedly happening, and back here, where ice chinks in glasses at six and hoses play on the gardens of Gezira.

'Nothing for you at the moment, my dear, I'm afraid,' says the Press Officer. 'Cast your eye over the latest casualty lists if you like . . .'

'. . . A picnic at the Fayoum on Saturday,' says Camilla. 'Heavenly. Eddie Masters is coming, and Pip and Jumbo. I say, Claudia – is something up? You look frightfully seedy – would you like an aspirin?'

First there is disbelief, resolute disbelief. No, it is not possible. Not him. Others but not him. And then there is hope because missing does not necessarily mean killed, missing men turn up – wounded, taken prisoner. Or they walk in out of the desert days later, unscathed; Cairo is full of such tales.

Hope becomes endurance – moving through the day, and the next and the one after; lying sleepless through the nights – with this hollow ache within, this tumbling down a cliff-face of fear each time you allow yourself to think, to remember.

Praying. Praying shamefaced in the Cathedral.

'Mademoiselle Claudia, on vous téléphone . . .'

127

'Claudia? Drummond here – Press Office. You asked us to let you know if there was anything on Southern. Captain T. G. Southern – reported missing. Is that right? There's a signal here – apparently he's been picked up now. Killed, I'm afraid, poor chap. Was he a chum of yours?'

The nights are worst. The days pass, somehow, because there are certain actions to be performed. The nights though are not seven or eight hours long but twenty-four – they are days unto themselves, hot black days in which she lies naked on the sheet staring at the ceiling, hour after hour after hour.

'I've sent Abdul out for some more milk,' says Camilla. 'The stuff in the jug was foul – I'm sure he's been topping it up with Nile water. Did we wake you up last night? Eddie brought me back from the Moffats' party and *insisted* on coming up for a drink. Aren't you having any breakfast?'

How? Where? Instantly? Or slowly, lying bleeding into the sand, alone. Too weak to fire the Very pistol. To find the water flask. Just lying waiting.
Please may it have been instantly.

Madame Charlot pounces from her lair. '*Un instant, Mademoiselle Claudia . . .*' An outpouring in her maverick combination of French and English – an impassioned account of rising prices and the chicanery of shopkeepers, the deprivations of the moment – 'this 'orrid war-time' – necessitating a rent increase '*mais très peu, vous comprenez, très peu, c'est moi qui souffrirai, enfin . . .*' So that Claudia has to stand holding the bannister until at last the nausea overcomes her .and she excuses herself, runs up the stairs . . .

Don't think about it. However it was it is over now. However it was or wherever it was. He is not lying there any more. He is nowhere now. Nowhere at all. Don't think about it.

'Cicurel have got some heavenly new materials in,' says Camilla. 'There's a pink and blue crêpe-de-chine I simply can't resist. A two-piece, I thought, for garden parties. The little Greek woman's going to do it for me, from a *Vogue* pattern.'

Is nausea always a manifestation of grief? Who am I to know? I have never been thus before. Grief-stricken. Stricken is right; it is as though you had been felled. Knocked to the ground; pitched out of life and into something else.

The *khamseen* blows. The windows have to be kept closed. The hot wind rattles the shutters and the kitchen boy sweeps dust from the hall floor three times a day.

The map on the wall of the Press Room is decked out with little flags: red, green, yellow, blue, brown, white. Brigades and divisions make gay patterns upon the contours. The Press Officer's pointer moves among them, reducing everything to orderliness and elegance. Noise, smoke, heat, dust, flesh, blood and metal are gone; it is really all quite simple, a child could grasp it, a question of dispositions and manoeuvres, flanks and pincer movements, lines and boxes.

> ' "There is a blessed home
> Beyond this land of woe," '

sings the cathedral congregation. The women sing loudest, in the clear clean precise voices of their race and class; a few tenors and baritones ring out also, confident but not assertive.

> ' "Where trials never come
> Nor tears of sorrow flow." '

And when they have done with singing they pray, to the Lord God of Hosts. Gloved hand to their brows, one knee upon the stone floor, they humbly beseech Him to abate the pride of their enemies, assuage their malice and confound their devices. And, that done, they rise, discreetly straightening trouser creases and smoothing silk dresses over knees, to sing once more.

' "Onward Christian soldiers,
Marching as to war ..." '

'You ought to get away for a bit,' says Camilla. 'Go to Alex
for a few days. You must be run-down, the way you keep being
sick all the time. There's a sweet little *pension* near the corniche
I can give you the address of.'

It is like travel. You journey from the event and as it
becomes more distant it becomes less potent and more poignant, like a remembered home. As the weeks go by the knife
turns differently.

And there is something else now to think about. With
amazement at first, then with apprehension, with wonder and
with awe.

'Oh my *goodness* ...' says Camilla. 'Well I mean I did
wonder you did seem to be ... um, well sort of filling out a bit
and of course you seemed so run down, I *see* now ... But
somehow the last person one would expect ... I mean not like
Lucy Powers or the Hamilton girl – with them one honestly
wasn't surprised, but you, Claudia ... What rotten bad luck.
How absolutely foul for you. But why didn't you ... I mean,
couldn't you have ... You're going to *have* it? Well, goodness I
do think you're *brave*.' She stares, incredulous; it is the most
extraordinary thing she has heard in weeks.

The nursing home is surrounded by a big shady garden.
Gravelled paths wander among palms – the stocky domesti-
cated kind with textured trunks – and casuarinas. Ambulant
patients wander also, and others recline on basket chairs on the
lawns and the verandah, patrolled by nurses. The nurses are all
very starched – coiffed in sparkling white like nuns of some
esoteric order. They are also unremittingly cheerful. Claudia is
received by a freckle-faced Irish sister whose uniform crackles
down corridors and into lifts. 'Not much further, dear,' she

keeps saying. 'We'll have you tucked up in bed in a jiffy. Not feeling too bad? How's the pain now?'

'I'm all right,' says Claudia, who is not. The pain in fact is intense; she clenches her stomach muscles, trying to hold it back.

There is the sound of a baby crying. They pass a door with a wide glass screen through which can be seen rows of cots. Claudia stops.

'Now then,' says the nurse, 'I wouldn't, dear . . . Better get yourself to bed.' Her cheerfulness wavers; this is an unforeseen hitch. 'Not that everything isn't going to be fine, Mrs Hampton, in a few months time we'll be popping your baby in there too.'

'Miss,' says Claudia. 'Not Mrs.' She stares through the glass screen. Only the babies' heads are visible, some fringed with hair, some not, so that they are just tiny scraps of red flesh at the top of a bundle of wrappings. 'Why do the cots all have their feet in tins of water?'

'It's because of the ants. If we didn't do it you'd have the ants getting to the babies. It's a terrible country, this. The climate and the insects, I never knew anything like it.'

She puts her hand on Claudia's arm, covering her discomposure with confidentiality. 'You'd hardly believe it, but I've been told – it was before my time, see, quite a few years ago – there was a girl didn't keep the tins topped up and they found one of the babies dead. The ants had got it. Eaten the little thing's eyes out. That was how they found it – the eyes gone and the ants all over it.'

Claudia moves away. She stands for a moment as though in thought and then turns to the bowl of sand in which people are supposed to put out their cigarettes; she is violently sick into it, in paroxysms that go on for several minutes.

'You're having a miscarriage my dear,' says the matron. 'As I imagine you realise. We'll make you as comfortable as we can.' She looks down at Claudia; her expression is blandly impersonal – a professional face. 'I imagine,' she goes on, 'that

131

under the circumstances you may be feeling it's the best thing. Doctor will be along to see you again in a few minutes.'

Claudia is lying with her legs clenched together. Some animal is gnawing her within. She stares at the woman and then rears herself up in the bed. 'No,' she whispers. She has intended to shout but her voice comes out as a hoarse breath. 'I'm not going to have a miscarriage. It is not the best thing and it is not for you to say so. You must *do* something.'

The matron's eyebrows have shot up now almost to her starched cap. Her tone is no longer quite so dispassionate. 'I'm afraid,' she says, 'that Nature has a way of taking its course, in these cases.'

'Then bloody well do something,' roars Claudia. 'I want this baby. If you don't save this baby I'll . . . I'll . . .' She sinks back, tears prick her eyes. 'I'll kill you,' she mutters. 'I'll kill you, you cow.'

And hours later, when they are doing things with bowls of water and pails and sheets she is aware of shouting again, shouting at them, swearing at them. ' 'Twas neither a girl nor a boy,' says the Irish sister. 'Over and done with now, it is. The best thing you can do is forget all about it.'

II

The aftermath of war is disorder. An example, incidentally, of the misuse of language: aftermath is a decent agricultural term, it has a precise meaning – the aftermath is the second crop of grass which appears after the mowing of the first. The aftermath of war should, correctly, be another war; it usually is. But the conventional aftermath is the struggle to set straight that which is awry: the taking stock, the counting of the living and the dead, the drift of the dispossessed back to their homelands, the apportioning of blame, the extraction of penalties and, at last, the writing of history. Once it is all written down we know what really happened.

I visited, late in 1945, a camp for Displaced Persons. I was to write a piece on them for the *New Statesman*. The camp was somewhere on the German–Polish border, in one of those bits of Europe where national boundaries make no sense, where the landscape has an impersonality and uniformity that makes it a nowhere. You are in the middle of a land mass; there are no edges – just sky, horizon. This area had been disputed for hundreds of years, scuffed about by armies over and over again. Once, presumably, there had been hayfields and little farms, cows and chickens and children. Now, after five years of abuse, it was a wasteland; and in the middle of it was the camp – line upon line of concrete block-houses among which people disconsolately wandered or queued for yet another interview with yet another harassed official surrounded by card-index boxes. I sat in on some of these interviews. Most of the people were old, or they seemed old, their faces belying the figures on their cards; some, though, were young – peasant girls transported as slave labour, their plump country faces grey and scraggy, seventeen turned forty. And they spoke with tongues – you never knew which language would come next: Lithuanian, Serbo-Croat, Ukrainian, Polish, French . . . Interpreters bustled to and fro. I talked to an old woman whose given nationality was Polish but who spoke French – an elegant drawing-room French. She wore a battered grey coat, a shawl round her head and she smelled a little; but her speech was an echo of some gracious home, of cut glass and silver, of music lessons and governesses. Her husband had died of typhoid, one son had been shot by the Nazis, another had perished in a labour camp, her daughter-in-law and grandchildren had vanished. '*Je suis seule au monde*,' she said, gazing at me. '*Seule au monde . . .*' And all around us the people shuffled past or stood patiently in endless lines.

I wrote my piece for the *New Statesman*, I suppose; perhaps I mentioned the old Polish woman. Presumably they tidied her away somewhere; sorted her out to an appropriate country, ticked off her card. She would not be one of those loose ends that cause trouble for years, those perennial matters for international reproach: a Volga German, a Crimean Tartar. At least they knew who she was and where she was.

For a nation, it is a great historical convenience to have edges. Islands do disproportionately well. I remember thinking about this when I first saw the cliffs of Dover again in 1945. There they were, those cliffs, conjuring up Shakespeare, the dry squeak of chalk on school blackboards and that song about bluebirds. They had barbed wire at their feet and pill-boxes on their tops. There were demobbed soldiers everywhere, conspicuous in their ill-fitting new suits; everyone was grumbling about something. If this was victory, it hardly seemed worth it. I sat in a train that rocked its way slowly through the fields of Kent; the windows were still partially blacked-out, the paint scratched away in wide runnels so that the landscape flickered by in snatches. I thought about those potent cliffs.

And Gordon was at Victoria to meet me. In a demob suit, with an aggressively short haircut and that mark on his cheek that only I would have noticed.

From halfway along the platform she can see him. It is as though no one else were there. She halts six feet from him; he is the same and not the same, this is the face she knows better than any face but it is also the face of a stranger. It has new strata; there are accretions and adjustments. The space between them acknowledges this – the six feet of grey station platform; she cannot cross it. To do so is to step back – back into other Claudias, back towards other Gordons. But those Claudias and Gordons are no longer there; they are wiped out just as that known face has been wiped out and another substituted. She is fascinated and alarmed. She searches herself for familiar signals. And then she steps across the six feet of platform, touches him, and the signals flash. But distantly now, distantly, overlaid by too much else.

He sees that she is smaller and thinner and she has red hair. She is wearing clothes that are not the dingy shoddy garb of everyone else around; her coat is glowing orange, distinctly un-English, she wears a little feathered hat. He was looking at her before he realised this was Claudia (others also glance, or openly stare). She advances towards him, neither smiling nor waving, and then stops. He would think she had not recognised him if it were not that her eyes are fixed upon him.

And then she steps forward and kisses him. She smells foreign and expensive, but beneath the Chanel or whatever it is there is a whiff – a rich emotive whiff – of unreachable moments. Within him something stirs, raises its head and sniffs. And Claudia is talking about a mark on his face.

'That's my war wound. Some repellent Indian skin disease. Is it that conspicuous? You, I'm glad to see, are quite unscarred.'

'Am I?' she says. 'Good.'

'But your hair's red. I remembered it brown.'

'My hair was always considered red. It was one of the things Mother held against me, from infancy. How is she?'

We went to some café and drank dense reeking tea out of those cups half an inch thick. I kept staring round me; London, the buildings, the people, the buses and taxis, had the same unreal quality as Gordon himself – as though it were an invented landscape suddenly made manifest. Only when I saw bomb-sites, and the gutted interior of a house with fireplaces airily exposed and the marks of ghostly staircases, did it strike home that time had passed here also. But I felt like a visitor, not the returning native.

We talked. We told each other as much as we were ever going to tell of what we had seen and done, of where we had been and with whom. I peered into the spaces in Gordon's account and he, I suppose, listened to the silences in mine. After an hour or so we were back five years – skirmishing and competing, bidding for one another's attention. Gordon, I gathered, had been involved with an American girl in Delhi. I asked 'Why didn't you get married?' He laughed and said he hadn't time to get married. He was going back to the research project he was involved in before the war, there were offers of jobs from all sides, he was going to be in the thick of things.

A year later he met Sylvia. I was never jealous of Sylvia. It would have been ridiculous. That unknown American girl, though, gave me a nasty twinge. For a year or so I used to imagine her.

Until I was in my late twenties I never knew a man who interested me as much as Gordon did. That was why it was as it was between us. I measured each man I met against him, and they fell short: less intelligent, less witty, less attractive. I tested myself for the *frisson* that Gordon induced, and it was not there. It seemed profoundly unfortunate that there was no one else in the world to match up to me except my brother.

Incest is closely related to narcissism. When Gordon and I

were at our most self-conscious – afire with the sexuality and egotism of late adolescence – we looked at one another and saw ourselves translated. I saw in Gordon's maleness an erotic flicker of myself; and when he looked at me I saw in his eyes that he too saw some beckoning reflection. We confronted each other like mirrors, flinging back reflections in endless recession. We spoke to each other in code. Other people became, for a while, for a couple of contemptuous years, a proletariat. We were an aristocracy of two.

The schoolroom has been turned into a dance studio. The sofa and chairs are pushed back against the walls, the carpet rolled up, the gramophone stands upon the old baize-covered table.

Gordon smells now of man. In her nostrils, as she presses up against him, breasts to his shirt-front, hair brushing his cheek, is a full-blown male scent, almost anonymous, no longer Gordon but something else. It is delicious, and there flows through Claudia the most strange and interesting feeling.

'Slow, quick, quick, slow . . . Other foot, you idiot . . . Start again.'

People at Cambridge are all doing rag-time now, Gordon says. But that is boring. So is the Charleston. Hopping about like loonies, says Gordon. No – the only thing worth doing is a slow foxtrot. And a quickstep. And you have to be better at it than anyone else, that is the whole point. You have to be so expert that you stop the room – you are left alone on the dance floor. That is what they plan – at the Molesworths' do next week.

'When I press your back we'll go into reverse. Now . . .'

And firmly, warmly, Gordon's hand manipulates the small of her back and they swing expertly sideways, hip to hip. Slow, quick, quick, slow. 'Oh, *very* nice . . .' says Gordon. '*Very* stylish . . . And again . . .' Slow, quick, quick, slow. Across and across the room, again and again, more adept each time, moving as one . . . A dash to the gramophone when it begins to run down . . . then body to body again, thigh to thigh . . . oh, heavenly, this is . . . let's go on for ever, we're getting better and better, let's never stop . . .

And so, for a long time, they don't. Dusk creeps into the room; they break off only to change the record or wind up the gramophone; neither says a word. Oh bliss, thinks Claudia . . . Goodness what bliss . . . She savours this extraordinary feeling, this excitement . . . She has never felt like this before. What is it?

They stop, eventually, by the window, in the blue cool twilight, and look at each other. Their faces are so close they nearly touch. And then they do touch – his mouth against hers, his tongue between her lips, her mouth opening. The gramophone needle sticks in the groove, the same note hiccupping out over and over, again and again.

'And another thing,' says Mother. 'Apparently at the Molesworths' on Thursday you danced with Gordon the entire evening. Mrs Molesworth says it wasn't that you hadn't other partners, either – she says Nicholas asked you at least twice, and Roger Strong. It's so rude. And apparently Gordon never asked Cynthia Molesworth once. You're too old to behave like that now.'

She lies on the grass of the river-bank, quite naked. The shadows of the willow leaves make fretted patterns on her body. Gordon rises from the water; he heaves himself up on the bank and comes to sit beside her. His thighs are streaked with mud, his hair plastered to his head. After a moment he reaches for his jacket, takes a pen from his pocket. He traces around the edges of the leaf shadows, on her stomach, her arms, legs, breasts; she is marbled all over in pale blue ink. 'And how am I going to get all this off?' she enquires. 'Don't be so prosaic,' says Gordon. 'This is Art. I'm turning you into an *objet trouvé* . . . Turn over.' She turns onto her stomach and laughs into the grass; the pen wanders insect-like over her skin.

'You're both very silent this morning,' says Mother. 'Pass me the marmalade please, Gordon. And Claudia dear, I don't think that dress you had on last night is at all suitable for down here. Wear it when you're in town if you must but it is simply not the thing for the country. People were looking at you.'

'Good serve,' says Gordon. 'Forty–love.' As they pass each other he murmurs, 'Slam it at her backhand this time.'

They have trounced all. The rest of the tennis party sit around amid the rose-beds, watching them with dislike. Claudia saunters to the back of the court, admiring as she does so her bare sunburned legs. She turns; she takes her time over the serve, savouring for a moment Gordon's back, the way his hair lies on his shirt collar, the shape of him.

'The children are off to Paris for a few days,' says Mother. 'Mind, I do feel Claudia is young yet for this kind of thing but she has Gordon to look after her.'

'It's Pernod,' says Gordon. 'And you'd jolly well better get to like it. You can't come here and not drink Pernod.' And presently when they get up and move on she realises that she is floating, not walking but most agreeably floating down the street, holding his arm. 'We must come here often,' she says. 'Naturally,' says Gordon. 'All civilised people spend a lot of time in France.' It is his birthday; he is twenty today.

'Claudia is going to Oxford,' says Mother. 'Of course quite a lot of girls do now and she has always been one for getting her own way.'

A summer. Two summers, perhaps, and a winter. Time out of mind ago – at least not out of mind but shrunk to a necklace of moments when we did this or that, when we said this or that, were here or there. When we were at home, sprawled side by side in the schoolroom, absorbed in one another while downstairs Mother sings to herself as she does the flowers. Or in Gordon's rooms at Cambridge, or at a theatre in London or roaming the Dorset landscape, arrogantly bored. I don't wonder people looked at us with dislike. A year, perhaps two . . . And then we both began to look beyond each other, to wander away, to take an interest in the despised proletariat beyond. That time went; it is also forever there, conditioning how we are with one another. Because of it, other people are still excluded. Most of them never knew this; only Sylvia, poor stupid Sylvia, who got a whiff of it but never knew what it was she smelled. Later, much later.

There is roast chicken for Sunday lunch, bread sauce, bacon rolls, all the trimmings . . . Mother has done everything herself, valiantly, with little self-deprecating comments. She has taught herself to cook, brave Mother, since the defection of the last of the village helps. Claudia gave her Elizabeth David's *French Country Cooking* for Christmas which was received politely but without enthusiam; no *coq au vin* or *quiche lorraine* has appeared on the table at Sturminster Newton.

'It's *lovely*, Mrs Hampton,' gushes Sylvia, the good daughter-in-law. 'Absolutely delicious. I do think you're clever.'

Mother sits at the head of the table, Sylvia at her right. Claudia is opposite, Gordon at the end. Mother and Sylvia continue to discuss bread sauce, butchers, and, in more muted tones, the absorbing progress of Sylvia's first pregnancy.

Claudia hears this as background noise: the buzzing of flies, a lawnmower. She has not seen Gordon for a couple of months. There is an unresolved argument to be taken up and a couple of scurrilous anecdotes to tell, one of which makes Gordon laugh uproariously. Sylvia breaks off what she is saying to Mother and turns. Her eyes are jumpy. She cries, 'Oh, what's the joke – do tell!' and Gordon, getting up .to carve himself more chicken, says it's just something about someone we used to know, not all that funny really, anyone else want some more? 'Meanie!' pouts Sylvia. 'Claudia, you tell me . . .' and Claudia focuses for the first time on her sister-in-law, who is wearing what appears to be a vast billowing flowered pillow case from which sprouts her pink, pretty face, her golden hair.

Sylvia arouses, really, no emotions in Claudia at all, beyond a certain incredulity. She does occasionally wonder what Gordon talks to her about.

'Oh – just a bit of gossip,' she says. 'Nothing really . . .'

Sylvia turns to her mother-in-law. 'Were they always like this, Mrs Hampton? So . . . so *cliquey*?'

'Oh no,' says Mother tranquilly. 'They squabbled dreadfully.'

'So did we!' cries Sylvia. 'Desmond and I. We *loathed* each other. We were absolutely normal. We still are. I mean, I'm fond of Desmond but really we haven't got a thing in common.'

Gordon sits down again with a plateful of food. 'Claudia and I will do our best to be abnormal in privacy in future, then. OK, Claudia? We can stage a good fight for you now, if you like.'

Sylvia is flustered. Her hand flies to his arm, kneads it, her face becomes even pinker. 'Oh heavens, I don't mean you're *peculiar*, just it's funny a brother and sister being so kind of intimate. Lovely, really.'

All through what she was saying to Mrs Hampton she could hear them – or at least, maddeningly, not quite hear them. Gordon talking in that tone he uses to no one else. Claudia's deep voice, a voice that can be so sarcastic, so unnerving, but to Gordon is so confidential. And when she tries to join in they clam up, fall silent, Gordon changes the subject, offers second helpings.

Claudia is wearing a red dress, very tight round the waist and hips. She is skinny thin these days. 'I love your frock,' says Sylvia determinedly. 'I wish I could get into things like that.' She pats her tummy and eyes Claudia: Claudia who is not married, not going to have a baby. She feels a little comforting glow of complacency. Thus bolstered, she is able to become gay and joky, to ask Mrs Hampton – who has been sweet, with whom there is never any problem – about when Claudia and Gordon were children, to chatter amusingly about herself and Desmond. And then Gordon says something in his shutting-out voice, his cool as-though-to-a-casual-acquaintance voice, and she is no longer bolstered, no longer glowing. 'I don't mean you're *peculiar*,' she wails. 'It's lovely, really.' She has not got it right. They are both looking at her now, Gordon and Claudia; she has got their attention all right, but not in the way she wanted. Are they laughing at her? Is that the tilt of little smiles at the corners of their mouths?

'Gracious!' says Claudia. 'You make us sound exotic. I don't think we've ever felt particularly exotic, have we?'

'Incestuous, don't you mean?' says Gordon, tucking into roast chicken. 'Though come to think of it I suppose incest is a bit exotic. Classical, though. Very high class. Look at the Greeks.'

'And look at Nellie Frobisher in the village,' says Claudia. 'Knocked up by her dad before she was seventeen. Dr Crabb used to say he could tell which village people came from in central Dorset from the shape of their heads.'

'Claudia, *really* . . .' exclaims Mrs Hampton.

And Sylvia can endure it no longer. Suddenly she isn't feeling very well. She pushes her chair back, puts her hand on her tummy, says with dignity that she is going to lie down for a bit – she's sure everyone will understand.

As she climbs the stairs she can hear Mrs Hampton scolding them.

12

'Thank you,' says Claudia. 'It looks nice and expensive. Fortnum's, I see. Put it on the table, will you. The nurse on florist duties will see to it later.'

She is propped up on pillows. A board is tilted at an angle in front of her; she has pen and paper.

'You're writing something,' Jasper states. He lowers himself into the bedside chair, which creaks betrayingly. Jasper is a substantial figure nowadays in every way. 'What are you writing?'

'A book.'

He smiles. Indulgently? Disbelievingly? 'What about?'

'A history of the world,' replies Claudia. She slides a look at him. 'Pretentious, eh?'

'Not at all,' says Jasper. 'I shall look forward to reading it.'

Claudia laughs. 'I doubt that, for various reasons.' There is a silence. She adds, 'I prefer to remain occupied, even when allegedly dying.'

Jasper makes a gesture of dismissal. 'Nonsense, Claudia.'

'Well, we shall see. Or, more probably, you will. So . . . You're still busy making expensive travesties of the truth, I gather. *The Life of Christ* in six episodes, is that right? With commercial breaks.'

Jasper starts to speak, takes a breath, stops. Starts again. 'This isn't the time or the place, Claudia. Pax, eh? I've come to see you, not to cross swords.'

'As you like,' says Claudia. 'I thought it might be good therapy. This is one of my brighter days, they tell me. I always rather enjoyed our sword-crossings, didn't you?'

He smiles – placatingly, charmingly. 'I have never regretted anything, my dear. The times with you least of all.'

'Ah,' Claudia looks sharply at him. 'Well, there I would agree with you. Regretting is always pointless, since there is no undoing. Only the sanctimonious go in for breast-beating. Do you want a cup of tea? Ring that bell if so.'

I suppose it is because I sense a compatibility that I have been fascinated by the exploiters of historical circumstance. Political adventurers – Tito, Napoleon. Medieval popes; crusaders; colonisers. I don't like them, but I cannot help observing them. Traders and settlers have always intrigued me – those fearless ruthless opportunists inserting themselves into the cracks and crevices and channels created by politics and diplomacy. I cannot help taking a censorious interest in the spice trade, the fur trade, the East India Company. In all those beady-eyed, devious, amoral, indestructible fellows of the sixteenth and seventeenth and eighteenth centuries who risked their lives and lined their pockets in the wake of public events.

Greed is an interesting quality. Jasper is greedy; he has to have money for its own sake – not just for what it can buy but as pure possession: figures on pieces of paper. Cupidity centred on bank statements and shareholdings is more difficult to understand than the avarice of an Elizabethan trader with his haul of cinnamon, cloves, mace, nutmeg and, presumably, gold bars under the floorboards. Since no one, nowadays, gets closer to visible touchable wealth than their bank statement or the plastic rectangles in their wallet it is presumably atavistic instincts of this kind that are aroused by newspaper stories of treasure – coin hoards turned up by the plough, chests of doubloons at the bottom of the Solent. We all dribble a little at the thought of gold and silver, and make lust respectable by sermonising about concern for the past. Nonsense. It's not

Anglo-Saxons or medieval sailors people are interested in – it's money, cash, guineas, pieces of eight, sovereigns, ingots, stuff you can run your hands through and count and feel the weight of and stash away under the bed.

Jasper turned the war to his own advantage. He made sure that he was never in any danger nor indeed greatly inconvenienced and set about furthering his career. He shot up ladders, outstripped his contemporaries and, I daresay, contributed his mite to victory. Jasper is a patriot, of course, in his own way.

It could well be asked why, since I talk like this of Jasper, I ever became, and remained, involved with him. When are sexual choices ever rational or expedient? Jasper was excellent to go to bed with, and entertaining out of it. By the time he was Lisa's father we were linked for good. And for bad.

'I'm leaving the Foreign Office,' says Jasper.

They are driving through Normandy. This landscape, Claudia thinks, is surely mythical, some collective dream of Frenchness, of farms and cows and apples, of the past, of how the world ought to be but is not. It is surely invented, yet here am I sitting in Jasper's not-quite-new Jaguar while it flows past the windows: medieval, aromatic, complete with chateaux and petrol stations and tractors and old Citroens held together with string. 'Are you indeed? Why?'

'They were proposing that I should go to Djakarta.'

'Dear me. As Ambassador, I take it?'

'Not as Ambassador,' says Jasper, sweeping past a farm cart and a lorry, aiming the Jaguar up an avenue of poplars; a church with Romanesque door flies by on the right, a hoarding advertising Pernod on the left.

Claudia laughs. 'I can see that Commercial Secretary in Djakarta wouldn't do. Whose nose have you been getting up at the FO, then?'

'My dear girl, that is not how it works. There is a progression. A laborious progression for which I am not prepared to hang around.'

'I see. So what are you going to do?'

'I'm looking into various things. One should be thinking about television. I may do a column for *The Times*. NATO is a possibility.'

'Ah,' says Claudia. 'NATO. Which is why we're here.'

'Up to a point.' He takes his hand from the wheel and squeezes her knee. 'It's also an excuse for a jaunt with you, of which I don't get enough. Here we are, I suspect.'

He swings the car off the main road and through wide gates into a tree-lined drive through parkland. Gravel spits up from the wheels. A sign at the gate, so discreet and tastefully lettered that Claudia only glimpses it, says something in French, English and German about Château de Something Conference Centre.

'What are you, precisely, when we get there?'

'I'm an observer. I'm doing a piece for the *Spectator*.'

'And what am I?'

'You're my secretary.'

'No I'm bloody not,' says Claudia. 'You can stop the car right away.' She opens the door. The Jaguar swerves, slows.

Jasper reaches across her. 'Don't be an idiot. Shut that door. I'm joking. Well, I had to put you down as something, didn't I? Friend? Mistress?'

The car, now, has come to a halt, with Claudia half in and half out. He has her by the arm.

'I have a name, don't I?' snaps Claudia. 'Let go of me.'

He pulls. She pulls. And all of a sudden he glimpses in the driving mirror the interested faces of driver and passenger in a car behind them. He yanks Claudia into her seat, slams the door and starts the car off with a jerk that flattens her. 'Darling, you're being absurd. What does it matter? We're here to amuse ourselves a bit, that's all.'

'Well right now I'm not particularly amused,' says Claudia, but she is calming down, he sees (shooting a quick glance), with one of those typically Claudia switches of mood. Indeed, she becomes suddenly quiet, her attention grabbed it seems by the chateau, which comes into view now as the avenue takes a turn. Very handsome it is too, complete with moat, water-lilies, swans, and a lot of glossy official cars parked on the gravel sweep in front. Jasper feels his spirits lift; the sight of chauffeurs, uniforms, cars unavailable to the common man, national flags and the apparatus of power takes him back to the war years, when one had been in the thick of all that. Perhaps a NATO job is indeed the thing to be going after. By all accounts there are some satisfactorily unspecific senior positions, in which one could rove around and generally carve out something rather interesting. And he could undoubtedly land one, if he puts his mind to it. He starts to make a mental list of people to have a word with when he gets back to London. And this will be an excellent occasion to make oneself known in other influential circles – to parade discreetly one's record, to talk knowledgeably, amusingly and confidently in four different languages. He begins to tingle at the prospect. He is going to be busy. Maybe it wasn't such a good idea after all to bring Claudia along. Except that Claudia, provided that she doesn't turn recalcitrant, is an asset. People notice Claudia. People notice one's association with Claudia; men are envious – women are impressed.

The chateau seems to stem from the world of Disney rather than Louis Treize. Claudia studies it as they approach – its silly pepperpot turrets and its clean creamy walls and its moat with water-lilies – and continues to do so as they climb stone staircases to find their rooms. There are immense salons, lavishly carpeted, and an echoing dining-hall hung about with archaic weaponry, and a bathroom with shower and bidet to each bedroom. She dumps her case on the bed and goes to look through the mullioned window; a swan with wake of cygnets cruises the moat.

'All right, darling?' says Jasper. 'Good place, eh? I'll just go and check up on a few things – meet me downstairs when you're ready.'

Claudia picks up the brochure that has been placed on her

147

dressing-table and reads that the chateau, home of the Ducs de Rocqueville for four hundred years, has been converted (with the minimum interference to its historic features) into the Rocqueville Conference Centre. Rocqueville, she learns, is a study centre for the problems of the post-war world, specialising in conferences attended by experts in academic, military, diplomatic and political spheres. The wording of the brochure is both high-flown and evasive: it hints at powerful international backing, attempts some mild intimidation by way of economic jargon, and throws in a lot about peace and understanding and the hopes of mankind. Distinguished visitors to Rocqueville since the centre opened in 1948 include Winston Churchill, John Foster Dulles, General de Gaulle, Professor John Kenneth Galbraith and Dag Hammarskjöld.

Claudia changes her clothes and descends the stone staircases. This week's experts from various spheres are by now gathered in the main reception room drinking pre-lunch aperitifs beneath crystal chandeliers and a billowing ceiling fresco of the *seizième* in which cherubs tow ladies in *déshabille* around on powder-puff clouds. She stands in the entrance for a few moments, taking in first the ceiling and the spindly gilt-limbed furniture and then the experts: there are military uniforms (uniforms so high-ranking that they admit only the occasional scrap of ribbon or chaste insignia), academic tweeds, political and diplomatic pinstripes. There are not many women – a few severely clothed donnish figures, various secretarial-looking girls who hover self-effacingly around the edges of the room, a recognisable Italian woman politician, and an administrative figure who steps forward now, with hostess smile. Claudia sidesteps neatly and moves off into the crowd, at the opposite side of the room to Jasper whom she can see with some uniformed Americans. She heads purposefully towards the window and comes to rest beside a solitary man who is contemplating the ceiling.

'Inappropriate,' says Claudia. She takes a glass from a proffered tray.

'On the contrary,' says the man. 'It is we who are inappropriate. The painting was here first.'

Claudia looks at him more closely. He is nondescript, a short dapper man with toothbrush moustache, the sort of person who goes unnoticed in a crowd, which is perhaps why no one is talking to him. 'You're right. Incongruous, I should have said.'

The man tosses back his drink, reaches for another from the retreating tray. 'And who are you?'

Claudia starts to bristle. But there is something about him to which she responds; the demand is direct rather than rude, and Claudia approves of direction. She tells him her name.

'I've read your book. The Tito thing.'

Claudia glows. She is vain enough (oh, quite vain enough), and new enough to mild fame, to appreciate recognition. She bestows on this man her full attention, to the exclusion of the babbling room, the cherubs and the ladies in *déshabille*. His appearance, she now realises, is deceptive; he has about him a sense of unswerving purpose. He is also a man used to asking questions, getting answers, and telling people what to do. She asks his name.

Jasper talks late in smoke-filled rooms. He shares a bottle of whisky with two Americans, an Englishman, an Italian and a Belgian, all of them men of influence and many connections. He has made, he knows, a good impression. When eventually they get up and leave the empty glasses, the stub-filled ashtrays, the deep leather armchairs, he is feeling good, very good indeed. He wants Claudia, who disappeared earlier. He saw her at dinner in animated conversation with some chap (a chap of such sexual anonymity as to be no threat, so that one could smile benignly) but when he caught up with her later on she murmured something about going to bed early.

Jasper, work over for the day, makes his way – a touch unsteadily – along the chateau's wide passages.

Claudia lies in bed with the light on and a book in her hand. The book is a pretence that is not working, and presently she lets it fall. She lies in this alien room and aches. Her mind and body howl. All that she can normally keep tamped down springs into life. She aches and howls for Tom. It is not that he is ever forgotten, but mostly emotion is dormant; it lies quiet, biding its time. And then every so often something brings it raging forth, and she is back ten years ago, back in that Cairo summer, back with the raw new truth of it.

She should not have allowed herself to talk about the war. She should not have let herself be made unwary by wine, flattering attention, questions and the temptation to expand on her own achievements.

And now here is a knock on the door that can only be Jasper. She stiffens. Jasper's body, tonight, would be an offence. The body of any man would be an offence. Any man who is not Tom. And Tom is dead. Ten years dead.

Jasper comes in. He is in his dressing-gown. 'I was afraid you'd be asleep. I got talking to some people. Sorry to desert you, darling, but I got caught up with that NATO general at dinner. Who was your pal?'

'A man,' says Claudia, staring at the ceiling.

Jasper, by now, has his dressing-gown off and is pulling back the sheet.

'No,' says Claudia. 'Sorry, Jasper – not tonight.'

'What's the matter? Have you got the curse?'

'Yes,' says Claudia. Simpler like that.

He continues to get into the bed. 'I don't mind.'

'Well I do,' says Claudia. 'Leave me alone, Jasper, please.'

Jasper prepares to raise objections and then suddenly capitulates; his head is foggy with whisky anyway, desire is beginning to ebb. He yawns; 'All right, sweetie, I understand. See you in the morning. I must say, it was well worth coming. I think I may have landed a thing or two.'

'Really?' says Claudia, without looking at him.

But it was I, as it happened, who had landed something. And quite without setting out to do so. Hamilton – anonymous Hamilton whom Jasper dismissed at a glance and never spoke

150

to throughout the weekend – was a newspaper proprietor. Not one of the flashier Fleet Street figures of the time, he was a man more reticent but none the less forceful, and blessed with the kind of physical greyness that allowed him to move about unrecognised. Hence Jasper's failure to curry favour.

Hamilton said, 'And what are you going to do now?' I had talked of Egypt; he had read, it turned out, some of my despatches. I said I was going to write history books. He said, 'You're not going to find yourself more wars? There should be a fair supply in the next few years.' I said I never wanted to see a war again; I said also that I didn't want to be a journalist. 'Pity,' said Hamilton. 'I was going to offer you a job.'

Write for me from time to time, he said. Write for me when you feel like it. Write when you like about whatever you like, and make it as cussed as you like. Provoke. Fly kites. Start hares. You can do it, I can tell.

When the first of my pieces came out – an attack on the latest work of a leading academic historian – Jasper was astonished. He felt upstaged, too. There was my name in big letters across the centre page of one of the quality national papers. How, he demanded, had I managed that? Jasper was himself doing quite a bit of journalism at the time. 'Hamilton asked me,' I said. 'How the hell do you know Hamilton?' 'Oh,' I said airily, 'I ran into him that weekend at Rocqueville. Man I was talking to at dinner, remember?'

Jasper never did get a job in NATO. It occurred to him in time that while this might be a route to power, of a kind, it was not a route to riches. He did the opportunist thing and put a finger in the television pie, got on to the board of a merchant bank and began generally to spread himself around. He was jealous of my successes. Men like Jasper do not really favour women like me; they are fascinated by them and obliged to associate with them, but their real taste is for compliance and subservience. Jasper should have had a Sylvia.

Enough of Jasper. But it is a satisfying irony that it should have been Jasper who inadvertently supplied me with a public pulpit, and was thus indirectly responsible for a great deal else.

151

At the time, it was neither Jasper nor Hamilton who were the central features of that odd visit, but something quite other – the place itself, and the way in which it seemed, at that particular moment, a physical manifestation of history as illusion. I experienced there the most violent outrage. I lay in bed mourning for Tom, but during the hours of daylight, the hours in which I listened to well-fed complacent men and women designing the future and re-arranging the past, I was infuriated. Now, I would be cynically amused. Then, young – well, relatively young – I wanted to assault them with their own blueprints and statistics and assessments. And the chateau itself, as fake as a film set, seemed to make a mockery of its own past, as frivolous as the cherubs and wantons on the *salon* ceiling. History is disorder, I wanted to scream at them – death and muddle and waste. And here you sit cashing in on it and making patterns in the sand.

13

'How did you sleep?' enquires the nurse.

'Indifferently,' says Claudia. 'I had a nightmare. In which I now realise I was present at one of the more gruesome moments of the early sixteenth century. The flight of the Spaniards from the Aztec capital of Tlacopan.'

'Gracious,' murmurs the nurse, shaking pillows. 'I'll put the back rest up for you, shall I?'

'Along the causeway. Horses clattering on the paving-stones. Arrows. Screams. Blood, steel, muskets firing. Smoke. Yells. And the boats swarming, swarming, the water thick with them, and the Indians coming out of the boats up the sides of the causeway, wave upon wave of bodies. Men being dragged from the horses, rolling into the water, the Indians falling on them. Arrows like rain. The noise.'

'Sounds like a film,' says the nurse, 'the way you tell it.'

'Now it's interesting you should say that,' says Claudia, 'for one reason and another. But it was much more real than that, I assure you. I too was sweating and screaming. And the curious thing about this nightmare – the impenetrable way in which evidently the subconscious works – is that it started as a vision of the Thames. London Bridge. With buildings – those little ramshackle cantilevered houses – and a mass of barges and other boats below, almost covering the water. An image, obviously, of some painting I've seen and forgotten except in the mind's eye.'

'Dreams are funny,' says the nurse. 'I once . . .'

'And while I was a spectator of the London scene – a kind of benign omniscient eye – I became a participant in Mexico. It was I who was going to be gashed, blown apart, sliced open, stabbed, impaled at any moment. I was fighting for my life. But was I a Spaniard or an Aztec?'

The nurse, who has had enough, cranks the bed a few inches higher, gathers up sheets and pillow-cases and leaves the room.

I wrote my Mexico book out of incredulity. Hernando Cortez cannot be true. There cannot have been a human being so brave, charismatic, obstinate and apparently indestructible. How could anyone be so greedy, fanatical, and unimaginative as to lead a few hundred men into an alien continent of whose topography he was ignorant, swarming with a race devoted to the slaughter and sacrifice of strangers, in order to take prisoner their leader in his own capital city? And succeed. And then, when the tables are turned and he is driven out, set to and build thirteen vessels of war and carry them back one hundred and forty miles across mountains because the only way you can tackle a city sited in the middle of a lake is with superior shipping. And succeed again. Is a man who is impelled to do such things a hero or a maniac?

Prescott, peering back from Boston in 1843, thought him the mirror of his time. And wrote great history about him. History which is also, of course, a mirror of the mind of an enlightened, reflective American of 1843. Just as my view was that of a polemical opinionated independent Englishwoman of 1954.

No wonder it all hangs around in the subconscious, surfacing in dreams. Here is one of the most extraordinary confrontations of people and of cultures there has ever been. It is also a dark hint of the world to come: technology triumphs. Cortez is outnumbered by fifty, a hundred, a thousand to one – but he has armour, he has gunpowder, he has ships and cannon. More than that, he knows what it is he has got and the

154

Aztecs do not. At first they, who have never seen horses, think the mounted Spaniards are strange magical Centaur-like creatures. They also think that they are immortal; the Spaniards, feeding this belief, bury the corpses of their slain in secret and by night. Cortez has technology and he has what Prescott calls the pale light of reason. Pale because of the inferior strength of reason in 1520? Or pale because of what it was up against? Either way, it is going to be too much for the Aztecs. They will disintegrate before a few hundred bigoted avaricious adventurers – armies, cities, the whole ancient fragile fabric of their society. Civilisation comes to Mexico.

The victory, in a way, is of one mythology over another. The Aztec – Prescott's 'untutored savage' – has to cope with gods who require continual appeasement if day is to succeed day and the sun is to go on shining. The Spanish God requires sacrifices too: an expanding empire of converts plus good conduct on earth as a passport to eternal life. Each appals the other. It is interesting to note that the Aztecs, who sacrificed captives to their gods by carving their living hearts from their bodies, were deeply shocked by the Spanish custom of burning transgressors at the stake. Cruelty, evidently, lies in the eye of the beholder.

My book was a success. It reached best-seller lists. I was interviewed by journalists. A well-known scholar attacked me in the *TLS*, which did me an inordinate amount of good. And two years later a film producer telephoned me. I listened to him with almost as much incredulity as I had first read about Cortez. When I put the receiver down I began to laugh.

'I have grave doubts about the feathers,' says Claudia. 'Some of them look like ostrich to me. There aren't ostriches in Central America.'

'Check those feathers,' says the producer to a minion. 'What about the general effect, though? Powerful, isn't it?'

'The general effect is . . . remarkable.'

It is indeed. For here in this Spanish valley are assembled the opposed armies of Montezuma and Cortez. In the background are mountains and also the rooftops of the little Spanish village that will of course remain out of shot, along with the telegraph poles along the road, the collection of parked cars and the three immense catering vans. In the foreground is Cortez's troop, all flashing armour and jinking harness and stamping hooves, and the Aztec hordes, brilliant in their plumed head-gear, their quilted tunics, their gold-trimmed boots and their dubiously feathered cloaks. Admittedly, corners have been cut on the hordes; the forty thousand cited by the researchers are represented by a hundred odd extras who – since this is one of the interminable breaks from filming – are sitting around smoking and drinking Coca-Cola. Montezuma himself is having his make-up fixed in his personal caravan. Claudia had dinner with him yesterday in a Toledo restaurant; he is an actor of Venezuelan extraction, a man of devastating sexuality and unbelievable stupidity. At one point during the dinner, struggling to make intellectual contact at any level whatsoever, she came to the conclusion that such a person must be thought of not as human but as an exquisite animal endowed with limited powers of speech and reason.

Claudia's name will appear on the credits of this film as Historical Adviser. She thought long and hard – well, for ten minutes or so – about whether or not to agree to this. Avarice won, in the end, along with curiosity. She could not afford to pass up the interestingly large sums of money offered by the film company for the tag of her respectable name (plus a little token respectable advice); and besides, it might be amusing – at least it's something different. Claudia at forty-six is restless. Even more restless than she has always been.

The director is now bawling at the extras through a megaphone. Cigarettes are stubbed out; feathers are adjusted. Montezuma emerges from his caravan and Cortez from his.

'They're doing the confrontation scene again,' says the producer. 'There was trouble with the horses in the last take.'

'I suppose you realise they never actually met in battle?' says Claudia.

The producer gives her a look. 'Well, we're stretching a

point, eh? Besides, you gave me a long lecture yourself about conflicts of evidence. This is a bit of conflicting evidence. Looks good, doesn't it?'

And out on to this barren valley battlefield of scrub and rank grass rides Cortez, a chunky figure whose face is instantly familiar. One has seen him peering out of oilskins over the wheel of destroyers, lurking under lamp-posts in fedora and belted raincoat, shooting it out in frontier towns – an international cipher of the century, known to all and to none. Claudia, meeting him just now, had the curious feeling that the hand he held out might be made of cardboard; it was disconcerting to touch ordinary warm flesh.

The armies are deployed; they form up and wheel around and hurtle upon one another; there is tumult and shouting; stout Cortez is seen to fall and rise again; Montezuma flees; trucks bearing cameras and frantic cameramen circle around and around. Claudia, the wind in her hair and the sun in her eyes, watches with interest and a kind of disbelief. The disbelief has nothing to do with the authenticity of the Aztec feathers, or the cleanliness of the combatants, or the sound of megaphones and combustion engines but with something quite else; she cannot believe her own presence at this expensive charade. She is amused but also a little queasy. She thinks of those wretched real Mexicans and Spaniards, who have furnished the story and lined many pockets including in a small way her own.

Jasper was to fling that point at me, years later, over a breakfast table in Maidenhead, when I had attacked his own traducing of history. I defended myself as a spectator, no more. Well, yes; up to a point. *Touché*, Jasper.

My Mexico book was a sober, if controversial, piece of narrative history. It told the tale. In my history of the world the fall of Tezcuco will be differently seen.

Or perhaps not seen but heard – told in a Spanish dialect that we have lost and Indian languages of which we have no notion, against the chanting of the Latin mass and the irretrievable rituals of that other hideous creed that demanded human blood day after day after day. Yes, that is how it should be done. Sights one can conjure up in the head; sound is more elusive. My readers shall hear, at this point – they shall become listeners. They shall hear the tramping of Cortez's long march to the interior, the rain, the wind, the swearing and the grumbling, they shall hear the awful hiss of Popocatepetl into whose smoking maw the Spaniards descend – having inconveniently run out of sulphur for gunpowder. They shall hear the sounds of the massacre at Cholulo, when the Spaniards, becoming short-tempered, dispose of three thousand Indians – or maybe six thousand, or maybe more, again we have a slight problem with conflicting evidence, but the noise would have been much the same. They shall hear the gardens of the Aztec city of Iztapalapan – the jungle sounds of the birds in the aviaries, the purr of humming-birds and bees feeding on the aromatic shrubs and the creepers that cover the trellises, the rustle of the gardeners' brooms sweeping the paths. They shall hear Montezuma's welcome to Cortez, and Cortez's affirmation of friendship and respect. They shall hear the clink and clatter of the gold and silver gifts heaped upon the Spaniards – the collars and necklaces and bracelets and other ornaments, the drinking vessels and platters. They shall hear the interested comments of the Spaniards upon the workmanship, the weight, the probable value. They shall hear the scratch of pen upon parchment as Cortez reports back to base, and perhaps even the mutterings of the Emperor Charles V in Madrid wondering if he controls the whole of the New World yet, or only part of it, which would not be enough. And at the end they shall hear the concerted howl of the mass of humanity – Spaniards and Indians, men, women, and children – who died because they were unfortunate enough to be around at a climactic moment in history.

And what, you may ask, does that moment in history have to do with me, Claudia, except that I wrote a book about it? Added a few more to the millions of words already written. How does it defy chronology and mesh into my unimportant seventy-six years?

Like everything else: it enlarges me, it frees me from the prison of my experience; it also resounds within that experience.

The smell of leather. The expensive smell of the upholstery of the chauffeur-driven car in which she sits with Cortez. Stout Cortez. Unarmoured now and wearing the off-duty dress of a very rich mid-twentieth-century actor, but stout none the less. James Caxton is pushing fifty, but plays down ten years, or fifteen at a pinch with a good cameraman. He is not exactly fat, but has the tight, glossy look of a man whose skin fits a little too well. His shirt, his trousers, his navy blazer are all craftily cut to give the impression of a body more lithe than it actually is. He holds himself carefully. His face, unmade-up, has a most peculiar texture – it continues to look as though someone has been at it with eye-liner and grease-paint; the light suntan does not seem natural, the brows and lashes are too sharply defined. His voice is a rich compelling bass; it makes everyone else stop talking, as though anything he said would be of great significance. In fact, as Claudia is learning, he is a profoundly uninteresting man. He seldom says anything of any note whatsoever; it is simply that his voice is hypnotic. He is talking, right now, about the scenery.

'I adore mountains.'

'Ah,' says Claudia. What else could one say?

'Thank God they didn't decide to shoot this movie in Mexico. The climate's appalling. The coast is tolerable. I've taken some vacations at Acapulco. Super beaches.'

Claudia considers saying 'Ah' once more. The landscape cruises by as the chauffeur swings the car down the hairpin bends. Instead, she asks James Caxton if he has ever seen any of the Aztec sites – the pyramids, the temples.

James Caxton ponders. He thinks not. Not absolutely sure. Possibly. One has been to so many places.

But one could hardly have failed to notice such things, Claudia thinks. Never mind. She persists for a while, talking of pre-Columban sculpture. The poor man is monumentally bored but he is, way back, despite Hollywood and Pinewood Studios and Cinecittà, an English gentleman and he knows how to behave to a lady; he arranges his famous face into an expression of interest and allows her to finish. Then he counters with a long story about when they were shooting his Napoleon film in Egypt (Claudia can see the train of association, though pyramids and temples in fact do not feature in the story). He has done his Napoleon, and his Francis Drake, and his Mark Antony, and his Byron. They are all, in his head, jumbled into a mosaic of disassociated personalities who have nothing to do with anything except an isolated dramatic sequence. Napoleon is mixed up with Josephine, and supervises battles. Drake has a prickly relationship with Elizabeth, and must be played with a Devon accent. In fact it becomes apparent that his grasp of chronology is extremely weak. He can hitch Napoleon to the nineteenth century, but is vague as to which end. Dates mean nothing to him, since he cannot relate them to each other. Here is a man, Claudia gleefully realises, who is adrift in time – a historical innocent. How did he achieve this purity? Cunningly, she probes (not difficult, since she is inviting him to talk about his favourite subject – himself); he was privately educated, it emerges, or rather, barely educated at all, because considered delicate as a boy. No wonder directors find him so pliable; a man without conditioning is without preconceptions.

He glances at his watch. 'Mike'll be having kittens. We're shooting the banquet scene this afternoon. Step on it a bit, can you, Charlie.' The chauffeur nods; the landscape flows by a little faster. They have been lunching in a town some distance from the location site because James Caxton was not needed in the morning and is fed up with canteen meals. Claudia is his companion because he does not hit it off with Montezuma (appropriately enough), his leading lady has a migraine and other members of the cast are required for a run-through. The meal was lavish and lengthy; the conversation laboured. At least so far as Claudia was concerned it was barely classifiable as conversation. For Caxton, she realised, it might have seemed

160

quite adequate. He is totally incurious. In three days she has rarely heard him ask a single personal question of anyone. This insularity seems to be not so much egotism as a deficiency induced by years of having other people intensely interested in his every word or action.

He approves, evidently, of Claudia. He has been affable, positively gracious, since first she arrived. He is impressed by her status as patron intellectual; she lends *cachet*. But she is also not the sort of woman to whom he is accustomed. Over lunch, he became almost inquisitive.

'What took you into the stuff you do – the sort of books you write?'

'Ignorance. Immodesty. *Hubris*. And fate, of course. I was a war correspondent during the war. That rather put me off reporting on the present.'

Caxton nods. 'I was in the Far East. ENSA. Not exactly the front line, but things were a bit dodgy once or twice. Convoy we were on was torpedoed off Singapore. I was bloody glad to get home.'

'All the same, we neither of us appear to have suffered unduly.'

This does not go down very well. He says stiffly, 'Well, possibly . . . In any case, I've always believed in taking the rough with the smooth.' His incomparable voice invests the words with distinction, for a moment.

'Very wise,' says Claudia.

'Don't you?'

'Not really. Probably more a matter of temperament than belief.'

'Women,' says Caxton, 'are always less philosophical about the ups and downs of life. My wife . . .'

'They also deal them out, of course.'

He stares at her. 'What?'

'The Fates,' says Claudia, 'are traditionally represented in Greek mythology as women. Three of them. Spinning.'

'As I was saying, my wife . . .'

'The Furies too. Remorseless atavistic maternal punishment.

161

But also the Muses. In fact we have all the best parts. I'm sorry – your wife?'

'I've forgotten what I was going to say about her. You're a very peculiar person, Claudia. You don't mind my saying that?'

'It's been said before.'

'Unusual, perhaps, is what I mean.'

'Peculiar will do.'

The focus has switched to Claudia. Both recognise that this is unacceptable. 'Greece,' says Caxton, conditioned to take up a cue, 'is a wonderful country. One of my favourite stamping grounds. Do you know Hydra?'

Claudia does not, which enables him to tell her at length about this tedious piece of rock on which he considers buying a villa. She thinks about the Fates, cackling over their looms or, presumably nowadays, if they move with the times, over their self-operating machinery – cackling, anyway, as they set in train wars, famines, disasters and a million random unimportant conjunctions such as that between herself and this unexceptional but celebrated man.

And so, eventually, the meal had ended and they had emerged from the restaurant into the hot and dusty afternoon and stepped into the limousine to be driven back over the mountains to the location valley. Claudia sits sunk into the squashy upholstery of the back seat, alongside Caxton, snuffing the leather and some esoteric after-shave of his. Talking. Listening. Observing from time to time the well-behaved landscape that slides past, this way and that, as the chauffeur negotiates the twists and turns of the road. And Caxton notices the time and asks the man to hurry, which he does so that the tyres screech now at the next corner, and at the next they are flung against each other and Caxton says 'Watch it!' but with a laugh so that the driver continues thus, swirling them down the mountainside.

She does not know at first what it is that has happened. One moment the car is smoothly gliding round a bend, Caxton is saying something about bull-fighting – and an instant later the landscape is no longer well-behaved but spins sickeningly around them, uncontrollable trees and mountains swinging and lurching; she is thrown forward and back, there is a thump, a bang and at last nothing at all.

She fights her way out of some deep buzzing sea. She is back in the car which is slewed right off the road into a bank. The chauffeur is hanging forward over the wheel; the windscreen is shattered; the engine is still running. Into Claudia's head comes the single thought that she must turn it off – something to do with fire and petrol. She has forgotten James Caxton, and where she is or why. She heaves herself up and leans forward over the seat, groping round the chauffeur's arm. She finds the ignition key. And now there is silence. She opens the door and staggers out on to the verge. She sits down. All is wonderfully peaceful; cicadas rasp and a bush rustles in the wind. She has no feelings or thoughts; there is a pain in her side but it does not seem important. She is in a state of suspension, and sits thus on a rocky platform staring at a little plant with tiny jewel-like flowers. She looks up; just above her head a bird floats against the deep blue backdrop of the sky. It hangs there, she can see the sheen of its wings; and then the sky becomes grey, the outline of the bird turns fuzzy, and just before she passes out she sees it slide away sideways and down into the valley.

The chauffeur died. James Caxton fractured his skull, broke a collar-bone and an arm, and cost the insurers some million dollars in lost time. I had concussion and two broken ribs; the Fates were taking only a mild interest in me. The *Evening Standard* carried a headline – JAMES CAXTON IN CAR CRASH WITH WOMAN COMPANION. Jasper, with whom I was still living off and on, said various things on the telephone, not all of them sympathetic. I lay for a week in a Madrid hospital; on the fifth day Gordon walked into my room and I burst into tears.

'If I'd known I'd have this effect,' he says, 'I wouldn't have come.' He takes out a handkerchief and wipes her eyes carefully. 'Now blow . . .'

'Oh, shut up,' says Claudia. She pushes his hand away, reaches violently towards the bedside table, yelps. 'Christ . . .'

'Then don't thrash around so. Keep still. You don't look too bad, anyway.'

'Why are you here? You're in Australia.'

'Sylvia reported. I switched planes. For God's sake stop *crying*, Claudia. I haven't seen you cry since you were about six. What's the matter with you?'

'It's called delayed shock. It's what happens to people when they realise they're not dead. Perfectly rational, if you think about it.'

'Don't talk like that,' says Gordon. He sits down by the bed. He reaches out suddenly and takes her hand. Holds it. Looks at her. She feels the warmth of his hand, sees his eyes and what is in them until she cannot take it any longer and looks away. He has not touched her for years, except inadvertently. They do not kiss when they meet.

He gets up and walks over to the window. 'Not the most distinctive of views. But presumably that won't have bothered you.'

Claudia lies looking at him. He is more inaccessible than anyone in the world, she thinks; more intensely known and more inaccessible.

She is sitting up in bed with a bruise on her forehead and no make-up on. She looks not like dauntless quarrelsome unquenchable Claudia but some pale unstable ghost of herself. And when he sees that she is crying the old proximity is there, it is years ago again, the time when there were only the two of them, before they noticed the rest of the world. He looks at her for a moment with the eyes of then, and she looks back. Neither wishes to return there; both celebrate, in silence, what will never be lost. Gordon stands up. He goes to the window and sees a boulevard with oleander trees, a crowd of people piling into a gaudy yellow bus, posters advertising cigars and

164

washing powders. It occurs to him that Claudia is both closer to and further from him than anyone else, and that he wishes it were otherwise.

▲▲▲▲▲▲▲▲▲▲▲▲▲▲▲

14

▼▼▼▼▼▼▼▼▼▼▼▼▼▼▼▼

My body records certain events; an autopsy would show that I have had a child, broken some ribs, lost my appendix. Other physical assaults have left no trace; measles, mumps, malaria, suppurations and infections, coughs and colds, upheavals of the digestive system. When I was young I carried on my knee for many years a patch of delicately puckered pink skin preserving the time Gordon pushed me down a cliff at Lyme Regis (or, he would claim, did not); I can no longer find it – the body obliterates, also. A pathologist would learn little more than an archaeologist contemplating ancient bones. I once read an excavation report that described, in the precise and uncommitted language of such documents, the skeleton of an Anglo-Saxon woman found face down in a shallow grave with a heavy rock resting upon the spine; the contorted position of the body and the placing of the rock suggested that she had been buried alive. From far away, beyond bare descriptive words and the silence of bone and stone, comes the roar of pain and violence. On a lesser scale, my pathologist, if given to fancy, might spare a passing thought for the groans of that birth, or speculate about those ribs.

My body records also a more impersonal history; it remembers Java Man and Australopithecus and the first mammals and strange creatures that flapped and crawled and swam. Its ancestries account, perhaps, for my passion for climbing trees when I was ten and my predilection for floating in warm seas. It has memories I share but cannot apprehend. It links me to the earthworm, to the lobster, to dogs and horses and lemurs and gibbons and the chimpanzee; there, but for the grace of God, went I. Being the raging agnostic that I am, of course, I consider that God had nothing to do with it.

My body has conditioned things, to some extent. The life of an attractive woman is different from that of a plain one. My hair, my eyes, the shape of my mouth, the contours of breast and thigh have all contributed. The brain may be independent, but personality is not; when I was eight years old I realised that people considered me pretty – from that moment onwards a course was set. Intelligence made me one kind of being; intelligence allied to good looks made me another. This is self-assessment, not complacency.

I came back from that Madrid hospital with bruises, a healthier bank account than I had ever had and a wonderfully concentrated mind. The world astonished me. I looked at the green water of the Channel, at the seagulls hanging above the ferry, at the rust of a railing and the curve of a deck-chair and these things had the intensity of great art. In Cairo in 1942 I raged at the continuing universe; I walked, on that appalling day, beside the Nile and the whole beautiful place was an offence – the life, the colour, the smells and sounds, the palms, the feluccas, the kites endlessly circling in the hard blue sky. Now that it was merely myself who was still alive, I forgave the universe its indifference. Magnanimous of me. Expedient also, you may say.

Back in London, I sent for Lisa, who was at Sotleigh with her grandmother. I wanted to compensate for being the kind of mother I was; I also wanted to see her.

Claudia, Jasper and Lisa walk along one of the wide avenues of London Zoo. It is Lisa's eighth birthday. The Zoo is Lisa's choice; she has been offered the whole of the city – the Tower, Madame Tussaud's, Battersea Fun Fair, a boat trip to Greenwich – and has opted for the Zoo, partly because she observed

Jasper flinch at the suggestion. Power does not often come Lisa's way. So here they are; one family amid many. And who would know? thinks Claudia. She looks at other groups, other superficial conformities of man, woman and child; she wonders what other histories are concealed beneath appearances.

Lisa wants to see the bears and the lions and the monkeys. They spend a long time in the Lion House; it is full of shrieking children, all of them, Claudia sees, indulging atavistic terrors. The big cats pace up and down or lounge impassively. The smell is appalling. 'Now I know what it was like underneath the Coliseum,' says Claudia. 'Please, darling, have you had enough lion?' And Lisa allows herself to be persuaded onwards, to the bear enclosures, where Claudia is silent.

'Don't you like polar bears?'

'Quite,' says Claudia. 'Not specially.'

'Well, I like polar bears,' says Lisa. She hangs on the railing, staring at the bear which neurotically swings its head, to and fro, slapping its way from one end of its concrete ledge to the other, like an old man in carpet slippers.

Jasper yawns. 'What about lunch, sweetie?'

'I don't want any lunch yet,' says Lisa. 'I want to find the monkeys now.'

So they find the monkeys, a whole tribe of brown monkeys in an outside enclosure, leading lives of careless abandon.

'What's that one doing?' says Lisa. She looks at Jasper.

'Mm . . .' says Jasper. 'I'm not quite sure.'

'Really!' explodes Claudia. She gives him a look of contempt. 'It's a male monkey, and it's making the female monkey have a baby.'

'How?' enquires Lisa.

'Yes, how?' asks Jasper, with equal interest.

Claudia glares at him. 'It puts the thing you can see sticking out underneath it inside the female monkey and sends a seed into her. The seed grows into the baby monkey.'

Jasper turns aside, apparently choking.

Lisa contemplates the monkeys for a while. 'Does the mother monkey mind him getting on top of her like that?'

168

'She doesn't seem to,' says Claudia. Furiously, she kicks Jasper, who composes himself.

'I saw Rex do that once with the dog at the farm. Granny Branscombe was cross with him.'

'Poor old Rex,' says Jasper.

Claudia takes a breath. She says, 'That's how people make babies too, you know. The same way.'

Lisa turns and stares at her. 'Like that?'

'Yes,' says Claudia determinedly. 'Just like that.'

Lisa looks from one to the other of them. 'How perfectly disgusting,' she says.

'Shut up,' says Claudia. 'She'll see you. It's not *that* funny.'

Jasper wipes his eyes. Lisa is several yards away now, absorbed by gang warfare in the monkey kindergarten. 'She is becoming most amusing. I should see more of her.'

'Because she's amusing?' says Claudia.

Claudia is looking very fine today. There is still the faint smudge of a bruise on her forehead, but her face is glowing, her hair bright, her body trim; she turns heads, as always, she is a woman one is satisfied to be seen with. Pity, Jasper thinks, that the child has turned out so unlike. Unlike himself either, come to that.

He takes Claudia's arm. 'Anyway, thank God you're here safe and sound.'

'Jasper, there's something I'm going to tell you.'

'You're pregnant again?'

'Don't be facetious. After Lisa's gone back to Sotleigh I want us to stay apart.'

He sighs. He allows her to glimpse his Russian soul, what there is of it.

'Darling . . . You're cross with me for some reason. If it's that Italian girl I assure you it's over. Finished and done with. She was never anything.'

'I don't give a damn about the Italian girl. I just want to be on my own.'

'On your own with whom?' He lets go of her arm.

169

'On my own with no one.'

Jasper feels himself flame with irritation. He looks down at her; she has turned from handsome entertaining Claudia to maddening intractable Claudia. It does not suit him, just now, to do without her; at another time, it might. He would prefer to make the time-table himself. He says, 'My dear, for the sake of the child I think we should talk about this in a sensible way at some other point.' They both look towards Lisa, who is apparently absorbed by the monkeys.

The baby monkeys – the tiniest baby monkeys – have faces like pansies, with bright black eyes. She wants one so badly that she can hardly bear it. She wants to have one for her very own, carry it round with her all the time, have its little hands holding on to her like it holds on to the mother monkey. The baby monkey is the best thing she has ever seen, better than baby chickens, better than puppies, kittens, better than anything ever. But it is no good – they would never let you have a baby monkey. Claudia would say 'Don't be silly,' Granny Branscombe would say no, Helga would say no.

One of the grown-up monkeys is eating a nut. It cracks the nut with its teeth and then picks the shell away with its fingers, just like a person. It drops the nut; one of the big baby monkeys tries to snatch the nut and the grown-up one makes chattering noises at it and chases it away. Then all the big baby monkeys play a chasing game, round and round. The father monkey who was doing that thing to the mother monkey has stopped and is looking for fleas, just like Rex does but with his fingers instead of his nose. Lisa looks at the mother monkey to see if she is having another baby yet, but she does not seem to be; she simply squats on a rock, doing nothing.

Lisa remembers what Claudia said just now, about people. She turns round and looks at them, at Claudia and Jasper. There they are, just as they have always been, Claudia and Jasper whom she does not call Mummy and Daddy because Claudia thinks those are silly names. Once upon a time she came out of Claudia's tummy; she knows that because Granny

Branscombe told her, in the garden, when she was getting roses for the house, and said it was something you shouldn't talk about. If Granny Branscombe knew what Claudia had said just now she would be very very shocked and hurt.

Lisa observes Claudia and Jasper. She thinks again about what Claudia said; she stares at them as she stared at the monkeys, but with less sympathy.

When Lisa visits me these days she talks always of mundane things; she is carefully dispassionate. She tells me about the weather, about the boys' school reports, about a play she went to. She is pretending that what is happening to me is not happening, but she is also avoiding dissension, because you do not quarrel with someone in my condition. I find all this trying, but I can see that there is no alternative. Self-exposure is anathema to Lisa; she is perfectly entitled to feel that way. I love Lisa. I always have, after my fashion; the trouble is that she has never been able to realise this. I don't blame her; she wanted a different sort of mother. The least I can do is try to behave now in a way that she would consider decent. And decency consists in leaving things unsaid, ignoring the inescapable, applying oneself to inessentials. She has a point, of course. All the same, where did she acquire this circumspection? Not from me. Not from Jasper, either. Nature, nurture. The latter, in Lisa's case. My mother and Lady Branscombe fashioned her according to their lights. My fault, again.

Yesterday she read bits from the newspaper to me, doing her best to select what would amuse or inform. She left out, though, the best item. I saw it later, when the *Observer* was lying on the bedside table. The remark attributed to Miss World 1985: 'I think destiny is what you make of it.'

Does she indeed. Discuss. With special reference to the careers of *a*) Hernando Cortez *b*) Joan of Arc *c*) a resident of Budapest in 1956. Use as many sides of the paper as you like.

1956; that year of Lisa's eighth birthday and of other more sonorous events. The year of the Canal; the year of Hungary.

Jasper and I parted company, as we had done before and as we would do again. Lisa went back to Sotleigh. I saw her as often as I could. I was writing a column now for Hamilton's paper, a roving commitment that sent me hither and thither – just what I needed in that curious time of mid-life rebirth. I wrote about whatever I liked, whatever aroused my passions. There was plenty, at that point. As the year unfolded I and those who thought like me listened to Eden's pronouncements first with incredulity and then with outrage. As those extraordinary weeks hurtled the government from rhetoric into apparent lunacy we felt for the first time what it is like to live in more demanding political climates. People shouted at each other; friends ceased to speak; families were split. I had the power of print but I also, in indignation and anxiety, joined those marches of duffel-coated and college-scarved young, spoke in crowded church halls and common rooms. And then in the middle of that week of cascading events came the cruel cynicism of Hungary; while the world was arguing about oil and waterways the tanks rolled into Budapest. I tore up the piece I had written for the next day's paper and wrote another. I forget what I said; I remember only that feeling of being the helpless detached spectator of murder. It was as though Hungary were not another place but another time, and therefore inaccessible.

Which of course was not so.

'I am telephoning you,' says a faint voice, through a blizzard of atmospherics.

'I know you're telephoning me,' says Claudia.

'The newspaper is giving me your telephone number.'

Claudia sighs. The newspaper has no business to do any such thing. It knows that. Some stupid girl. And some tiresome nut pestering. 'Look,' she begins . . .

'From Budapest I am telephoning you.'

Claudia takes a breath. Oh. Oho . . . Hence the crackling. There is a noise now like a small bonfire somewhere along the line. 'Hello?' she says. 'Hello? Can you talk louder?'

'I am telephoning you for my son who is in Wimbledon. My son Laszlo.'

'Wimbledon?' cries Claudia. 'Do you mean Wimbledon, London?'

'My son is in Wimbledon, London for his studies.'

'Who are you?' says Claudia. 'Please tell me your name. Please talk slowly and loudly.'

And through the bonfire and the exploding fireworks and the oceanic gales there comes this voice – from another place but not, oh indeed not, from another time. '. . . I am university professor . . . my son Laszlo who is eighteen years old . . . student of art . . . visiting in your country before these events of which you write in your paper, do you know of what I speak?' ('Yes, yes,' cries Claudia. 'How did you . . .? No, never mind, go on, please go on, I can hear you fairly well.') '. . . I am telling my son he must not come back to his home, I am telling him to stay in your country . . . I think I am not able to speak to you for long, you understand, I am sorry to ask you this but I have no friend in your country, I think you are a person who is perhaps interested in what happens here . . . no money . . . eighteen years old . . . must not come back to his home . . . people who perhaps can help my son?'

'Yes,' says Claudia. 'There are people who will help your son.' The bonfire is roaring now; the gales howl. 'I can hardly hear you. Please give me the address. The address in Wimbledon. Please give me the address in . . . at your home. No – no, don't do that. Will you telephone me again?'

'I think that will not be possible. I think soon perhaps I shall not have address. Do you understand?'

'Yes,' says Claudia. 'I'm afraid I do.'

And so here is Laszlo, a child of his time, sitting in Claudia's Fulham flat on an October afternoon. Outside are the unremarkable London noises of feet on pavements, a throbbing taxi, an aeroplane overhead; Laszlo sits on the edge of the sofa with a small kit-bag at his feet. He has lank black hair, acne and a heavy cold. He owns nothing but the clothes he wears, a change of shirt and socks, a map of London, a pocket Oxford English dictionary and a handful of postcards from the Tate Gallery. He has also, of course, a passport which nails him for who he is and whence he comes.

'This is a terrible deciding,' he says.

'Decision,' says Claudia. 'Not deciding. I'm sorry . . .' she adds, '. . . as though it mattered. Damn words.'

'Words are not damn,' says Laszlo. 'English I must speak. Good English.'

There he sits, in his baggy kneed trousers and his too-tight sweater. And Claudia is consumed by a surge of that most stark of all emotions: pity. You poor little sod, she thinks. You poor little wretch, you're one of those for whom history really pulls out the stops. You are indeed someone who cannot call his life his own. Free will, right now, must have a hollow sound.

'If you decide to stay I shall do whatever I can for you. You can live here, for a start. I'll find out about places in art colleges.'

There is a silence. 'I shall never see again my father,' says Laszlo. His mother, it appears, died when he was a child.

'*Never* is perhaps too strong . . .' murmurs Claudia.

'Never. I have also aunt and grandmother and cousins.'

Claudia nods. And what are you offered instead? she thinks. This airy concept called freedom which cannot at the moment seem anything of the kind. All the eighteen year olds I know are worrying about sex and examinations: that is freedom.

'I think I go back to Budapest,' he says. He looks at her with hang-dog eyes, beseeching her to prescribe.

Claudia gets up. 'I'm going to make some supper. You go and have a nice hot bath. Lie in it and think about nothing, if possible. You aren't going to decide anything until the morning, anyway. Or the next day or the one after.'

For several days Laszlo agonised. He sat around the flat in a fog of misery, or walked the streets. His cold ripened. When I found myself irritated by his sniffing I knew that our relationship would endure. Someone had evidently brought him up nicely; in the thick of that anguished time he remembered to say 'please' and 'thank you' and kept trying to do the washing up. And when his father's letter reached him, six closely-written sheets posted before the telephone call, he gave in. He spent three hours alone in my spare bedroom with the letter and then came out and said, 'I stay here.'

'Good,' says Claudia briskly. 'Then we must get on with seeing about things. Do you want to go to art college in London or somewhere else? I'll take you to look at some places. There's a committee collecting people like you. We'd better get in touch with them. There are quite a few of you, apparently. And you'd better go out and buy a coat and a thicker sweater before the weather gets any colder. You can't go on walking around clad as for the central European summer.'

Good grief, she thinks, who is this talking?

Thus came Laszlo, washed into my life by the Kremlin. I remember feeling a curious satisfaction, as though one had been enabled to frustrate Fate. Hubris, of course; I too was Laszlo's fate. And what did I – forty-six-year-old busy committed Claudia – want with a disturbed artistically inclined adolescent boy speaking fractured English?

'I should be dead,' says Laszlo. 'I should better be dead like Hungarian people.'

He stands wearing the coat bought with money she made him take (a loan, it is called, entered sternly by him in a Woolworth's notebook). The coat is a size too large and hangs down his thin shanks. The acne is worse than ever. He stands in the front hall of the flat, glowering.

'You are very kind to me. Always you are being very kind to me. I am most grateful.'

'That's OK,' says Claudia. 'Hate me if you want to. You're

175

perfectly entitled to hate someone, and I'm handy. Go ahead.'
'What means handy?' snarls Laszlo.

Laszlo gets drunk. He learns about pubs and goes one night to the King's Road where he falls in with some gang of young sparks, returns to the flat after midnight and is copiously sick on the bathroom floor. The next morning he comes to Claudia with his kit-bag packed and offers to leave. Claudia says that will not be necessary.

Laszlo draws. He covers sheet after sheet of rough grainy paper from the grocer round the corner with huge wild charcoal drawings of guns, of tanks, of shattered buildings, of huddled people. Claudia pins some of them up on her walls. 'These are good,' she says.

'No, they are not good,' says Laszlo. 'They are terrible, bad, awful.' He takes them down when she is out and burns them in the kitchen bin. The flat reeks of charred paper. Claudia says, 'Do what you like with your pictures but you've no damn business setting my flat on fire.'

Lisa, when she comes to the flat, is cool towards Laszlo. He offers to take her to Battersea, but she will not go. 'Why not?' says Claudia. 'I thought you wanted to go on the Big Dipper.' 'I don't like his spotty face,' mutters Lisa. Claudia, through clenched teeth, says in that case she can do without the Big Dipper, once and for all.

Laszlo gets a letter, posted in Austria. It is from his aunt. His father is in prison. There is no address any more for his father. Laszlo tells this to Claudia, handing her the letter because he has forgotten for the moment that she cannot read Hungarian. He has been weeping, Claudia sees. Claudia asks him to translate the letter for her because it will give him something to do. As he does so she thinks intensely of this woman who is a whole life for Laszlo but just a voice for her, and of this faceless man, another whole unimaginable life.

*

Laszlo gets drunk again. Alone, this time, in the flat. Claudia invades his room, finds the empty whisky bottle and plonks it on the sitting-room table. 'Next time you want to do that,' she says, 'tell me and I'll join you. As it happens I'm not particularly partial to whisky but we have a tradition in this country that no one gets sloshed on their own. OK?'

Claudia sets Laszlo the task of learning London. She makes him ride bus routes from end to end, walk miles every day. Laszlo complains. 'Do it,' she orders. 'It's the only way you're going to grow a new skin.'

On Claudia's birthday Laszlo presents her with an enormous bunch of daffodils. He has picked them, it emerges, in Kensington Gardens. Amazingly, no one noticed.

Guided by me, Laszlo inspected London art colleges and eventually selected Camberwell. He could have gone wherever he wished; the whole of the western world wanted to compensate for the Russian tanks. Laszlo was made a fuss of by both teachers and fellow students. Within a few weeks he was wearing a French beret and a silk paisley scarf tucked into the neck of his shirt. He started smoking Gauloises and going to films at the Curzon. He had a grant now and some money from the committee set up to supervise the Hungarian students. Sometime in the spring he moved out of my flat to live with friends south of the river. Periodically he would quarrel with the friends, or they would all be thrown out for not paying the rent, and he would move back in with me again until some new arrangement was sorted out. I became used to late-night calls from phone boxes, to Laszlo's lanky figure on the doorstep. My small spare room – as opposed to the one usually occupied by Lisa – became known as his room. He would drift away for weeks on end, neither writing nor telephoning, and then come bounding back.

It was to go on like that for ten years or so.

I watched Laszlo mutate. I watched him turn from a

177

disoriented boy to a volatile adult. To be honest, I have never been certain how much of Laszlo's instability can be attributed to history and how much to temperament. Perhaps he would have been like that anyway. And to be fair he himself never for one moment blamed circumstances for anything. What he did do was cleave unto his adoptive country. Within two years Laszlo was speaking a more demotic English than his peers; he became aggressively insular. He cultivated the most English friends he could lay hands on – a bizarre mixture of working-class boys with strident London accents and laconic offcuts of the upper class, with double-barrelled names. He seldom talked about Hungary and became irritated when the subject came up; whatever was going on went on within. He avoided the overtures of fellow expatriates – that mildly *louche* and mysterious Eastern European sub-culture that lurked then in South Ken and Earls Court. He flirted for a while with Anglo-Catholicism. Then he dropped that and joined the Labour party. He took up, in turn, bird-watching, vegetarianism, judo, gliding and every passing artistic fashion. His attitude towards me varied from amiably patronising to effusively affectionate.

Laszlo is a little tipsy. He lies on the sofa with his feet on the arm.

Claudia says, 'You might take your shoes off.'

'You are being bourgeois,' says Laszlo. He removes his shoes. 'You are my mother, Claudia.'

'No, I'm not, thank God. And you shouldn't talk like that.'

'No,' says Laszlo, after a moment. 'You are right. But I want to say something. Who else can I say it to? It is this. I like men. Not girls.'

'So?' says Claudia. 'If that's the way you are, then that's the way you are.'

Lisa never accepted Laszlo. When she was a child she watched him suspiciously. Was she jealous? Did she think of him as my surrogate son? Was he, indeed, my surrogate son? I think not. But who am I to say – all I can do is record what I felt about Laszlo. And what I felt was compunction, responsibility and, eventually, great affection. Which is quite a lot. But Lisa had no need to be jealous. When she was older – seventeen, eighteen – she was polite but distant with him. Nowadays, on the rare occasions when she meets him, she behaves as towards a second cousin who has fallen upon hard times and might be going to ask for a loan.

By the time Laszlo was in his early thirties he had simmered down, insofar as he ever would. He went to live with an older man in Camden Town – an up-market antique dealer with one of those shops that has nothing in it but three pieces of expensive furniture and a couple of Chinese pots. I have never cared for the fellow but he has looked after Laszlo, endured his moods and provided him with somewhere to work. Laszlo is not a successful artist. I can quite understand why few people want to buy his paintings; they are too uncomfortable to live with. They howl of *malaise*; they jar the eye; they are discordant and disturbing. Nightmare creatures stalk through surreal landscapes; things fall apart; anguished people scurry in broken cities. They hang on my walls, but then I have no choice: if I won't honour them, who will? Anyway, I'm used to them.

▲▲▲▲▲▲▲▲▲▲▲▲▲▲

15

▼▼▼▼▼▼▼▼▼▼▼▼▼▼

'For God's sake . . .' says Claudia. 'You're supposed to jolly me along, not sit there wringing your hands.' It is a bad day; her voice comes out as a whisper.

'They didn't tell me,' wails Laszlo. 'We have been in France and then I went to New York and when I came back I telephoned you and there was no one there so I telephoned again later and still no one and then I telephoned Lisa. Why didn't they tell me?'

'They tried,' says Claudia. 'Lisa phoned you. As you say, you were away.'

Laszlo leans forward and stares intently at her. 'So how are you?'

'Still here.'

Laszlo prowls to the window. He is thin, his elbows poke out of holes in his sweater, his black hair is streaked with grey. Claudia watches him.

'What can I do? What do you need? What can I get for you? Books? Papers? I shall come every day.'

'No,' says Claudia, rather too promptly. 'Every now and then will do fine. Tell me about France.'

Laszlo makes a dismissive gesture. 'France . . . France was for Henry. Fireplaces. Everything now is old fireplaces for rich silly women who pay the earth.'

'New York?'

'I had an exhibition.'

'Aha. Sell much?'

The door opens. 'Visitor for you!' cries the nurse.

Claudia turns her head. 'Hello, Sylvia,' she murmurs.

And no, no, no, she thinks, it is my privilege now to turn away from inappropriate conjunctions. She closes her eyes and leaves them to it, Sylvia and Laszlo. Who have never, in any positive sense, inhabited the same world. She hears Sylvia saying that actually she's never been *desperately* fond of New York; she hears Laszlo muttering that no, he didn't go to the theatre much and yes, it was quite cold.

We all act as hinges – fortuitous links between other people. I link Sylvia to Laszlo, Lisa to Laszlo; Gordon links me to Sylvia. Sylvia always retreated from Laszlo by saying he was rather a difficult boy and Claudia was awfully good with him. Laszlo, in his frenetic twenties, used to imitate Sylvia, cruelly and accurately. Gordon found him interesting but exasperating; Laszlo has always allowed his soul to hang out like his shirt-tails and Gordon found this uncongenial. He did not object to people having souls but preferred them tucked away out of sight where they ought to be. But he took Laszlo on, in his way. He left Laszlo a small legacy.

Claudia opens her eyes. Lisa is there, taking off her jacket and hanging it tidily over the back of the chair.

Claudia contemplates her. 'It's all go today. Laszlo came. And Sylvia. Now you.'

'No,' says Lisa. 'That was two days ago. You're a bit muddled up. You've not been too good.'

'What have I been doing for two days, I wonder?' says Claudia. 'They seem to have passed me by. Or taken me with them.'

'You look better,' says Lisa.

Claudia raises a hand and studies the back of it. 'I wouldn't say so. I've never got used to the fact that they have brown spots all over them. They look to me like someone else's, to be frank.'

Lisa, who does not like the turn things are taking, asks after Laszlo.

'Laszlo was as ever. He has always been consistent, that you must admit.'

Lisa inclines her head, noncommittal.

'I'm sorry, you know,' says Claudia.

'Sorry about what?' enquires Lisa, cautiously.

'Sorry I was such an inadequate mother.'

'Oh.' Lisa searches for a response. 'Well ... I wouldn't exactly say ... You were ... Well, you were who you were.'

'We're all that,' says Claudia. 'It's something one has to overcome. By conventional standards I made a bad job of being a mother. So I apologise. Not that that's much use now. I just wanted to put it on record.'

'Thank you,' says Lisa at last. She has no idea, she realises, what she means by this. She wishes Claudia had not said what she has; now it will always be there, complicating things.

I never expected to see Lisa grow up. For years, when she was a child, I waited for the Bomb to drop. As the world lurched from Korea to Laos to Cuba to Vietnam I was simply sitting it out. And Lisa's existence sharpened the horror. What might happen to the whole of humanity became concentrated on Lisa's small limbs, her unknowing eyes, her blithe aspirations. I may have been an inadequate mother, but I was still a mother; through Lisa, I raged and feared. I would never have admitted to those dark nights of the soul. Publicly, I behaved like a rational responsible being – I argued the pros and cons of unilateralism, I wrote my column, I marched and demonstrated when I felt it appropriate. I kept to myself that curdling of the stomach I felt during the nine days of Cuba, and at a dozen other times over those years. On some days I could not turn on the radio or pick up the newspaper, as though ignorance might insulate me from reality.

Lisa has grown up. Her sons are growing up. From time to

time my stomach still curdles, but not as it used to; I no longer shrink from the newspapers. Now why should this be? The world is no safer than it was twenty years ago. But we are still here; the monster has been contained, so far – with every year that passes the hope grows that it might continue to be contained, somehow; daily expectation of calamity is too exhausting to sustain. The monks at Lindisfarne must have whistled while they worked when they stopped looking out to sea; people made love in cities under siege.

We expect Armageddon; the Bible has trained us well. We assume either annihilation or salvation, perhaps both. Millennarian beliefs are as old as time; the apocalypse has always been at hand. People have lain quaking in their beds waiting for the year one thousand, have cowered at the passage of comets, have prayed their way through eclipses. Our particular anxieties would seem on the face of things more rational, but they have an inescapable ancestry. The notion that things go on for ever is recent, and evidently too recent to attract much of a following. The world being what it is, it has always been tempting to assume that something would be done about it, sooner or later. When I went to Jerusalem in 1941 I stayed in a small *pension* run by American Seventh Day Adventists, elderly people who had sold up in Iowa or Nebraska in the 'twenties and taken themselves off to the Holy Land with all their savings to be on the spot for the Second Coming, due in 1933. The Second Coming never came; the savings ran out; there they still were, sensibly making the best of it by managing a hotel. It was a delightful place with a shady courtyard in which tortoises ambled among rosemary bushes and pots of geraniums.

Gordon and I, over the years, have argued about disarmament more than about anything else. When I was a member of CND he was not; his pragmatism has always been an antidote to my pessimism; he has always been able to produce arguments and figures when I have brandished emotions and struck attitudes. I can say this now. The last time we were together, in a taxi in London, two days before he died, he looked down at the headlines of the evening paper on his knee and said, 'One resents being axed from the narrative, apart from anything else. I'd have liked to know the outcome.'

Gordon, of course, has been one of those who have a share in outcomes. He has made things happen, from time to time. It is given unto economists to interfere with the narrative, in their small way; peasants in Zambia, small shopkeepers in Bogota, factory workers in Huddersfield have been, at one time or another, affected by Gordon's professional activities.

Gordon, a week before he died, gave evidence before a Royal Commission on Broadcasting whose report he knew he would never see. Sylvia and I took him there in a taxi, Sylvia squeaking and clucking, her eyes pink-rimmed, shreds of damp Kleenex all over her clothes; Gordon was ill-tempered, impatient, pumped full of drugs and slung around with plastic tubing. The doctors said, 'If he wants to, he should do it'; I agreed. He gave his evidence, staggered back into another taxi and sat there talking about the forthcoming election. He set out to provoke and I took the bait, knowing that I must not do otherwise. We argued. Sylvia burst into tears.

She sits beside Gordon and Claudia sits opposite, on the jump-seat. He shouldn't have come, those wretched doctors should never have let him come, none of them should be here at such a time bumping through horrid December London in a taxi. Gordon's breath rasps and he has these tube-things strapped to his leg at which she cannot bear to look, they make her feel so woozy. And he is talking talking which cannot be good for him, getting worked up about the stupid election when who in the middle of all this cares about the election? Gordon will not be . . . By the time the election comes Gordon will have . . .

Sylvia stares out of the window, biting her lip.

She is going to be terribly brave about it. She is not going to break down. When it happens. She is going to be brave and sensible and see to all the things that will have to be seen to and keep calm and dignified.

And as she thinks this there stream through her head other thoughts that ought not to be there she knows but that she cannot keep out . . . thoughts about afterwards and selling the house, she's never really liked north Oxford anyway, one could move to somewhere more countryish, not right in the country which could be a problem but a nice little market town with the sort of people one would get on with, and one need never ever go to the States again, one might even find a little job, voluntary work maybe, an Oxfam shop or something like that, just to have an interest . . .

'Rubbish!' says Claudia. 'Absolute rubbish!' And Sylvia jumps, staunches the flow of thought, turns to here and now. In which Gordon and Claudia are arguing. To and fro, just like the old days: but listen you don't really mean to tell me . . . you only say that because you know nothing about . . . let me finish what I'm saying . . . you're simply *wrong* there Claudia.

How *can* Claudia! Coming back at him like that when he's so ill. Interrupting. Raising her voice. Typical Claudia. It's appalling. When he's . . . when he's going to *die*.

And the tears come welling up, spilling over, so that she has to turn to the window again and rummage for her hankie, and she sees her own face in the glass, superimposed on shop fronts and pavements, a round pink *old* face with puffy eyes and streaked cheeks.

'Rubbish!' says Claudia. It sounds vehement enough; it sounds almost as though she means it. Her eyes meet Gordon's, and she sees that he is not fooled, but he goes on talking and she goes on talking and interrupting and beneath what is said they tell each other something entirely different.

I love you, she thinks. Always have. More than I've loved anyone, bar one. That word is overstretched; it cannot be made to do service for so many different things – love of children, love of friends, love of God, carnal love and cupidity and saintliness. I do not need to tell you, any more than you need to tell me. I have seldom even thought it. You have been my *alter ego*, and I have been yours. And soon there will only be me, and I shall not know what to do.

Sylvia, she sees, is weeping again. Not quite silently enough. If you don't stop that, thinks Claudia, I may simply push you out of this taxi.

It is a grey winter afternoon, glittering with car lights, street lights, gold, red, emerald, the black rainy pavements gleaming, the shop windows glowing Wagnerian caverns. Gordon, talking, sees and takes note of all this. He talks of events that have not yet come about and sees light and texture, the kaleidoscope of fruit outside a greengrocer, the mist of rain on a girl's cheek. A newspaper kiosk is a portrait gallery of pop stars and royalty; the traffic glides like shoals of shining fish. And all this will go on, he thinks. And on, and on. What do I feel about it? What do I care?

His eyes meet Claudia's. 'Rubbish,' she says. 'I've always given theory its due. It's just that I have preferred to write about action.' 'Mad opportunists,' says Gordon. 'Tito. Napoleon. That's not real history. History is grey stuff. Products. Systems of government. Climates of opinion. It moves slowly. That's why you get impatient with it. You look for spectacle.' 'There is spectacle,' says Claudia. 'All too much of it.' 'Indeed yes,' says Gordon, shifting on the seat, wincing. 'Of course there's spectacle. But the spectacle may mislead. What's really happening may be going on elsewhere.' 'Oh come on,' cries Claudia. 'You'd tell the prisoner on the guillotine that the action is really somewhere else?' And as she speaks he hears and sees a hundred other Claudias, going back and back, woman and girl and child. You, he thinks. You. There has always been you. And soon no longer will be.

He feels, beside him, Sylvia's turned head, her shuddering shoulders. He reaches out and puts a hand on hers. It is the least he can do. And the most.

Gordon died five years ago. I am separate from him now. No day passes in which I do not think of him, but I can do so with detachment. He is complete; he has beginning and end. The times in which we were together are complete. I do not mourn him any the less, but I have had to move away: there is no choice. We were children together; we made narcissistic love; we grew up and depended upon one another. From time to time we loathed each other but even in hatred we were united, exclusive, a community of two. I knew Gordon as ruthlessly as I know myself – and as indulgently. What I felt for Gordon was classifiable as love for lack of a better word: he was my sense of identity, my mirror, my critic, judge and ally. Without him I am diminished.

In the beginning there was myself; my own body set the frontiers, physical and emotional, there was simply me and not-me; the egotism of infancy has grandeur. And when I became a child there was Claudia, who was the centre of all things, and there was what pertained to Claudia, out at which I looked, the world of others, observed but not apprehended, a Berkeleyan landscape which existed only at my whim – when it ceased to interest me it no longer existed. And eventually, or so I am claiming, I grew up and saw myself in the awful context of time and place: everything and nothing.

She swims up from some tumultuous netherworld. She sees Laszlo, sitting beside the bed, his brown gaze fixed upon her. 'Ah,' she says. 'You again. Sylvia's gone, then?'

'That was three days ago,' says Laszlo. 'You are confused, dear.'

Claudia sighs. 'I shall have to take your word for it. And don't call me dear – it sounds unnatural, you never have before.'

'I am sorry,' says Laszlo humbly. 'Is there anything you would like?'

'Lots of things,' says Claudia. 'But it's too late for them now.'

'You mustn't talk like that.'

'Why not?'

'Because . . . Because it isn't like you.'

Claudia eyes him. 'I'm dying, you know.'

'No!' says Laszlo violently.

'Yes. So don't pretend. You're just like Lisa. If I can cope with it, so can you. Not that I am going particularly quietly.'

'What do you mean?' enquires Laszlo, with caution.

'Nothing. All in the mind. I'm not proposing to attack the nice kind doctors.' She closes her eyes and there is a silence. Laszlo gets up and roams the room. He examines the flowers ranged on the table – the scarlet poinsettia, the shock-headed chrysanthemums, the red roses with unnatural long thornless stems. 'Lovely roses.'

'Jasper.'

Laszlo turns his back on the roses with a sniff. 'He has been then?'

'He has.'

Laszlo dumps himself down in the chair again. 'Jasper I have never understood. When you could have had . . . any man.' He raises his eyes to the ceiling, spreads his hands, sheds his English top-dressing.

'So you've said before.'

'Anyone. You who were so beautiful . . . Are,' he adds, hastily.

'And I don't much care for Henry,' says Claudia. 'That's life, isn't it? Anyway, Jasper was a long time ago.'

'How many men have asked you to marry them?'

'Not a lot. Most had too strong an instinct for self-preservation.'

Laszlo pulls a face. 'Always you make yourself out so . . . formidable. To me you are not formidable. You are wonderful, simply.'

'Thanks,' says Claudia; she has closed her eyes again. Laszlo sits watching her: the profile with the high sharp nose, almost translucent at this moment in the light from the afternoon sun that pours through the window, and in which the flowers blaze, brilliant red and orange. She turns suddenly towards him: 'There is one thing I should like, if you are coming again.'

'Of course.'

'At the flat,' she says carefully, 'in the top drawer of my desk. A brown envelope tied up with string. Addressed to me. Quite thick. Just something I'd like to look through again, if you could bring it along.'

I can't exactly say that Laszlo has been a comfort to me in my later life: he has been alternately a liability and a source of interest. Also we are fond of each other. I have subsidised him, baled him out, consoled him; he has given me affection and entertainment. I have found his temperament, which sends a lot of people running, more intriguing than alarming. Laszlo's histrionics, which induce pursed lips and heavy silences in Lisa or in Sylvia, have been for me the breath of alien other worlds; they evoke the tumultuous unfettered society of Eastern Europe – languages I do not speak, cities I do not know, saints and tyrants and forests and vampires, a past that is more myth than history and all the better for it. When Laszlo was in his roaring twenties I used to put my feet up and become an appreciative spectator as he ranted up and down the sitting-room of the Fulham flat, bewailing his latest love affair, quarrel, betrayal, his creative struggles, the casuistry of critics and art gallery owners. He was always in a state of triumph or despair; he always arrived with a bottle of champagne or to tell me that he proposed suicide. I can't help respecting such responses; they seem an appropriate commitment to life.

Lisa, though, finds his personality excessive and embarrassing; despite (or maybe because of) her own ancestry. When she was young and obliged to consort with him from time to time because still within my orbit, she was as stiff and aloof as she could get away with. After her marriage she distanced herself firmly from him, and saw him only at unavoidable family events: birthdays, weddings and funerals. Laszlo, who would like to love and be loved by her, always leaps at her like a friendly puppy, and withdraws bewildered and hurt; he never learns.

*

'Many happy returns of the day,' says Lisa. She lays the parcel on the table and puts her cheek, for a moment, against Claudia's, drawing back even as she does so.

Claudia opens the parcel. 'Just what I need. Thank you.'

'I hope the colour is right.'

'The colour is perfect. Black goes with everything, after all.' They both consider the sensible matronly handbag.

Lisa sits down. 'I thought Laszlo was coming.'

'He is. He'll be here any minute. I've booked a table at the Greek place.'

Lisa looks around the room, infinitely familiar and in which she has never felt at home. It is Claudia's room, full of Claudia's things, thick with Claudia's presence; as a child, she used to feel as though she might stifle in it.

'What are all those enormous boxes in the hall?'

'Wine,' says Claudia.

'*Wine*?'

Laszlo's present. Seventy bottles. One for each year.

Lisa feels outrage well up within her. 'But you'll never . . .'

'I'll never get through it? I daresay not.'

Lisa flushes. 'Typical Laszlo.'

'Quite. But stylish, you must admit. It's rather good wine, too. Perhaps you should take a bottle back for Harry.'

'He has a regular order with the Wine Society.'

'Ah,' says Claudia. 'Then best not to interfere.'

The doorbell rings. Lisa sits tensely listening to the sounds of Laszlo's arrival, his greeting of Claudia, their laughter. He comes in, cries, 'Lisa darling it is so long since I saw you, and looking so . . . so fine in that pretty dress.' He advances on her to embrace but she has withdrawn behind the fence of a long low coffee table and he is reduced to blowing a kiss across it. Lisa says, 'Oh, hello, Laszlo. How are you?'

'I am well. But never mind about me today – it is for the birthday we are here, the celebration of seventy Claudia years! Isn't she terrific!' He flings his arms out towards Claudia, like an impresario with a discovery.

'Yes,' says Lisa, looking at the floor.

'So we are this nice cosy party,' says Laszlo. 'Just us three. Excellent. And this wonderful article in the Sunday paper, Henry brought it for me – did you see it, Lisa? Your mother writing so wonderfully of the war, of Egypt, all these things of which you talk so little, Claudia. Practically never do you talk of that time. And now this article. And this photograph. Young Claudia, so beautiful, sitting on a lorry in the sand. Wonderful!'

Lisa, who has also read the article with attention, looks at her mother. 'I'd never seen that photo.'

'I found it at the back of a drawer,' says Claudia. 'Thought they might as well use it.'

Laszlo carefully folds the crumpled sheet of newspaper. 'I was very proud. I have shown it to everyone. It is so long since you wrote a piece like this.'

'Why did you?' asks Lisa.

'Oh, an editor had been badgering me,' says Claudia. 'And I felt like it. All my generation seem to be busy turning their pasts to good account, so why not me?'

'So now you will tell us more,' says Laszlo gaily. 'Over dinner. All the interesting things you did not write for the newspaper. All the officers who were running after you, all the boyfriends. Promise!'

Lisa clears her throat. 'Oughtn't we to be getting to the restaurant?' She rises, gathers up her possessions. 'Have you had any other nice presents, mother?'

Mother. Thus, in mid-life, has Lisa won a small victory. Claudia prickles with irritation but is amused all the same. Lisa is conferring dowager status, determinedly. Well, if it gives her pleasure . . .

But no, she thinks, as they walk to the restaurant, I am not going to tell you about my other present, my undreamed of present, not now nor ever, not you or anyone. Nice is certainly not the word, though what the word would be I do not know, because I am still swept up by it, I can't yet think coherently about it, I am disordered.

And to fend off Laszlo's teasing, to forestall his questions, she talks loudly of other things, becomes involved with waiters and menus, with who is going to have what and what there is to be had; if I am to be cast as a matriarch, she thinks, I may as well do the thing properly. And somewhere beyond or within, another Claudia looks on with amusement. And regret. And disbelief. Is this true? This strident bossy old woman; these blotched veined hands opening a napkin; and these companions – who are they?

For a moment she is someone else, and then she returns and sees Laszlo looking across the table at her, asking something.

'So who took the photograph?' he says. 'Which of the handsome officers? Who is it you are smiling at so beautifully?'

She is smiling now, she has the look of the girl in the photograph, now in the dim warm light of the restaurant, but as he speaks the smile is switched off and she becomes another Claudia – oh, a Claudia he knows all too well – tart dismissive Claudia, and she says, 'I forget,' and turns to Lisa and asks about the grandsons, the dreadful grandsons who thank goodness are away at school so cannot be here, and boring Harry cannot be here either because Claudia probably did not ask him so there is just poor pale Lisa in her safe prim dress, all on edge as she always is with her mother. Better it were just Claudia and me, thinks Laszlo, but never mind. Lisa is after all the daughter, though goodness knows how, never would you think it, so mousy, like a shadow beside Claudia, but of course that is the trouble. And he remembers, kindly, indulgently, spiky fifteen-year-old Lisa and distracted maternal Lisa with her yowling babies. You could not imagine Claudia with a yowling baby, and perhaps that too is the trouble, he thinks wisely, Lisa of course was looked after by the grandmothers, perhaps there is a problem there too.

Always I have been a little in love with Claudia, he thinks. Always Claudia has seemed brighter cleverer more entertaining than other people, always I could talk to Claudia about anything, always when you leave Claudia you go flat a little.

Henry does not like Claudia, he is jealous, also he is afraid of her – lots of people are afraid of Claudia. But not me. I am not clever like Claudia but never has she squashed me like sometimes she squashes people, always she has listened to me, even if she laughed at me too. We have quarrelled, but always we have become friends again at once.

Lisa is speaking now of Jasper, coolly; she has taken the sons to visit him, he gave them money for bicycles. Rich, benevolent Jasper. At the thought of Jasper Laszlo curdles with dislike; never should Claudia have been involved with a man like Jasper, a hollow man, an *entrepreneur*, not worth her time. For an affair, perhaps, a little love affair, but not for so long, off and on, years and years, why do people make such mistakes? But Claudia has not good taste in men – for a woman so brilliant, so handsome it is extraordinary. Laszlo reviews, silently, various men, and his disapproval must be reflected in his face, for Claudia asks him what he is looking so ferocious about. 'Not ferocious,' he says. 'Not ferocious at all. Just I was thinking about some people.'

Except the brother, with whom she was so close. Laszlo thinks about Gordon, and his expression changes yet again. There was something strange there – Claudia and Gordon, something not quite like sister and brother, they seemed set apart when they were together, they made you feel you were not there. And I was a little afraid of Gordon, Laszlo tells himself, if I am honest I was always a little afraid, I had to try to please, to be careful.

'And now you've got your hangdog expression on,' says Claudia. 'I thought we were celebrating my seventy misspent years. Entertain me, please!'

16

'Someone brought this,' says the nurse. 'You were asleep so he just said to tell you Laszlo left it.'

And when she has gone Claudia unties the string, opens the envelope and takes out an old exercise book, stained, dog-eared. Her movements are slow, her hands fumble. She stares at it for a moment, then reaches out to the bedside table for her glasses, which takes more time, and effort. She puts them on and opens the exercise book.

The first time I saw it – recognised the handwriting – I felt as though I had been struck. I went numb. Then hot. Then cold. I put it down and read the letter, his sister's letter, brief and to the point: 'Dear Miss Hampton, Having seen your article on being a war correspondent in the Western Desert I realise that you must be the C. referred to by my brother Tom Southern in his diary. He spoke of you in letters to us, but never gave your name. I think you should have the diary, so here it is. Yours sincerely, Jennifer Southern.'

After that I read the diary, as I do again now.

It is a light green exercise book with CAHIER on the front in black letters. Ruled paper, rough and grainy. He has written in pencil. The entries are undated, and separated from one another by a wavy line.

This written God knows where, on a day in 1942. At an hour's notice to move off. So time to draw breath, have a brew-up. Fitters cursing over new tanks, two delivered last night, Grants, which we haven't had, half the equipment missing, guns still swimming in oil. Not my headache though – our troop came through yesterday unscathed. Can't put down yesterday as it ~~happened, what we did, who we met, who did what to whom –~~ *so let me try to record what it was like. For C., perhaps – what I tried to tell her that first time we met, and failed I think.*

The blackness of moving out of leaguer before dawn. Sandstorm too, so howling blackness full of sound and smell – rest of the squadron roaring away out there, interminable whistle and crackle of one's headphones, fuel stink. Then grey light turning to pink, orange. Moment of uplift when you see everyone else, long shapes of the Crusaders riding ridges – going fifteen–twenty miles an hour – sense of the whole place being on the move, more of us than there really are. Last call-up from the CO, then hours of wireless silence during advance. Hours? Or minutes? Time is not time any more, in any proper sense. Becomes simply the hands on one's watch, the CO's voice – 'Report to me in figures five minutes – we move off at figures 0500 hours – fire in figures three minutes.' You don't remember further back than half an hour. You don't anticipate except in your stomach.

Fear. Worst always before battle, not during. The fear of fear. Of being paralysed with it when the time comes, not being able to function, doing something bloody silly. In action it becomes something else. Keys you up. Saw my own hands shaking yesterday, once, looked down and saw them as someone else's, juddering on the edge of the turret, but my head quite clear, voice coming out normal or thereabouts, telling driver this, operator that, reporting our position, reporting tanks spotted at seven thousand yards, recording assessing predicting all as though some other self takes over. Only the hands a giveaway. Banged them down on the cover to get them under control and burned them on the hot metal. Which maddened me the rest of the day.

Sunset now. So we leaguer here, get some sleep pray God, we had damn all last night, everyone doing repairs till all hours, racket like an assembly line, and explosions every few minutes from enemy ammunition dump going up in the next wadi. Lay looking at stars and thinking. No, not thinking. You don't think, just fetch out some images and have a look at them. Other times, other places. Other people. C. Always C.

A week on. I think. During which not a moment for this – either going flat out, in the thick of it, or too exhausted to do anything but collapse till the next move. Even if it were expedient I couldn't say now what came before what, where we were when, how this happened or that, in the mind it's not a sequence just a single event without beginning or end in any proper sense simply a continuity spiked by moments of intensity that ring in the head still. Looking down to see that my loader is hit, blood pouring from his neck but he doesn't seem to realise is still loading still shouting something and I have to reach out and touch him to get his attention. Dust in the turret so thick that we can't see each other's faces, I can't see the map unless I hold it inches from my nose. Sick flop in the belly when one of my own troop brews up, that awful belch of orange then thick black smoke, and watching to see if anyone bales out and no one does, not one. Different sick feeling when what I thought was an enemy derelict comes to life and starts firing. Flare of exhilaration when enemy reported retreating, we are to pursue – sitting up on the turret squinting through field-glasses searching for tell-tale dust on the horizon I feel nothing but primitive lust for chase, no fear, that bone-cracking exhaustion gone, just this instinct like a pack of hounds. And, later, am ashamed and amazed.

Burying the crew of a Crusader from C squadron. They dropped behind with engine trouble during an attack and later we found the tank shot up and burnt out, all dead, the driver and commander still inside, a bloody mess fuming with flies that we took out as best we could, in pieces, the gunner and operator lying near in the sand, shot when they'd tried to bale out, hardly a scratch on them, just stiff on the sand in that absolute unreachable silence of the dead.

Battle noise that reverberates in the head long after it has ceased – noise to which one responds like an automaton, not identifying but blowing with it, one jump ahead, seeing in the mind's eye the field-guns and rifles, accounting for a burst of high-velocity fire, assessing range and distance. And the voices always in one's ears, the disembodied to and fro of the squadron as though we roamed the sand like tormented spirits, calling to one another in a mad private language – 'Hello, Fish One, Rover calling . . . O.K. off to you . . . All stations Fish . . . Advance on a bearing of figures ten degrees . . . Move now . . . Can you confirm . . .' – and sometimes the pitch changes, the tempo becomes frenetic, the voices shriek and wail against each other in the tight box of one's head – 'Fish Three where the hell are you . . . bloody well get off the air when I'm talking . . . Fish Three, blast you, where are you? . . . Hello, Rover, I am hit, repeat, I am hit and withdrawing.' It is as though one existed on different planes: that of sight – the confusing treacherous spread of the desert, smoking and flaming, flinging up tracer and Very lights, vehicles crawling hither and thither like ants, and that of sound – which comes from everywhere, above, around, beyond, within – the whine of aircraft, the bangs, clatter, screech and the voices which seem to come not from what one sees but to be detached, a commentary, a ghost chorus.

I've just seen a gazelle. Usually we shoot them when we get the chance – they make a fine change from bully beef and tinned bacon – but I couldn't bring myself to this time. It hadn't seen me, just stood there flicking its tail, ears pricked, sand-coloured but somehow brilliant in the rock and scrub, in the deadness of the place, rusty petrol tins and barbed wire and a burnt-out lorry near and in the middle of it this scrap of life. And then it scented me and went bounding off.

Sleeping after being in action. Either a black pit of extinction or one skates around just below the level of consciousness, having wild manic dreams, surrealistic dreams in which crazy things go on that you never question. Apt reflection of what we're in the middle of, come to think of it – preposterous world of sand and explosions that becomes the only one you've ever known and therefore banal, mundane, normal.

The moments that rear up, when one stops, the pictures that stay in the head . . . My gunner squatting in the sand over a fry-up in a respite between actions, intent, absorbed, the sky-line exploding all around, smoke streaming, 'Here we are, sir, try a bit of this,' small wiry chap with a Midlands accent, in the building trade pre-war. Staring into heat-shimmer unable to make out line of vehicles on a ridge, what are they? Tanks or lorries? Enemy or not? They hang quivering just out of reach and I am hunched in the turret gripping field-glasses so intently they mark my hands. Italians scrambling out of a gun-emplacement, being herded together by an Aussie infantryman with cigarette glued to his lip, bawling at them occasionally, the blue-green Italian uniforms looking suddenly alien, foreign, intrusive against the khaki – and now I see them again and think of the expedient simplistic way in which war conditions thought of us and them, ours and theirs, good and bad, black and white, no confusing uncomfortable indeterminate areas.

Except the desert, of course, which is neutral. Not on our side or on theirs, but simply on its own. Going about its business of hot and cold, sun and wind, cycles of days and months and years for ever and bloody ever. Unlike us.

More moments. Padre setting up altar for Sunday service in the back of a ten-ton lorry, tail-board let down, men standing round in half-circle, apologetic unsynchronised murmur of prayers and hymns, column of armoured cars moving past behind. God being said of course to be on our side.

Looking down into a weapon-pit with what seems to be a heap of torn clothing in the bottom and it is not clothes but a corpse, resolving itself suddenly into twisted limbs and flung-back head with open eyes crusted in dust, and again that remote silence of the dead, almost a superiority, as though they knew something you don't. Walking off to some rocks for a shit and finding oneself eye to eye with a little snake, coiled up as still as a stone, just its tongue flicking, beady black eyes, bright zig-zag markings down its back. These two sights separated perhaps by days but they come together now and seem to complement one another, to say something about the potency of life, its charge, the way in which death is total absence.

Air attack on enemy anti-tank guns dug in at the neck of a shallow valley, blocking us for hours, CO's voice on the headphones saying 'Friends up above, thank God, at last,' and then the bombs showering down like white skittles. And before that – after – I don't know – a hideous time when what I thought were rocks turn into a line of Mark IIIs, hull-down a couple of hundred yards off and I have seconds in which to decide whether to get into reverse bloody quick and withdraw or find the range and take them on, have they seen me yet? Can I hold them off long enough to call up support? And then they solve the problem for me by opening fire, the first shells whistling past thank God and I report my position to command, bawl at my gunner to fire, all at the same moment it seems and stuttering with the effort to keep panic out of my voice.

The desert lifting around me as someone walks into an 'S' mine a dozen yards ahead. He is killed. I am deafened for half an hour and have a small flesh wound in one leg. Everyone has their tale of a miraculous escape – that I suppose is mine, except that miracles don't come into it, just blind chance. But no one likes the idea of chance, so they play games with language and talk about miracles instead.

Nights. The noisy illuminated darkness full of aircraft, ack-ack guns, thuds and bangs off-stage, orange flashes, the silver rise of shells, great glowing furnaces – a Gotterdammerung above which the stars preside, the same icy glitter night after night, Orion, Sirius, the Plough, the Bear. Periods of truce in which we leaguer (odd, that term, reaching back to other wars, other landscapes) – soft vehicles within defensive ring of armour, draw breath, take stock, get orders for tomorrow and, occasionally, sleep.

Two weeks later. Nothing doing for days now – pitched from frenzy into boredom, apathy – the capricious way of this campaign. Rumours that we will advance, withdraw, be sent on leave, sit here for months. So we sit – dispersed untidy city of vehicles and tents and dug-outs. Shanty-towns of petrol tins spring up. People lay out a cricket pitch. Supplies are brought up. We repair kit, equipment, ourselves. Pass round tattered magazines. Write letters. I write this.

To whom it may concern. C., I hope. Myself, maybe, in some future that at the moment seems frankly incredible. We all talk about 'after the war' but it is almost an incantation – a protective device: touch wood. One thinks about it, one day-dreams, makes plans – something like the day-dreaming of childhood: When I'm Grown-up. So I say to myself: when I'm grown-up in this mythical world in which there are no more tanks, guns, mines, bombs, in which sand is stuff on beaches and the sun is something one appreciates – when I'm let loose in this playground I'm going to . . . What am I going to do? And then the mythologies take over because what one conjures up is a place stripped of imperfections, a nirvana of green grass, happy children, tolerance and justice which never existed and never will. So one shoves that out of the way and summons up more wholesome stuff like hot meals, clean sheets, drink and sex. All those things one took for granted a bare three years ago which now take on almost holy significance. Which seem at times to be what we are fighting for.

'Tell me a story,' C. said in Luxor. I never told her the other story, in which she stars, in which she is always the heroine – a romanticised story full of cliché images in which I am telling her all the things there has not been enough time for, in which we are doing all the things there has not been enough time for, in which this damn thing is suspended and we are living happily ever after, world without end, amen. To such indulgences have I sunk. Well, perhaps I am telling her this now, and if I am, may she be tolerant and understanding, may she perceive the extravagance into which one is pitched by war, the suspension of ordinary common sense except that aspect of common sense needed for

doing what has to be done, for telling other people what to do, for moving a lot of heavy metal around and trying to kill people with it while avoiding being killed oneself.

May we, eventually, contemplate all this together.

And now I want to get yesterday down while I still have the awful taste of it.

Orders to move off before dawn again – objective enemy tanks in large numbers reported twenty miles east. Felt keyed up during midnight briefing in CO's HQ, even glad at prospect of something positive after days of sitting around. Walked back to my tank – brilliant starry night, quite still, men moving about against the pale sand, black hunched shapes of vehicles. Settled down for a few hours sleep and was seized by something I've not known before – sudden paralysing awareness of where I am, of what is happening, that I may die, so savage that I lay there rigid, as though in shock, but the mind screaming, howling. Fear, yes, but something more than that – something atavistic, primitive, the instinct to run. I told myself to snap out of it, take a grip on things. I tried breathing deeply, counting to a hundred, going over the codes for the day yet again. No bloody good. All that I can think of is that the morning is riding at me full tilt and I am pinned down with no escape and shit-scared as I've never been before and I don't know why. So I try something else. Tell myself I am not really here. That I am moving through this place, this time, must do so, cannot avoid it, but soon I shall come through and out beyond into another part of the story. Thought of the gazelle I saw, flicking its tail carefree amid heaps of rusty metal, that I envied for a moment; but the gazelle has no story, that is the difference. Pinned down and shit-scared, I have a story, which makes me a man, and therefore set apart.

So I make myself move backwards and forwards, lying there huddled in the sleeping-bag on the cold sand – backwards to other places, to childhood, to a time I climbed a Welsh mountain, walked the streets of New York, was happy, not happy, was by the sea in Cornwall long ago or on a bed in Luxor with C. last month. Forwards into obscurity but an obscurity lit by dreams which is another word for hope. I make myself dream, push away the night and the desert and the black shapes all round me, push past the morning and tomorrow and next week and make pictures, dreams. I dream of green fields. I dream of cities. I dream of C. And at last the primitive paralysing thing loosens its grip and I even sleep, to be shaken awake by my driver. 0500 hours; I am tense but sane.

And then the rest. Advanced all morning, patrols reporting enemy position and direction, then contact lost, much swanning around looking for them, at one point they appear to have melted into the sand, or were never there in the first place, then my headphones jammed with excited orders, they are spotted again at 7000 yards. Relieved to find I am still sane, functioning O.K., almost calm. Switch over to talk to the crew. We have a new gunner, Jennings. He is fresh from the Delta – his first time in action, which I hadn't realised till the night before, a stocky lad from Aylesbury, barely into his twenties I imagine. Hadn't had much time to get to know him, he seemed efficient enough, a bit silent I thought but we were all too busy in the usual flap of last-minute checks to do much about him. And now I realised there was something wrong – first I couldn't get an answer out of him at all, then he didn't make sense, went on muttering things I couldn't catch. I said 'Jennings, are you O.K.?' – but the CO's voice was coming over now on the other set and I had to switch off and the next fifteen minutes or so were chaos – orders and counter-orders, our B squadron in action against a bunch of German Mark IIIs, we were told to move up and give support, then had to wheel round to take on another lot they hadn't spotted. I told Jennings to get the range and be ready to open fire, and all I could get from him was a whimpering noise, terrible, like a tormented animal. And then words – the same thing over and over again: 'Please get me out of here. Please get me out of here. Please get me out of here.' I tried talking to him calmly and steadily, not bawling him out, telling him to take his time, steady up, just do the things he'd been taught to do. But now I could see the enemy tanks, coming on fast, and a couple of shots slammed past us and seconds later my sergeant's tank was

hit and brewed up at once. We couldn't carry on like this, a
sitting duck, so I pulled back both remaining tanks to a hull-
down position in a dip behind us and tried once again to
persuade Jennings to get a grip on himself. But it was hopeless.
All the time he was moaning and whimpering – out of his mind
clearly poor little blighter.

God knows why we weren't hit. The Mark IIIs kept on firing.
There was nothing I could do – short of throwing Jennings out
of the tank and taking over the gun myself. But then the
commander was saying there was another of them coming up
and we were to pull back for the time being until he could bring
up support from our friends to the east. We withdrew out of
range and the Germans chased for a bit and then held back and I
reported that my gunner was a casualty and asked for the MO,
the CO saying angrily 'What the hell's up with you – you
weren't hit?'

I got Jennings out of the tank. The rest of the crew hung about
awkwardly, not wanting to talk about it, lighting cigarettes.
Jennings sat slumped with his head in his hands – he'd been sick
and his battle-dress was flecked with yellow vomit. I tried
talking to him, told him not to worry, he'd be all right presently,
things like that, but I don't think he took anything in. He looked
up at me once, and his eyes were like a child's, but a child that's
seen some nameless horror, the pupils swollen, black pits in a
white face. So I stopped trying and we hung around there
fidgeting and presently the MO's truck came bustling up and the
doctor jumped down and took one look at Jennings and said
'O.K., old chap, come on then.' And as soon as he'd taken
Jennings off the rest of the crew began joking, exaggerated,
feverish, like I've seen men do after a near miss, and I felt myself
as though I'd shaken something off, something unlucky,
contaminating – I didn't want to think about him: his face, his
voice.

Our squadron had lost three tanks that day. The crew had
baled out of one and the gunner transferred to mine. The next
day was unmitigated hell – to and fro actions from dawn till late
in the afternoon. By the end of it I was functioning like an

automaton, beyond feeling or caring, but then when we leaguered we were told the scale of enemy losses and that we'd pushed them right back from their positions and exhilaration took over and we sat around congratulating ourselves in a sudden tide of confidence and bonhomie. No one mentioned Jennings again except the CO who said 'Chap of yours cracked up, I gather – bad show,' in an embarrassed sort of way. And I remembered that men were shot for cowardice on the Somme. Now it was just a bad show, which seemed like progress of a kind.

I have put this down – Jennings, my own duel between mind and matter – because one day I am going to want to think about it. This is as it was, raw and untreated. At some point I shall want to make sense of it – if there is sense to be made. C. asked me once – the first time I met her – what it was like out here. I found it hard to explain. Well, at one point it was like this. So this is for her too, perhaps. Maybe one day she will help me make sense of it. She intends to write history books, after all, so it will be within her line of business.

That was last week. The story continues; I am still in it. Stagnation again, sitting around, waiting for supplies and reinforcements – rumours that there will be a big push at any moment. Time to think again – a kind of thinking that is on two different planes, one taken up with here and now, with the tank, the men, the equipment, the CO, with what this man has said and that one has done, with the way a brother officer eats with his mouth open (and how in the middle of all this one can be irritated by someone's table manners God only knows). And the other – the other level of thought – so far removed that it is as though one were two people; I think of how once I was brash enough to believe I could dictate to life instead of which it has turned on me with its fangs bared. I think of all the things I haven't done and all the things I intend to do still. I think of C., who features in most of these. I read a tattered copy of DOMBEY AND SON hunched in a bivouac in the shade of the tank, crawling with flies, and am lost, transported, for hours on end, beyond all this, anaesthetised – ah, the miracle of words, of narrative. I make idle, childish lists, to amuse myself: the Greek gods, English wild flowers, American presidents, French novelists.

P.M. – same day. My tank has an oil-seal gone. I'm told I can take it back and get a replacement from Field Workshop. A welcome break.

Here the diary ends. Below the last entry Jennifer Southern has written, in now faded ink, 'My brother was killed in an enemy air attack while undertaking this task.'

▲▲▲▲▲▲▲▲▲▲▲▲▲▲

17

▼▼▼▼▼▼▼▼▼▼▼▼▼▼

And so, eventually, we contemplate this apart, years apart. We are no longer in the same story, and when I read what you wrote I think of all that you do not know. You are left behind, in another place and another time, and I am someone else, not the C. of whom you thought, the C. you remembered, but an unimaginable Claudia from whom you would recoil, perhaps. A stranger, inhabiting a world you would not recognise. I find this hard to bear.

I am twice your age. You are young; I am old. You are in some ways unreachable, shut away beyond a glass screen of time; you know nothing of forty years of history and forty years of my life; you seem innocent, like a person in another century. But you are also, now, a part of me, as immediate and as close as my own other selves, all the Claudias of whom I am composed; I talk to you almost as I would talk to myself.

Death is total absence, you said. Yes and no. You are not absent so long as you are in my head. That, of course, is not what you meant; you were thinking of the extinction of the flesh. But it is true; I preserve you, as others will preserve me. For a while.

You asked me to make sense of it. I can't. Your voice is louder now than the narrative I know – or think that I know. I know what happened next; I know that Rommel was pushed out of Africa and that we won the war. I know all that has ensued. This dispassionate sequence explains – or purports to explain – why the war happened and how it evolved and what its effects have been. Your experience – raw and untreated – does not seem to contribute to any of that. It is on a different plane. I cannot analyse and dissect it, draw conclusions, construct arguments. You tell me about gazelles and dead men, guns and stars, a boy who is afraid; it is all clearer to me than any chronicle of events but I cannot make sense of it, perhaps because there is none to be made. It might be easier if I believed in God, but I don't. All I can think, when I hear your voice, is that the past is true, which both appals and uplifts me. I need it; I need you, Gordon, Jasper, Lisa, all of them. And I can only explain this need by extravagance: my history and the world's. Because unless I am a part of everything I am nothing.

It is late afternoon. Claudia lies with her eyes closed; she breathes loudly, an irregular rasping that makes the bed from which it comes the focal point of the room, though there is no one but Claudia to be aware of this. But she can feel it, drifting in and out of some pounding sea that is full of the din of her own existence. She comes to the surface, opens her eyes, and sees that it is raining. The sky has darkened, and the room with it; the window is struck as though by tiny pellets and water slides down it in bands so that all beyond is distorted – the branches of a tree and through them rooftops and more distant trees. And then the rain stops. Gradually, the room is filled with light; the bare criss-crossing branches of the tree are hung with drops and as the sun comes out it catches the drops and they flash with colour – blue, yellow, green, pink. The branches are black against a golden orange sky, black and brilliant. Claudia gazes at this; it is as though the spectacle has been laid on for her pleasure and she is filled with elation, a surge of joy, of well-being, of wonder.

The sun sinks and the glittering tree is extinguished. The room darkens again. Presently it is quite dim; the window is violet now, showing the black tracery of branches and a line of houses packed with squares of light. And within the room a

207

change has taken place. It is empty. Void. It has the stillness of a place in which there are only inanimate objects: metal, wood, glass, plastic. No life. Something creaks; the involuntary sound of expansion or contraction. Beyond the window a car starts up, an aeroplane passes overhead. The world moves on. And beside the bed the radio gives the time signal and a voice starts to read the six o'clock news.